GUNMAN'S
DAWN

GUNMAN'S DAWN

Gary Wayne

Library of Congress Control Number: 2003092106
ISBN: Hardcover   978-1-4010-9428-7
                 Softcover   978-1-4010-9427-0

Cover photo courtesy of Bones Forman.

Website information: www.gunmansdawn.com

Print information available on the last page.

Rev. date: 02/08/2023

To order additional copies of this book, contact:
Xlibris
844-714-8691
www.Xlibris.com
Orders@Xlibris.com
534849

Acknowledgment

The author wishes to thank Rachel Tilley
for her invaluable assistance in editing this book.

In memory of my brother Roy,
who never read Westerns

CHAPTER ONE

John Howard checked his guns. He had just reined his Appaloosa stallion to a halt when they arrived at the top of a tree-shaded hill. That was when he first heard the noise. He frowned, and as he did, his stark features were highlighted by caution in the rays of the unusually warm October sun. Straining, he listened, as he heard the sound again. After hearing it a second time, he had no doubts. Beyond the rim of the next hill arose a steady rumbling that was growing in intensity. It was the sound of horses.

He was concerned about the identity and purpose of the riders he heard. The year 1876 was a dangerous time to be riding alone in the Black Hills of the Dakota Territory. Crazy Horse and Gall had recently rubbed out Custer and more than two hundred and fifty troopers of the Seventh Calvary. The high plains were ablaze with rumors of a full-scale Indian uprising, threatening every white man, woman, and child between the Yellowstone and the Mississippi Rivers.

Howard raised his Confederate hat and wiped sweat from his brow, fixing his eyes on the area below. As he continued to study the terrain around him, several riders suddenly came into view as they skirted the base of a low hill located a quarter of a mile away. He was able to get a clear look at them through his field glasses, noting with alarm that it was a small contingent of Union soldiers. Howard counted twenty-one men in the group.

Though he bristled at the approach of the soldiers, he had no intention of running from them; he was confident that he was not on any wanted posters. Without conscious thought, he loosened the thong that kept his Smith and Wesson .44 revolver secured in its holster and with his knee felt that his Winchester "Yellow Boy" rifle was easily accessible. He reached into his saddlebags and pulled from them a second Smith and Wesson .44, and stuck the handgun in his belt behind his back. He even verified the position of a small two-shot .41 Remington derringer concealed under his shirt. As a final precaution, he located a second scabbard underneath the Winchester, and touched the stock of a Remington single-shot, breech-loading .44-90 caliber rifle. Howard doubted he would use the .44-90 that day, because it was for long range work, and if shooting started with the soldiers, he would rely on the firepower of the Winchester and the speed of the revolvers.

After verifying the position of his guns, he eased his horse a few paces forward in front of the trees. Though he could then be seen by the soldiers, he was still close enough to the trees that he could take cover behind them if shooting started.

The soldiers drew rein about forty yards away and slowly spread out into a semicircle, facing him as the horses slowed to a walk. One of two troopers in front, a large, grizzled sergeant with gray sideburns, spoke to Howard in a voice that clearly indicated his dislike of anyone wearing any part of the uniform of the late Confederacy.

"Aw'right, rebel scum, who are you and what you got in them saddlebags?" he demanded.

"The War of Northern Aggression has been over for more than a decade, Corporal," Howard replied. "As far as I know, wearing part of a cast-off Confederate uniform is not a crime. I'm a civilian riding on open range and am minding my own business. You would do well to do the same."

The soldier cursed violently. He followed with, "It's 'Sergeant,' you rebel trash, not 'Corporal.' So you've got a big mouth and talk like you think you're somebody special. Mebbe you think you're some kinda professor or some such thing. But fancy words don't keep you from being a stinkin' Johnny Reb." He looked closely at Howard. "Say now, you look kinda familiar. Where in hell have I seen you before?"

"That depends, Corporal. What part of hell are you from?"

Several soldiers snickered, and a couple laughed outright. The noise quickly subsided as the sergeant swivelled in his saddle to glower at the men behind him. Then he turned his attention back to the rider in front of him.

"Think you're pretty funny, huh? Well, Reb, maybe I think we just ought to teach you respect fer your betters. Open them bags right now or we'll knock you down off that Appaloosa and take a look fer ourselves. How 'bout that?"

With that statement, the sergeant spurred his mount forward. He had every intention of seeing this belligerent stranger comply with his order. The soldier wanted Howard to suffer humiliation at least, and a physical beating at worst if he didn't immediately obey. While the sergeant's sadistic nature made him hope that this man would resist, he really didn't think that a lone rider facing more than twenty carbine-carrying troopers would be foolhardy enough to put up a fight.

His horse had not taken more than two steps before Howard spoke again. "Well 'Corporal,' or 'Sergeant,' or whatever you call yourself, I think it would be funny to see you go through my saddlebags."

The sheer gall of this statement caused the soldier to momentarily pause and ask the obvious question.

"And just whadda you mean by that?"

"It would be funny to see a man with a bullet in his head search my saddlebags or anything else of mine."

This particular sergeant was not the brightest soldier on the frontier. But even as slow-witted as he was, he recognized that Howard's threat was serious. However, he also felt that only an insane individual would try to face down twenty-one armed soldiers. While this rider might be a hardcase, he didn't seem to be crazy.

Taken aback though he was, the trooper was nonetheless pleased in the situation that had arisen. Now he thought that he had an excuse to teach this rebel just who had won the war. Secure in his superior manpower, the sergeant doubly resolved to also teach this arrogant Southerner respect for the Union Army and its noncommissioned officers. He knew that he had to be decisive in front of his lieutenant, who, so far, had said nothing. He smugly thought that he would give the rest of the lads something to talk about back at the barracks.

He was right in one respect—he gave the other soldiers something to remember, but it was not what he had intended. In reality, when the rest of the men talked about the event later, they would all agree on two things: they had never seen the sergeant so swiftly and neatly put in his place, even by a commissioned officer, and they had never seen a gun put into action so fast. As the sergeant spurred his horse again and Howard's right hand hovered over his holster, a cocked revolver seemed to magically appear in Howard's left hand. A moment later, the stunned soldier realized that the .44's muzzle was pointed directly at his own head.

Howard spoke in a low voice. "Hoka-hey. That's Sioux for 'this is a good day to die.' Do you agree, Corporal?"

On the heels of Howard's question, a new voice rang out. "Stop right there, both of you!"

Shifting his glance slightly, Howard looked at the soldier who had just spoken. He saw a trim soldier wearing the insignia of a second lieutenant. Although the officer was very young, probably two or three years younger than Howard, he spoke with the assurance and confidence of one trained to lead men.

The lieutenant barked another quick order. "Sergeant Reilly, stand fast!" Directing his attention to Howard, he spoke again. "You sir, holster your sidearm. I'm Lieutenant James Campbell, and I won't have anyone threaten my men." He cast a disapproving glance at the sergeant. "Even if they might deserve it."

Howard eased his horse a single step forward. "Don't try to tell me what to do, Lieutenant. You have no reason to harass me. So I suggest that you call off your dog unless you want him shot. If he tries to lay hands on me, I'll kill him."

The lieutenant clenched his jaws. He tried to think of a suitable reply, desperately wishing that a proper response to this particular situation had been covered at West Point.

"It's obvious that you're not going to be bullied, sir," responded the lieutenant. "The sergeant has stopped, as you see. He's not going to touch you or your possessions, and he was wrong to try to do so. However, you're equally wrong if you think that you can threaten the United States Army. I'll tell you only once more, holster your gun. If you do, you won't be bothered. If you do not, my men will open fire on my command."

As if on cue from Lieutenant Campbell, the soldiers raised their Springfield rifles and trained them on Howard. Reilly was the only one who didn't move. The sergeant sat motionlessly on his horse, his hands clutched tightly on the reins.

Lieutenant Campbell kept his eyes locked on Howard. "It appears that you have unusual skill with firearms, so if shooting starts, you may put down several of us. But understand this, regardless of how many of us you get, we'll kill you. Now, for the last time, holster your gun!"

Howard suppressed a smile as he deliberately returned his revolver to its place under his belt. "Interesting," he thought. "I've finally met a Yankee officer with courage and wisdom. I didn't know they existed."

Once Howard no longer held his revolver, Campbell ordered his men to put away their rifles.

Howard was impressed enough with the officer to tell him his name. He thought he detected a slight change in the officer's facial expression at the mention of his name, but he wasn't sure. The moment passed and Campbell addressed the gunfighter.

"Mr. Howard, I'm glad we stopped before this situation got too far out of hand. I'd like to avoid any further problems if we can, and I think it will help if I explain some things. We're members of the Second Cavalry on temporary assignment to Fort Pierre. We're on patrol, warning civilians that the Sioux are riding the war trail. They beat the Seventh Cavalry this summer, and now anyone away from the settlements is taking his life in his hands. In fact, we've been looking for a war party of about one hundred warriors that are rumored to be in the vicinity."

"Do you think you have enough men to take on one hundred Sioux?" queried Howard. "There's no better fighting man than a Lakota warrior. Most of the Yankee soldiers I've seen will only fight if the odds are drastically in their favor, say, at least, twenty to one."

Campbell ignored the jibe. "Mr. Howard, the army feels that one soldier can handle at least five or six Indians." Lieutenant Campbell paused and adjusted his holster to a more comfortable position before he added, "Besides riding patrol, we've been asked by the civil authorities to assist in looking for the thieves who held up a money shipment last week that was going from Fort Pierre to Gold Valley and Deadwood. That's why Sergeant Reilly wanted to look in your saddlebags. He's looking for stolen gold. Now that you understand his motive, I'll ask you if you'll give us permission to look in your bags. But remember, I'm asking you, not telling you. The choice is yours."

Howard folded his hands on the pommel of his saddle before answering. "Since when does the army have authority to enforce civil law?"

"Normally it does not. However, part of the shipment contained an army payroll."

"I see. If you put it like that, I'll consider letting one of your men look in my bags; anyone except him, that is," answered Howard, as he motioned toward Reilly.

Campbell directed a private to go forward. Abruptly, Howard visibly tensed. He slowly dismounted and grasped the grip of his Remington rifle.

As he extracted the big rifle from its scabbard, he said, "But I think that we've got a much bigger problem than deciding who will search my saddlebags. The bigger question is whether any of us will live through the next few minutes."

CHAPTER TWO

Howard motioned to the rear of the troopers and said, "We've got company. It looks like you found your Indians. It also looks like your estimate of their numbers was low."

Upon hearing Howard's words, the soldiers turned and surveyed the plains behind them, where they had been just a few short moments before. What they saw caused a wide range of reactions, varying from startled surprise and fearful uneasiness in the case of veteran troopers, to sheer terror among the new recruits. Spreading out across the horizon was a group of at least two hundred Sioux warriors in battle formation. The Indians were less than half a mile away.

Through the brass telescope on his .44-90 Remington rifle, Howard could see what they all suspected. The Sioux were painted for war. Howard was no expert on Indians, although he had spent the better part of 1867 among the Sioux and spoke some of the language. However, he didn't have to be an authority to recognize that many of the hostiles in front of him had recently fought with the army, because he saw several bits and pieces of blue uniforms among the Indians. He also thought that he saw the tattered guidon of a cavalry unit among them. Scanning the Indians, Howard abruptly stopped the telescope on a massive warrior who was out in front.

"No, it's not possible. It can't be him," thought Howard incredulously.

Nevertheless, he was forced to conclude that there were probably not any other Sioux warriors the size of the man he saw. Consequently, he continued moving the telescope and settled the cross hairs on the chest of another warrior as the Sioux slowly advanced toward the white men.

Lieutenant Campbell wasted no time in issuing orders. "Philips, Benson, Sutherland, O'Brien . . . hold the horses. Sergeant Reilly, form the rest of the men in a skirmish line. We'll wait until they get to that red rock. When they do, on my command, commence firing and continue firing at will. It looks like we're up against it. Mark your target and squeeze the trigger. Wait for my order to fire."

The lieutenant had momentarily forgotten Howard. Had he looked at the gunfighter, he would have seen him preparing a stable shooting rest on the ground with his saddle roll. He would have also seen him carefully adjusting the Remington while he assumed a steady prone position.

As Howard positioned the stock of his Remington into his shoulder, he spoke to the soldiers in general and to Lieutenant Campbell in particular. "If you wait until they get to that red rock, it may be too late. That rock is within one hundred yards of us. Unless they break ranks, they'll charge right over us. We have to stop them before they get too close. We've got to break their spirit to have a chance of stopping them, even if your men are good shooters. What do you think?"

"Mr. Howard," said Campbell, "your point is well taken, but there's not a lot we can do until they get closer. I only have fifty rounds of ammunition for each man's rifle and twenty-four rounds for each pistol. Even though my men are some of the finest marksmen in the Army, I don't have enough ammunition to randomly throw bullets downrange without a chance of doing damage to the enemy. The best we can do is to fight well, and if we have to die, at least we'll die with honor."

"Lieutenant," replied Howard, "I agree with your sentiments but don't necessarily hold the same conclusion."

As he finished speaking, Howard gently took out the remaining slack in his Remington's three pound trigger. The report of the rifle had already died down when one of the Indians clawed at his chest and dropped off his pony. The advancing line of Sioux momentarily paused as they looked for what they thought had to be a hidden rifleman near them. Not one of them believed that the shot came from the small group of soldiers on the hill in front of them. After all, they were still more than seven hundred yards away, and none of them believed that any man could shoot well enough to hit his mark at that range. The second shot, which followed less than ten seconds after the first, caused them to rethink their position, because a second warrior fell to the ground, this one clutching his mid-section.

The Sioux were thoroughly confounded. After the second shot, several of them saw smoke rising from among the soldiers on the hill in front of them. They were forced to reluctantly conclude that among the soldiers there was a deadly sharpshooter with an incredibly accurate rifle.

Later, some of the warriors would speak in hushed tones of a "medicine gun," which was the only explanation they had for what they were experiencing but could not understand. But that discussion would come later, when the survivors of the fight were seated around their camp fires. At the moment, they wanted to not only wipe out the hated white soldiers they faced, but to count coup on the sniper who had already killed two of their fellow braves at an unbelievable range.

As a guttural cry lifted from among their ranks, the Sioux began to advance again. This time, they were not merely trotting their horses, but were galloping at full speed. It was a spectacular sight; a long line of some of the finest light cavalry on the face of the earth, riding in unison and sweeping across the open prairie in a colorful wave of death and destruction.

But the "medicine gun" continued to roar, with every echo producing another riderless horse. So incredibly effective was Howard's gunfire that in the space of time it took the Lakota to cover three hundred yards of the remaining distance, eight more men and two horses were shot down.

At slightly more than two hundred yards, Campbell could wait no longer. Forgetting about his instruction to wait until the enemy was one hundred yards away, he yelled at the top of his lungs, "Help him! *Volley fire!*"

At his command, the deafening boom of Howard's .44-90 was joined by the similar sounds of the .45-70 Springfields being fired.

It became immediately evident to Howard that the troopers on the hillside with him were better trained and more accurate marksmen than any Union soldiers he had seen. With the first volley, nine Indians toppled to the ground, only one the victim of Howard's Remington. A couple of horses also tumbled to the ground, throwing their riders so hard that they were incapacitated. With the second volley, fourteen more warriors fell, many with fatal wounds.

In spite of himself in the moments that followed, Howard began to feel a certain sense of grudging respect for the soldiers. Though badly outnumbered, they fought with courage and discipline. And while none appeared anxious to die, they were fighting like true warriors, prepared to make their deaths as costly as possible to the enemy.

The marksmanship of the soldiers created a difficult problem for the Indians. They desperately wanted to overrun the troopers in front of them, and all of their recent experiences told them that they should have been able to do just that. After all, they well remembered riding that summer against the troops commanded by Crook and Custer. Those soldiers had fought well, but still Three Stars Crook had been forced to retreat, and the seemingly invincible Long Hair had died, along with every man under his immediate command.

Yet now, in less than the space of two minutes, the Lakota had lost almost one fifth of their fighting force and had yet to inflict a single casualty or count a single coup. Such a thing had not happened since the Wagon Box Fight of 1867, when a small group of soldiers and civilians armed with breech-loading Springfield rifles fought behind a makeshift fort consisting of overturned wagons. Several hundred Sioux under Red Cloud had been forced to withdraw from the field that day.

And this day was worse. In the mind of more than one Sioux present that warm October afternoon, there was something positively supernatural in the ability of the enemy they faced. Surely, it was a true thing that this small band of bluecoats fought like devils with weapons that almost never missed. It was almost as if

Wakan Tankan, the Great Mysterious, was with the white eyes and against the Indians.

So although the Sioux were among the bravest fighting men ever to have ridden forth in war, they were good enough tacticians to unashamedly disengage when the odds were too much against them. At one hundred and fifty yards from the tiny island of soldiers, the sea of howling Indians broke and streamed into two separate lines that swept below and past the troopers. As they did, the cavalrymen continued firing with deadly results. By the time the last of the Indians had passed, there were almost a dozen more riderless ponies.

"Cease-fire, cease-fire!" shouted Campbell. "They've had enough, let them go."

The soldiers began to cheer, but were abruptly interrupted by the sharp report of Howard's Winchester. He had replaced the Remington with it when the Sioux were two hundred yards away and now continued to fire at the retreating warriors, downing two of them with as many shots before Sergeant Reilly knocked down the rifle barrel.

"The lieutenant said to let 'em go! He said to cease-fire!"

For the second time in less than ten minutes, the sergeant found himself looking down the barrel of a gun held by John Howard, except this time it was a Winchester, not a revolver.

"Reilly," said the gunfighter, "you're beginning to try my patience."

In the still that followed, Howard felt the barrel of a .45 Army revolver placed between his shoulder blades and heard the lieutenant's low but angry voice. "Mr. Howard, you've got exactly three seconds to put your rifle down. One, two . . . "

Howard slowly lowered his rifle before speaking. "Lieutenant, perhaps I overestimated you. I thought you might be a man of honor. You gave me your word that this ape wouldn't bother me anymore."

As Campbell lowered his revolver, he replied, "Mr. Howard, I meant it when I said that Sergeant Reilly won't bother you. You must understand that when he grabbed your gun a moment ago, he was only trying to enforce my command."

Howard looked at the officer. He began assembling a cleaning rod to run through the bore of his Remington and said, "But I'm not under your command. I don't answer to you or any other Yankee officer. So the next time you point a gun at me, you had better use it, because if you ever draw down on me again, I'll kill you."

CHAPTER THREE

The lieutenant blinked the sweat out of his eyes and felt his stomach muscles knot up while he thought of a suitable reply. There was no doubt in his mind that the man facing him fully intended to carry out his threat, and there was no doubt as to his speed and accuracy. Campbell had an analytical mind and he began to rapidly sort out the various aspects of the situation that had arisen. It was obvious that Howard was a Southern sympathizer or, more likely, a Confederate veteran. It was equally obvious that he held no respect whatsoever for the Union Army, and the rude and unprofessional behavior of Sergeant Reilly had made the situation worse. The lieutenant decided that had he been in Howard's position, he might have reacted in the same way, especially in the immediate aftermath of a life and death battle.

Campbell kept his tone even when he said, "Mr. Howard, I sincerely hope that we never point guns at each other again. I appreciate what you have done for us, and I believe what you say. Now I'll offer you the same advice you gave me. Don't you ever draw a gun on one of my men again, unless you're prepared to use it. Do we understand each other?"

Howard nodded his head. "Yes." He stopped the motion of the cleaning rod. "Understand this. I'm not looking for trouble, but I won't sidestep it, especially if it involves Yankees trying to push me. Everyone seems to say that the war is over, but that works both ways. If you leave me alone, I'll leave you alone. Besides, we've got enough to think about with those Sioux out there."

"Fair enough," answered the officer. Campbell then turned and faced his men. "How's everyone doing? Was anyone hit?"

Sergeant Reilly answered, "The lads are all okay. We didn't

have a single casualty. Collins got a bullet burn on the side of his neck, but he's cut hisself worse than that shaving." Then he added in a malicious tone, "Seems like the gunslick wasn't so lucky. Looks like his purty spotted horse caught a stray bullet. Reckon he'll just have to walk now. Do him some good. Mebbe it'll knock some of the starch out of him."

"That's enough, Sergeant. See to the men while I talk to Mr. Howard."

He turned and looked at Howard. The gunfighter had stepped over to his dead horse and was kneeling down beside it. Howard noticed that the bullet wound to the head had probably been instantly fatal, because there was very little blood seeping from it. Howard brushed away the flies that had already started collecting themselves around his dead mount, then he gently rubbed the animal's neck. It seemed highly coincidental that his horse was the only one hit during the battle. Howard did not believe in coincidences, and he was sorely tempted to take Reilly to task. The only thing that stopped him was that he had no proof, and he wanted definite proof before he drew on someone, even a despised Yankee soldier.

In the absence of tangible evidence, he could only bear his grief in silence. With his eyes slightly glistening, Howard softly muttered, "Good bye, old friend. I won't forget you."

As Howard wiped his eyes with his left hand, Lieutenant Campbell walked up beside him and said, "I'm sorry about your horse, Mr. Howard. He looked like he was a magnificent beast."

Howard paused before answering, "He was. I'll never own another like him again."

"Perhaps not, but I'll see that you get another suitable mount, compliments of the U.S. Army. It's the least we can do after what you did for us today. It looks like you put down almost as many of the enemy as the rest of us combined. I see now what you meant about breaking their spirit."

Howard glanced at the young officer. "We're not out of trouble yet. Those warriors aren't about to give up just because we killed some of them. You've probably got a long way to go between here and the nearest white settlement. The land around here looks like it's full of gullies and ravines, perfect places for an ambush."

Campbell gave a questioning look. "Do you really think they'll come back after what just happened? We just whipped them soundly."

Howard nodded. "Sure, we won this time. But that doesn't mean they won't be back." In response to the officer's doubting look, Howard added, "I don't know how much experience you've got fighting Indians, but I can assure you of one thing. These Indians aren't likely to quit until all of our scalps are hanging from their lodge poles and lances. We happen to be in the middle of a war, and the first rule of survival is to kill the enemy before he kills you. And it may be even worse than you think. Did you notice the big warrior out front? I think that I know him. If he is who I think he is, he hates the Army more than any other Indian on the plains, and he's also the toughest fighting man I've ever known. He may temporarily disengage, but he'll not give up without a very good reason."

Campbell didn't ask how Howard might be acquainted with a Sioux warrior. Instead he addressed the men. "You heard the man. Stay alert." He then issued an order to the nearest soldier, a sunburned young man who was reloading his gun. "Smith, dismount and ride double with Philips. Mr. Howard, you ride Smith's horse."

Reilly immediately challenged that decision. "Begging the Lieutenant's pardon, you ain't really serious, are you?"

"I am, Sergeant. The discussion is closed."

"But Lieutenant, you ain't expecting Smith to give up his hoss for that gunnie, are you?" persisted Reilly.

"Yes I am, Sergeant. As I said, the discussion is closed, that is, unless you want to give Mr. Howard *your* horse."

The noncommissioned officer turned and walked away, mouthing obscenities under his breath. Trooper Smith handed the reins to Howard without comment.

While Howard put his belongings on the Army mount, Campbell asked him, "What do you think our best options are at this point?"

"I don't care what you do. It's your problem, not mine."

"You're right, Mr. Howard. But I want your advice, and I'd like for you to ride with us." In response to Howard's look of skepticism, he added, "I'd like to think that I've got enough good sense to accept advice from someone who knows more about something than I do. Besides, it's in your best interest to ride with us, at least for a while. I doubt if those Indians out there will spare a white man just because he's not wearing a blue uniform."

Howard liked the officer's humility and directness, so he decided to answer the question. "The Sioux will probably have another go at you. If you leave, you give up the high ground advantage, so for now, you may want to just wait."

"Point taken. However, I've ridden this particular stretch of country before. The Sioux went down that draw to our right, which is in the opposite direction of the stage relay station we're riding to. We should be able to spot them before they get within half a mile. If they come at us again, I'm sure we could make it to that next rise, about two miles to the west. We could make another stand there."

Howard nodded in agreement. "If you do move out, keep your men together in a column of twos. Don't let anyone approach any Indians out there. I heard a couple of your men talking about taking up some souvenirs. That wouldn't be a good idea. We don't know how many of those Indians are actually dead or how many are still capable of putting up a fight."

Reilly walked over to where the two were talking and brusquely interrupted. "He's trying to talk like he's some kinda expert on Injun-fightin' tactics, just 'cause he can shoot some."

"That's enough, Sergeant Reilly," ordered Campbell in a blunt tone. "I asked Mr. Howard for his opinion. I don't recall asking for yours."

Reilly spat out the plug of tobacco he had been chewing. He opened his mouth to reply when the lieutenant spoke again.

"I agree with your assessment, Mr. Howard. Any other suggestions?"

"You should set out for the nearest settlement. If the stage relay station you mentioned is close, go there. Don't let your men get too far apart. Keep someone in the point position. You'll also need flankers on either side, as well as someone constantly watching to the rear. You're right in that you'll probably have a warning before they attack again. They need to attend to their dead and wounded, which will work in your favor. They may also take time to figure out why their medicine was not working today."

The officer nodded. "Our best marksmen should be in the front and rear of the column. That would be you, Mr. Howard and Trooper O'Hara. Will you ride out front?"

"Why do you think I'd be willing to ride point for Yankee soldiers?"

"Because whether you like it or not, we need each other right now. That's one of the reasons I gave you Smith's horse. And you won't be riding alone. I'll ride with you. Now what do you say?"

"I say that we had better get moving."

Campbell mounted his horse and turned to his men. "Nobody goes near those Indians. Brennan, you and Gallagher ride on our left and right flank. Stay within fifty yards of the column. The rest of you ride behind Sergeant Reilly in a column of twos. O'Hara, you ride at the rear and keep looking behind us. Everyone check your weapons and ammunition and be prepared to move out in two minutes. Any questions?"

"Uh, begging the Lieutenant's pardon again, do you think it's a good idea for you to ride ahead with that gunfighter?" asked Sergeant Reilly.

"Yes, Sergeant, it is a good idea for me to ride with Mr. Howard. If I'm ahead of the column, I can best lead the men. And regardless of what you may feel about Mr. Howard, I think that we need the best riflemen at the front and rear of the column. That's why Mr. Howard will be with me in the front, and O'Hara will be at the rear."

The lieutenant then turned his attention to John Howard. "We're about ten miles east of the stage relay station. If we don't run into any more trouble, we should be there by noon."

Howard adjusted the saddle on his temporary mount as he

considered the statement. "I think that we'll be very fortunate if we reach the station without more trouble. Like I said earlier, those Sioux aren't likely to give up. We should expect another attack, even though we have probably bought some time."

"Do you have any other ideas that might help us?" queried the officer.

"No. I think your plan is a good one under the circumstances, and considering their losses, they may think our medicine is stronger than theirs."

"I hope so," said Campbell. Upon further reflection he added, "You know, we do have strong medicine, especially in that big Remington rifle you just put up."

Campbell then nudged his horse forward and turned to the rest of the soldiers. "Stay alert, men, and keep about fifty yards behind us. Let's move out."

The column rode in silence for the next few minutes. The lieutenant noticed that Howard kept scanning some ravines to their right. He also noticed that Howard rode with his right hand on the Remington.

"Mr. Howard," he said, "you displayed the finest shooting that I've ever seen. I'm curious about how you got so good. I'm also curious about your weapons."

"How and where I learned to shoot is not something I'm willing to discuss right now."

"Fair enough. But what about your rifles? It looks like you've got one of the Remington rolling-block rifles and a Winchester. But I've never seen anyone able to shoot them like that. My men are good, in fact probably the best shooters in the Army, but not one of them, except maybe Trooper O'Hara, could have done what you did. And our rifles are not as accurate as yours. Is your Remington a .45-70?"

"No, it's a .44-90."

"I've heard of the .44-90 caliber, but have never seen a rifle chambered for it. I believe it was developed especially for the Remington Creedmoor rifle. Is your rifle a Creedmoor?"

Howard was impressed with the soldier's knowledge of the

rifle. Still, he preferred to answer a question with a question. "What do you know about Creedmoors, Lieutenant?"

"I understand they are specially made rifles that were designed to be used in an international marksmanship competition at Creedmoor, New York. The Creedmoor rifles were designed by Louis L. Hepburn, the foreman of Remington's mechanical shop and a member of the American rifle team."

"You're right. The difference between my rifle and the ones they used at Creedmoor is that mine has an optical sight as well as iron sights. The telescope was made in Germany, and it increases the size of the image you're looking at fourfold. In other words, a man four hundred yards away looks like he's only one hundred yards away. That's why if you know the trajectory of your rifle and can read the wind, it's possible to hit a man at a half-mile."

"After what I saw you do today, I believe that. Although I've heard of the Creedmoor rifles, I thought that they were very rare. How did you acquire one of them?"

Howard ignored that question and changed the subject. "You and your men are also good shooters," he said. "Most of the Yankee soldiers I've seen have very poor hand/eye coordination."

As they spoke, Sergeant Reilly spurred his horse up even with the gunfighter and the officer. He heard the last part of Howard's comment.

Reilly muttered an obscenity and added, "Whadda you mean by that stuff about hand/eye coordination? You saying we ain't no good with our guns? We was good enough to beat you Rebs in the war and them Injuns today."

Howard glanced disdainfully at the non-com. "Sorry, I didn't know we had company. Perhaps I should use terminology that the Corporal, er, Sergeant, can understand."

Howard then explained in very coarse and explicit language that most of the Union soldiers he had encountered couldn't hit the rear end of a bull ten feet away. He also was none too charitable in his description of Reilly's ancestry, making graphic reference to the sergeant's heritage being of the canine variety.

Reilly considered lunging his horse toward Howard, but

thought better of it when he recalled the earlier events of the day. In Reilly's mind it was not a good day to die, and he knew his brute strength was no match for Howard's guns. Still and all, he was unwilling to let an insult pass, so he tried to get in the last word. "Someday I'll make you eat them words, Reb. Nobody calls me that and gets away with it."

Howard smiled, but there was nothing friendly about it. "Anytime you think you can make me do anything, you have at it. On second thought, though, I may have been too harsh describing your ancestry."

"You trying to apologize, Reb?" asked Reilly in a suspicious tone.

"Yes, but not to you. Instead, I should probably apologize to dogs everywhere. I like dogs. Most are better people than some men are. I don't know of any self-respecting dog that would claim you for a son."

Reilly's face turned sanguine as he fought to control himself. His attempt to frame a suitable retort was interrupted by his commanding officer.

"Sergeant, don't say anything else. You asked for an explanation, and Mr. Howard gave you one. Now, do you need something?"

"Naw, I was just wanting to be sure that you was okay."

"I'm fine, Sergeant. Now return to your position and stay there unless I tell you to do otherwise."

After Reilly turned his horse Campbell continued, "Mr. Howard, I would consider it a favor if you would limit your conversation with Sergeant Reilly. As you said, we've got enough to worry about with those Sioux out there." He smiled, almost unnoticeably. "By the way, I like dogs myself." To avoid further discussion on that subject, he added, "You acknowledged that my men are good shooters. Would you like me to tell you why they are?"

"Yes, as a matter of fact."

"I believe in discipline and constant training. The Army doesn't allow practice ammunition, but I know that to be proficient at anything you have to practice. So I acquired extra ammunition so that my men could shoot. Each man fires at least one hundred rounds a week when we're not in the field. We may not have a flamboyant reputation like some of the regiments, such as the Seventh, but I'll put these troopers, even Reilly, up against the best soldiers anywhere in a fight. You saw yourself how they handle themselves."

Howard nodded his head in reluctant agreement. "They can fight, that's true."

The officer continued, "You also see that I wasn't far off saying that they're equal to five or six adversaries in a fight, at least on open terrain with a high ground advantage. But it's ironic that any of us are alive right now."

"It's not ironic, Lieutenant," said a puzzled Howard. "You said it yourself, it's because of good discipline and good shooting."

"No, Mr. Howard, you don't understand. I'm not referring to our fight with the Sioux today. I suppose you heard what happened to the Seventh Cavalry at the Little Bighorn this summer."

Howard nodded. He refrained from smiling, although the news of Custer's death had elated him when he first heard about it the previous summer. Months later, it still brought him a perverse sort of pleasure to visualize Custer dead. Howard also enjoyed remembering that the regiment that was the pride of the Union Army had been defeated and humiliated by an enemy it despised.

The lieutenant continued, "I said it's ironic because part of our regiment was supposed to be with Custer at the Little Bighorn."

"How was it that you avoided it?" asked Howard.

"Well," replied the Lieutenant, "I don't feel comfortable speaking ill of the dead, but the fact is that Lieutenant Colonel Custer refused to have the Second go with him. That was a huge mistake, but Colonel Custer was an arrogant officer who often boasted that his regiment, the Seventh, could whip all of the Indians in the northwest by itself. Perhaps things would've been different if he had let us go with him, and if he had taken a Gatling gun."

Before replying, Howard made a mental note that Campbell referred to Custer by his actual rank, rather than the brevet rank of "General" that had been given to him during the Civil War. Then he said, "I don't know. From what I've heard, there were simply too many Indians. Besides, the world is better off with that murdering bastard dead. Someone should have killed him long ago."

The sheer bitterness and intensity of Howard's last statement caused the officer to study him closely for several long seconds before he asked, "I don't suppose you would care to elaborate as to why you think Custer was a murderer, would you?"

"You're right. I wouldn't. But just ask yourself what you would have done if had you been in the Indians' place and your home was attacked and your loved ones killed so that the government could steal your land. Consider also that the U.S. government has never honored any treaty it made with the Sioux, or any other Indian nation, for that matter."

When the soldier failed to reply, Howard continued, "I notice that you didn't respond, Lieutenant. Is it possible that you actually agree with my last statement?"

"Mr. Howard, I don't make Indian policy. I'm just a soldier. I enforce policy. I can tell you, though, that whether you and I agree with it or not, the Sioux's way of life is finished. America is going to keep expanding. There are many people who honestly believe in the principle of 'Manifest Destiny;' that it is God's will that we bring civilization from the eastern seaboard all the way to the Pacific Ocean." Lieutenant Campbell then added, "But between us, if I were a Sioux Indian, I'd fight to the last drop of my blood to protect my family and preserve my way of life, even if I knew it was a lost cause."

"Then you would be branded a 'hostile', Lieutenant, and would be hunted down like a dog by the U.S. Army," replied Howard.

After that, they continued their ride in silence. When Howard periodically turned around, he noticed that all of the troopers, including Reilly, rode with an air of alertness and caution. Furthermore, he thought that although the Indians probably would attack again, they would be reluctant to try another frontal assault because of the results of the earlier battle. That meant that they might try an ambush, or perhaps some long-range sniping. His thoughts were proven correct by the sudden crash of two shots fired from behind.

He and Lieutenant Campbell wheeled their horses around and saw a young redheaded trooper at the rear of the column reloading his Springfield rifle. Looking out to the northwest, they saw a riderless pony at the edge of a small ravine they had just passed.

"Sergeant, what happened?" shouted Campbell.

"O'Hara spotted the Injun that was on that pony when he come out of a gully to try a shot. The Injun missed. O'Hara didn't."

Within a few seconds the officer and gunfighter had rejoined the column, so that it was no longer necessary to shout. Campbell then addressed the soldier who made the shot. "Very nice shooting, Trooper O'Hara," he said. "That was at least two hundred yards."

"Closer to two hundred-fifty," observed Howard.

Reilly glared at the gunman. "Always think you know more'n the Army, don't you? Well, you ain't nuthin' special. You ain't nuthin' more'n a saddle tramp who can shoot a little. If you didn't have them fancy guns, I expect you wouldn't dare to back talk an officer. I think that once we get to civilization, you'll have to take off them guns sometime. When you do, we'll see if you can fight with your hands. If you try to, I'll whup you like a dog."

Howard ignored the sergeant, and instead addressed Campbell, "If you want him to stay healthy, keep him away from me."

CHAPTER FOUR

"Lieutenant, come quick!" yelled the trooper who was standing sentry duty in front of the relay station.

The small band of soldiers had just arrived at the newly-built stage relay station, and the sentry had only been on duty for a couple of minutes. Remarkably, the trip had been made without further incident after Private O'Hara killed the single Indian sniper. The first thing Lieutenant Campbell had done upon arrival was to post sentries and assign men to attend to the horses. Noticing the Concord stagecoach that was standing by the front of the building, Campbell and Howard then went inside the building to check on the passengers.

The officer and gunfighter had just entered the room when they heard the sentry's call. Lieutenant Campbell sprinted to the door with John Howard on his heels. The other occupants of the building, both civilian and military, also followed.

Running outside, everyone looked in the direction where the sentry was pointing. In the distance they saw the Sioux. Apparently the band who had attacked the soldiers earlier had taken on reinforcements, because there now appeared to be about three hundred warriors facing them.

Two of the Indians separated themselves from the rest and approached the station. One of them towered head and shoulders above the other. In his right hand he held a rifle with a piece of white cloth tied to the end of the barrel.

"You reckon they want to talk, Lieutenant?" asked one of the troopers.

"It seems so," said Campbell. "And it's better to talk than to fight. There are too many of them, even more than before, and now we have the civilians to protect." He quickly issued an order. "You civilians stay inside. Troopers, look alive and keep your rifles trained on those Indians. But nobody, and I mean nobody, fires unless I say so. Is that clear, Sergeant?"

Before Reilly could answer, the two Sioux halted and slid down from their ponies at fifty yards in front of the building. Once their feet hit the ground, the unbelievable height and overall size of the larger one was even more pronounced. He appeared to be about seven feet tall and had no fat on his massive frame.

One of the soldiers said in an awed voice, "I ain't never seen no Injun as big as that feller."

Another replied, "I ain't never seen nothin' that big, except maybe a grizzly bear."

Then Howard whispered, "Lieutenant, remember what I told you earlier about knowing one of those Indians? You're going to find this hard to believe, but now I'm positive I know that big warrior. Do you want me to go with you to talk with him?"

In an astonished voice Campbell answered, "Sure thing, Mr. Howard. Let's go." He added, "By the way, it is hard to believe that you know him. Is he a friend of yours?"

"He was, many years ago. I hope he still is."

Walking slowly toward the Indians, Howard raised his right hand. "Touch the Clouds, it has been a long time. How is my brother?"

At the mention of the name, all of the white people within earshot stiffened. Touch the Clouds was a war chief of the Sioux whose reputation for ferocity in battle was equaled only by his undying hatred of the whites. He was a close friend and trusted ally of Crazy Horse, and it was said that he had played a major role in both the Battle of the Rosebud and the Battle of the Little Bighorn. In short, the huge Indian was one man who lived up to his reputation, and as an implacable foe of the bluecoats, he was without equal.

But even as the whites stood aghast at the sound of his name, a look of incredulity slowly spread over the normally impassive features of the giant warrior. It was several seconds before he spoke in surprisingly good English.

"Wambli-ska, it is your voice. Can the man standing before me be my brother, John Ho-ward?"

Howard was relieved that Touch the Clouds recognized his voice. He was also glad that he had given his correct name to Lieutenant Campbell. "It is, Touch the Clouds. I was but a child when we last rode together. I am now a man. My look has changed, but yours has not."

"John Ho-ward, you never were a child, not even as a boy," replied the Sioux.

"It has been nine summers," said Howard. "We have much to talk about."

"Truly," acknowledged the Indian. Then he continued, "We came with the white flag because of the medicine gun. Some said that it was you, or your spirit. Others believed it could not be so. Still, no white eyes or Lakota could ever shoot like you. And some said that your spotted horse was seen."

"My horse will be seen no more," said Howard sadly. "He was killed in the fight. Woe be to the one who killed him."

"I am sorry, John Ho-ward. But, now tell me, why do you ride with the bluecoats against the Lakota? Do you not still hate the bluecoats as much as I do?"

"I do not ride with them by choice. The Lakota attacked while I was with the bluecoats. I had to fight or die. And know that I have an enemy among these. Do you see that one, the large one with gray in his hair and hatred in his eyes?" as he motioned back at the relay station toward Reilly. "He would kill me if he could. He wishes to fight me."

"Then he is a fool, or does not know the medicine you have," replied Touch the Clouds with a disdainful gesture. "Does he not wish to live?"

"All people wish to live, my brother. Even the warriors who rode against me this day wish to live. Many have died. The rest may live if they do not attack us again."

The Indian's face changed ever so slightly at that last remark.

Anyone watching who knew him would realize that the expression he now held was as close to a smile as the bitter red man could manage. Then he spoke. "But I have many warriors and you are but a few. How is it then that the Lakota will die and not the bluecoats and other white eyes?"

"You may have had many warriors when you began attacking us, but you did not have nearly so many after the fight. And it is a true thing that should you attack again, you will lose even more. You know that I have strong medicine in my guns. These bluecoats have medicine almost as strong, for how else could they have rubbed out so many of the Lakota when not even one of them has been hurt?"

"John Ho-ward," replied that giant Sioux, "it is true that many warriors have been rubbed out this day. But know that others have joined us. I have three hundred warriors now."

"Ah," thought Howard, "That additional hundred or so must be the war party that the blue bellies were following when they first ran into me. The two hundred Lakota that we fought this morning were the unknown factor. No wonder Campbell said they were trailing about one hundred Indians."

Touch the Clouds spoke again, with curiosity in his voice. "They are your friends? The bluecoats are friends of my brother, Wambli-ska?"

"Perhaps some of them may be. I do not know yet. Do you see this one beside me? He is their chief. Even though he is a bluecoat, his heart is big and his tongue is straight. He speaks for these others."

Touch the Clouds looked at Lieutenant Campbell. "You must be a good soldier chief, or my brother would not say so. You are a worthy enemy."

Lieutenant Campbell saluted. Then he spoke. "I am Lieutenant Campbell. I have never met you, Touch the Clouds," he said, "but I know of your deeds, as do all the white soldiers. Now you know something of my deeds. We can fight again, but if we do, it will be as John Howard has said, and many more warriors will die. But it does not need to be so. We simply want safe passage for the stagecoach and ourselves. But know this. You may have beat Long Hair, but you will not beat me, even with three hundred warriors, for my medicine and that of John Howard is too strong."

Several moments of silence followed. Then Touch the Clouds spoke, never wavering his gaze from the officer. "Maybe so and maybe not. But it is a good thing to be able to speak without fear in your voice when facing death."

Then to Howard, the giant Sioux said, "Maybe Wakan Tankan has favored the wasichus because the Lakota warrior Wambli-ska rides with them. It is no good to fight against your own people."

Howard said, "Truly, my brother. And it would not be a good thing to keep fighting today. Why should more die? Even if you are able to rub out these pony soldiers and other white eyes, many more of the Lakota will die. And know that more bluecoats will follow. Remember the fight at the Greasy Grass? You killed Long Hair, and that was a good thing, but still it did not stop the rest of the bluecoats. And now, even more wasichus continue to invade the Lakota's land."

Touch the Clouds stood silent for several moments before saying, "We have lost many warriors this day, and the snows are coming. Maybe it is time now to ride north, John Ho-ward, to the land of the Red Coats, where most of our people have already gone. Or we may stay in our own country and still fight. You are a wasichu, but are still a member of the Lakota nation and my blood brother. Your tongue is straight. What do you say?"

As the giant Indian asked the question, the other whites looked on in wonderment at Howard. Who was this drifter, that a Sioux war chief like Touch the Clouds would ask him for advice?

As for Howard, he considered the question for several seconds before answering, "If I were my brother, I would ride north for now. There are too many bluecoats and other white eyes in the Lakota's country. And what about your women, children and old ones? Who will watch over them if many more warriors die? And more will die. You have seen that these bluecoats fight like no others."

Touch the Clouds replied, "Tatanka Iyotake has already led many of our people north. If there were only Lakota warriors, we would fight to the last man to keep our country. But you speak the truth when you say that we have many women, young ones, and old ones who need to live."

Howard nodded. "My brother still thinks of his people before himself. You do need to care for those who cannot take care of themselves. And know this. The white eyes will never stop coming. Truly, they are wasichus."

The giant Indian looked at the gunfighter. "So be it. We will fight no more with the pony soldiers who ride today with my brother. We go now to join Tatanka Iyotake. Do you ride with us, Wambli-ska?"

"I thank my brother for the offer. But this day I have killed many Lakota warriors. They made war on me first, but still, I cannot ride with you."

"So be it."

Suddenly, the other Indian, who had been silent up until then, spoke quickly to Touch the Clouds in his native language. Howard could not understand most of the words, but caught the gist of the conversation as the Indian motioned with his chin at the relay station.

Touch the Clouds then spoke again. "Crow Killer wants to trade for the woman."

"What woman?" asked Howard.

"The pretty one who has dark hair and wears a red dress. Will you trade for her?"

Before answering, Howard stole a glance at the officer beside him who stood with a look of blank astonishment on his face. He then looked back and saw that several of the stagecoach passengers had gathered outside by the front door of the building. Two were strikingly beautiful young women who looked like sisters. One wore a red dress. He also noticed that the occupants of the relay station had started talking excitedly among themselves in low, agitated voices.

"The soldier chief and I must speak of this in private," said Howard.

As Howard and Campbell turned and walked a few paces

toward the building, Howard whispered, "Apparently this particular situation was never covered at the Point, but I've got an idea that just might work. Do you want me to try it?"

"Whatever you think, Mr. Howard. I hope you can continue to talk as well as you fought this morning."

They turned and walked back to the waiting Indians.

With a gleam in his eyes and sidewards shaking of his head, Howard said in a slightly raised voice, "Crow Killer does not really want the dark-haired girl or her sister."

"He does," contradicted Touch the Clouds. "He said she will bring him many children and do much work."

"Ah, but her tongue is sharp like a sword or a skinning knife. And her temper is as red as her dress. She may be pleasant to look at, but within three days Crow Killer would be driven crazy. Why, he would probably seek refuge among the bluecoats. And her sister, well, her sister is even worse."

With a gleam in his own eyes, Touch the Clouds repeated in Sioux what Howard had said.

The smaller Indian smiled slightly and said something back to his huge companion.

Then Touch the Clouds said to Howard, "Crow Killer asks how do you know this thing. Is she or the other pretty one your woman?"

"They are not," said Howard. "But if they were, I would either have to beat them daily or go crazy myself and join the bluecoats or the thieving Pawnee, for surely the Lakota would not allow any warrior to live among them with such a one for a squaw."

Touch the Clouds made his decision. "The woman stays with the white eyes." He turned on his heel and started walking back to his horse.

Hesitating, he took the reins and looked back toward Howard. "Your spotted horse is dead. It was the same one you had when we last rode together?"

"It was," said Howard. "He was getting old. Even so, he was still strong like the bear and swift like the wind. The Nez Perce probably still regret losing him to the giant Lakota warrior and his small white brother. We counted much coup when we stole him."

"Truly," said Touch the Clouds. The Sioux leader paused when he started to mount, as if he were making another decision. Then he turned and led his own war horse to Howard. He handed Howard the reins, saying, "John Ho-ward, you will take my horse. I have only had him a short time, but already he is my favorite. He is swift and yet strong enough to carry me all day. He will serve you well."

Howard looked intently at the horse. It was a big sorrel gelding, with a deep chest and long legs. Its most interesting feature, however, was that it had horse shoes and a "U.S." brand on its flank.

"It is a fine gift, my brother. Tell me," he added with an ironic tone, "How long has it been that the Lakota have been shoeing and branding their horses?"

"Only as long as the bluecoats have been losing their horses," responded the Lakota slyly. "Perhaps it is as the white chiefs say, and the bluecoats are our friends. Yes, truly. For why else would they leave us gifts, such as their horses and their hair, when they attack our villages and kill our women and children?"

Howard smiled broadly, in contrast to Lieutenant Campbell, who maintained a neutral expression. Howard wasn't sure, but he thought he heard the click of a rifle being cocked at the relay station.

Remembering his Lakota protocol, Howard offered a gift in return, asking, "What may I give my brother for the horse, since you no longer want the girl?"

The huge warrior proudly raised his rifle that had the white cloth attached to it. The rifle was an 1866 Winchester with a brass frame, identical to the Winchester that Howard carried. "John Ho-ward, you see that I still carry the 'Yellow Boy' you gave me nine summers ago. Now I would like one of your pistols, if it would have the same medicine in my hands that it does in yours."

"Let us see," said Howard. He looked around on the ground, and spotted a rock about the size of a man's fist. He picked up the rock and threw it to the side about fifteen feet away. Then, as quick as a thought, he drew his .44 and shot underneath the stone, causing it to hurtle into the air. Just as the rock reached the apex of its ascent, he fired a second shot that disintegrated it into dozens of tiny fragments. It was a show-off stunt without a doubt, but one with a serious purpose.

Reversing the revolver so that he now held the barrel, John extended the .44 to Touch the Clouds and asked, "Does my brother think the magic in my pistol would work like that for him?"

Touch the Clouds stared at the firearm and almost imperceptibly shook his head from side to side. He grasped the grip of the revolver and continued to look at it. He then reversed the revolver and handed it back to Howard, grip first. When he did, Howard slid the Smith and Wesson back into its holster, securing it with the thong.

Then Touch the Clouds shifted his gaze to Lieutenant Campbell's sword and said, "When we rode at the Greasy Grass against Long Hair, his men did not carry their long knives. Why they did not, I do not know. But I think it would be big medicine to have a long knife such as the young soldier chief wears. I think the medicine in the long knife would work for me."

"We will speak of this among ourselves," said Howard.

The soldier and the gunfighter once again walked a few feet toward the relay station before Howard whispered to Lieutenant Campbell, "If I were you, I would give him the sword. In his mind it will be an even trade between warrior leaders and he and his men will ride away. If not, it will be a grave insult and the festivities of this morning may be repeated. What do you think?"

"I think that big Indian has just acquired himself an Army officer's saber."

Then the young officer turned and walked back toward the waiting Indians. He unbuckled his sword and offered it across his open palms toward Touch the Clouds.

"Use this only against the Pawnee or Crow. Do not use this against any white soldier or white civilian," said Campbell, "for if you do, I believe that the spirit that dwells inside it will surely slay one Lakota every time you kill a white man."

Grasping the sword with his right hand, Touch the Clouds

handed his rifle to Crow Killer. Then he vaulted onto the other pony from the right side. Crow Killer hopped up behind him.

The giant warrior transferred the sword to his left hand. Raising his right hand, palm outward, he said, "Now we ride, John Howard, to the land of the Grandmother and the Red Coats. There we join Tatanka Iyotake. I think this is the last time we will meet. Ride with care, my brother."

CHAPTER FIVE

As the Sioux rode away, Lieutenant Campbell raised his right hand to his forehead and with an unconscious gesture wiped the sweat away from under his hat brim. Howard also wiped the sweat from under his own hat.

Then Campbell remarked, "I'm glad that's over. Do you think the Sioux will do what Touch the Clouds said?"

"Touch the Clouds never lies," answered Howard. "If he says he's riding to Canada to join up with Tatanka Iyotake, you can bet your life he is going to do just that."

"Ah, so you believe in the notion of the 'noble red man' that James Fenimore Cooper wrote about?"

Howard patted the neck of his new horse as he considered the question. "Lieutenant, Cooper wrote fiction. But the fact is that Indians are just like whites. Some are good, and some are bad. Touch the Clouds is one of the good ones. And as far as the other Indians doing what he says, there's no one in the whole Lakota nation, including even Crazy Horse himself, who would openly defy Touch the Clouds. He's one of their greatest warrior leaders. If there were many more like him, the Union Army would never dare to rape another Indian woman or murder any more Indian children and old ones."

Ignoring the last part of the gunfighter's statement, Lieutenant Campbell replied, "I hope he's telling the truth, because we are betting our lives, quite literally, that he will do what he says. But I believe I'll have my men follow him for a few miles, at a safe distance, just to see what he does."

The officer and the gunfighter turned and walked back together toward the building, when Campbell continued speaking. "It seems you've done the Army another favor by keeping my command out of a battle with very bad odds, even worse than what we faced earlier today. You've also done the Army a great service by persuading Touch the Clouds to go to Canada with a sizable number of warriors."

"I didn't persuade him to do anything. I merely gave him my opinion when he asked for it."

"Nevertheless, I'm indebted to you," insisted Campbell. "I'll see that my superiors know about this and your role in the battle this morning. I'm going to recommend you for a civilian commendation."

Howard didn't bother replying. It was apparent to Campbell, however, that Howard wasn't overly impressed with the idea of a commendation from the United States Army.

Just before reaching the front of the relay building, Campbell spoke again. "By the way, what was the name he called you, if you don't mind my asking?"

"He called me 'Wambli-ska'. It means 'White Eagle.' A long time ago Touch the Clouds said I had to have the spirit of the eagle in me to shoot like I do, and to see the enemy so clearly in battle."

"An appropriate name. And what does 'wasichu' mean?"

"It means 'you can't get rid of them.' That's a name the Sioux use to describe all white eyes, good and bad."

"And who is Tatanka Whatever-his-name-is?"

"Sitting Bull."

"One more question. You told Touch the Clouds that you hadn't seen him in nine years. Do you mind telling me how you knew him?"

"Yes, I would mind. It's none of your affair. Just be glad he remembered me."

Stepping inside the compound of the relay station, the soldier and the gunfighter noticed that the inhabitants inside, both civilian and military, wore expressions of wonder mixed with relief. One of the passengers, a solid-looking, gray-haired man dressed in the black garb of the clergy, spoke up.

"That was very well done, gentlemen. I couldn't hear everything you said, but obviously the good Lord gave you exactly the right words to say. I think we probably owe our lives to you."

The other passengers echoed the words of the minister. All of them, that is, except the young woman who Touch the Clouds' companion had wanted for a wife. John Howard noticed that her lovely face was now drawn into hard lines. The other young girl simply looked at him with quiet admiration, and perhaps something else.

Then the girl in the red dress spoke. It was obvious that she was trying to control herself, but without much success. Her words were released in an angry outburst, pouring out of her mouth like white water cascading over a waterfall. "How dare you say those things about me? Who gave you the right to insult me like that? You don't even know me! I don't know who you think you are, mister, but you're obviously no gentleman. I normally try to reserve judgment, but I think I have to agree with what that big sergeant said about you. You're just a rude and boastful gunman." Turning to the minister she added, "Papa, are you going to let him get away with that?"

Howard was taken aback by the suddenness and ferocity of her verbal attack. The man who was normally never at a loss for words now involuntarily blushed and stammered out, "Uh, I'm sorry, Ma'am . . . um . . . it wasn't what you heard . . . uh, I mean . . . that is, I didn't mean what you thought I meant. I intended no offense."

"Uh, I'm sorry, Ma'am . . . um . . . it wasn't what you heard," she repeated mockingly. "Is the silver-tongued gunslinger actually at a loss for words? You certainly didn't seem to be when you said those hateful things about me and my sister. Do you think you can say anything you want because you're a gunfighter and killer? Oh yes, I heard what those soldiers have been saying about you, and I saw how you just had to show everyone how fast and straight you can shoot. Well, I'm not impressed, and I for one am not the least bit afraid of you. Besides, I know something about western behavior, and even a cold-hearted gunman like you wouldn't dare harm a woman. If you did, the soldiers would shoot you down. And anyway, if you tried anything, my papa would take those big guns from you and spank you like a child!"

Still off-balance, Howard could only stare in numbed silence in the face of this beautiful girl's onslaught. He was clearly chagrined and uneasy.

Before Howard could attempt to frame any type of response, the minister spoke up. "Just a minute, Rosa," he said, "I think you've got it all wrong. This young man was not trying to insult you or your sister. On the contrary, he was trying to save your life. You see, by saying those things about you that he did, he let the Sioux save face without turning you over to them, and he avoided a fight. I suspect that he knows quite a bit about diplomacy and negotiating. However, I also suspect that his considerable skill does not extend to doing verbal battle with such a lovely member of the gentle sex," he wryly added. "Is that not so, sir?"

Grateful for the unexpected defense and the time that it had bought him, Howard now organized his thoughts to launch a counteroffensive. His initial embarrassment was now giving way to anger. When he spoke, he chose his words with care, for maximum effect. "As your father and I said, ma'am, I intended no offense. The Parson was also right when he said I had to make you seem unattractive to the Sioux. I felt very fortunate to be able to come up with something on the spot that would overshadow your looks. But even so, had Touch the Clouds not been my blood brother, it wouldn't have worked, because the Sioux are like most other men. They would overlook almost any shortcoming to have a girl who looks like you. But you know, maybe I wasn't so far wrong in describing you. You surely do have a temper and your words cut me so sharply that I feel like the Lakota stabbed me with one of their war lances. In fact, now I'm halfway sorry that I didn't trade you to them. I never really did like Crow Killer. It might have served him right to give you to him."

Now it was the girl's turn to blush. A deep shade of crimson spread slowly over her face, while Howard looked on in appreciation.

The other girl still sat quietly. Howard felt the weight of her gaze on him. He admitted to himself that he didn't mind her attention at all.

The moment was broken by the minister clearing his throat before saying, "Touché. I think that about evens things up. Allow me to introduce my daughters and myself. I'm Jeff Hightower, a minister of the Gospel." Motioning to the girl who was staring at Howard he continued, "And this is my daughter Consuela. You've already met my other daughter Rosa."

Then to the lieutenant, Reverend Hightower said, "I heard you and Mr. Howard say that the Sioux are riding north. Do you think that it's safe for us to travel on to Gold Valley?"

"I don't know, Reverend," said Campbell. "I'm learning to trust Mr. Howard's judgement, but I still think it may be a good idea for my men to follow those Indians at a safe distance, just to see what they do. We're lucky that the terrain is fairly flat for the next five or six miles north of here. We can follow them and get back to the stage coach if they should circle around. I think it would be okay for the stage coach to move on to Gold Valley. Do you agree, Mr. Howard?"

"I think so."

The station-keeper nodded his head. "Yep, them Injuns is gonna go to Canady. Never would have believed old Touch the Clouds hisself could be talked into leavin'. I been on this job fer six months, ever since this place was built, and mebbe now I can rest easy at night. Mebbe you sodger boys can foller 'em while the stage goes on to Gold Valley. Y'all that'll be on the coach will only have to worry about them stage robbers that're operating hereabouts. But it ought to be okay, as long as you keep yer eyes peeled. Ought not to have no trouble a'tall, as long as the Parson here protects Howard from Miz Rosa," he concluded with a sly grin.

CHAPTER SIX

The stagecoach had six passengers inside, after being joined by Trooper O'Hara, who was heading to Gold Valley. His tour of enlistment with the Army had ended two weeks earlier. Due to the recent intensified trouble with the Sioux, his departure had been postponed. However, now that Touch the Clouds was riding to Canada, Lieutenant Campbell told O'Hara that he could leave with the stage.

Taking on O'Hara as an extra passenger made it necessary for John Howard to ride up in the box beside the driver. Howard was riding on the coach because he wanted his new horse to have a break from being ridden. His horse trotted at a leisurely gait beside the coach, its reins tied to the passenger door.

The gunman enjoyed the warmth of the sun and the wind in his face as he reflected on all that had happened earlier that day. He thought that it was particularly ironic that he and Yankee soldiers had fought side by side against warriors whose number included some of his own former friends. Howard allowed himself a rare smile when he further considered that one of the staunchest enemies of the white man had given his finest horse to one who had slain many of the Indian's comrades that very day.

He also considered how strange it was that a Yankee officer would offer his hand in friendship to a former Confederate guerrilla, as Campbell did when the stagecoach left the relay station. Before they parted company, the lieutenant told Howard that the troopers would stay awhile at the station before they shadowed the departing Sioux.

Most of the passengers were half asleep, lulled into drowsiness by the constant pounding of hooves. They had been traveling for an hour when Howard's horse suddenly snorted. This warning gave Howard barely enough time to draw his .44 before a bandit stepped out in the middle of the road. He was tall and thin, but beyond that no accurate description could be given of him, because his long duster was coated with grime and dirt, and his face was concealed by a blue bandana.

As the highwayman raised his cap-and-ball Colt revolver, John Howard immediately went into action. He saw no reason to wait for the bandit to start shooting or give orders for the passengers to throw out their valuables and guns. Further, he saw no reason to wait for the robber's associates, if any, to close with the stage. There were times for negotiation, but this was not such a time. Howard quickly aligned the front sight of his Smith and Wesson on the robber's chest. While he cocked and fired he never allowed the front sight to waver. As the shot sounded, the robber simply wilted to the ground with a bullet through his heart.

As the robber fell, the stage lurched to a sudden stop. This allowed Howard to jump from the coach and lay down flat between the wheels. In a low voice he advised everyone to stay inside. A few seconds later two other robbers appeared to his right. Like their fellow thief, both had their features concealed by handkerchiefs. Unlike the dead outlaw, they were armed with long guns, the first with a Spencer rifle, and the second with a muzzle-loading double-barreled shotgun.

The shotgunner let loose a blast at the stagecoach driver from a distance of fifty-five yards. He should have focused his attention on the prone figure beneath the coach, rather than the driver, because triggering the right barrel of his shotgun was the last thing he would ever do.

In the space of the next thirty seconds Howard fired five shots, all with telling effect. Since the range was more than fifty yards, it accounted for the fact that he required two shots to stop the shotgunner and an additional three shots for the rifleman.

Compounding the problem was that after seeing his two comrades fall, the rifleman decided that discretion was indeed the better part of valor. He also decided that he had chosen the wrong profession. Before he turned and ran like a jackrabbit toward the shelter of some nearby boulders, he hesitated to fire a shot at Howard. That was his fatal mistake. Although he was literally running for his life, he unintentionally proved the old adage that a man can't outrun a bullet, or in this particular case, three bullets, especially when the first one hits just behind the right knee. After falling, the wounded robber turned toward the stage and raised his rifle while he levered a fresh cartridge into the chamber. Doing so gave Howard time to carefully fire two more shots, which ensured that this particular outlaw would never commit another robbery or murder.

Howard surveyed the area around him while he broke open his revolver and reloaded all six chambers. He told the stage driver to hand him his Winchester rifle. Even though he was confident in his marksmanship, he knew not to approach the downed highwaymen too soon. He also didn't know if there were more outlaws with the three he had shot.

This gave the other passengers time to digest the events of the past minute. They reacted as many people do in similar situations. An elderly couple simply sat in their seats and looked at the carnage in front of them. Reverend Hightower and ex-Trooper O'Hara had jumped down from the opposite side of the coach. O'Hara held a Springfield rifle. Howard had expected the former soldier to be armed, but noticed that the minister was also armed. The minister held an old .44 Walker Colt revolver as if he knew how to use it. Rosa stared at Howard in horror and disgust.

When she spoke to Howard, it was in the monotone voice of one who still could not comprehend how fast death had come. "You're not just a bully. You're also a cold-blooded killer. You shot down those men like they were animals. As soon as we get to Gold Valley, I'm going to report you to the authorities. I hope you hang!"

Before Howard could frame a reply, the younger girl said, "Rosita, Mr. Howard couldn't have done anything else. Would you rather have had those vile men rob us or do even worse?"

"Oh, you think you know everything Consuela, but I know

you're just taking up for him because you think he's . . . ," began Rosa.

Whatever she thought her sister felt about Howard was never fully expressed because Reverend Hightower spoke up. "I'm afraid I have to agree with Consuela," he said. "Of course, you're entitled to your own opinion, Rosa, as we are to ours. I think the rest of us saw things differently. At least I know that I did. Those men were not the type to respond to reason or kind words. I'm convinced that Mr. Howard saved us once again, just like he did back at the relay station. I'm only sorry that I wasn't able to act fast enough to help him. I hope that you don't intend to swear out a complaint, but if you do, I'm afraid that the rest of us will have to tell what we saw."

Then turning to Howard, he said, "My friend, that was truly remarkable shooting. Have you ever considered serving your country in the military or as an officer of the law?"

"I had a brief military career, Parson. It's not something I would ever return to. Anyway, the last time I served my country, I was just a kid, and I shot soldiers wearing Yankee uniforms. Besides, if Rosa has her way, I'm not likely to have much time to do anything, other than walk up the steps of a gallows. If that happens, maybe you would consider saying a kind word over my cold-blooded murdering corpse, and maybe Consuela would put some flowers on my grave." Softening his tone he finished with, "I'd be pleased to have a clergyman who carries an impressive piece of artillery like that old Colt of yours officiate at my funeral. And it would be a relief to have a pretty girl do something nice for me, instead of criticizing me."

CHAPTER SEVEN

When the stagecoach finally pulled into Gold Valley, the day was almost spent. In the waning rays of the late afternoon sun, Howard noticed that the kerosene street lamps were already being lit. He decided to walk his horse to the livery for a rub-down and a bag of oats. He looked behind and waved to the preacher, who was helping the elderly couple down from the stage.

Reverend Hightower called after him, "John, after you get your horse settled, join us for supper."

"Thanks. I'll be at the hotel diner in a few minutes. I hope my presence doesn't spoil your oldest daughter's appetite."

A crowd of curious townspeople congregated around the stagecoach, looking at the bodies of the dead highwaymen. The driver, normally a quiet man, stepped out of character on this occasion to tell everyone within earshot how the man walking down the street to the livery had dispatched the robbers with unbelievable shooting.

"Of course," explained the driver, "he put on a shooting exhibition at the relay station that Wild Bill himself couldn't have outdone on his best day. And that ain't all. No sir, not by a long shot. He talked old Touch the Clouds himself and a heap of Sioux into not hanging around this neck of the woods. Them Sioux is gonna ride north to Canada."

The stagecoach driver was known by all present to be a solid individual not given to exaggeration. Therefore, this bit of information started all the old ladies present, both female and male, to speculate on the identity of this gunfighter.

A couple of minutes later, while Howard talked with the liveryman about his horse, the rest of the passengers walked toward the hotel. Reverend Hightower and former cavalryman O'Hara entered the hotel ahead of the other passengers, as they were carrying most of the older couple's luggage, as well as their own. No one seemed to notice that the minister handled the heavy bags as if they were weightless.

The passengers' movements were watched by a group of miners who were lounging on the steps of one of the town's numerous saloons. One of the miners, a bearded giant who stood almost as tall as Touch the Clouds, sauntered into the street directly in front of the passengers. Standing with his feet spread and his hands on his hips, he leered at Rosa and her younger sister Consuela.

"Howdy, you purty thangs. Come on in and let me buy you a drink."

Both young women ignored the comment and tried to walk around the giant miner. They had endured enough discomfort for one day and had no intention of replying to the vulgar man.

The scenario was being watched by several people on the street. One of the onlookers apparently anticipated trouble, because he had sprinted down the street to the town marshal's office as soon as the huge miner stepped into the street. Nevertheless, no one present said anything until the miner grabbed Rosa by her arm.

"Hey darlin', maybe you didn't hear me. I said I's gonna buy you a drink. But iff'n you don't want one, why that's okay with me. Let's just walk on down this here alley an' I'll show you both what a real man is like. An' since you think you're too good to talk to me, after I get done with you, I might just let some of my pards get in on the fun too."

Just then, two of the miners disengaged from the crowd and stepped forward. One spoke up. "C'mon now, Bull. These little gals don' want no trouble. Let's go back in an' I'll buy you a drink. They's saloon gals in there that'll drink with us."

"Meagher, my lad, stay out of the way. Nobody refuses to drink with Bull Jackson. Ain't you smart enough to know . . . "

The sound of a shotgun being cocked caused Jackson to stop in mid-sentence. He released Rosa's arm and turned toward the man holding the gun.

"Well howdy, Marshal Bates. Hey now, ain't no need to get all riled up. I didn't mean nothin'. Now you just put that scattergun down afore it goes off an' somebody gets hisself hurt."

The town marshal was an average-looking fellow named Frederick Bates. He was in need of a shave and was dressed in an ill-fitted business suit. He was also ill-fitted for his position and was clearly out of his element. He visibly hesitated before he replied. It required no great powers of observation to determine that he was very much afraid of Jackson, since he was unable to control his trembling hands, in spite of his best efforts.

This caused one of the saloon bums on the wooden sidewalk to shout, "Better watch it, Bull. He's got the shakes so bad, he's liable to blow a hole in you big enough to drive that coach through!"

Jackson's other companions began laughing as the lawman finally found his voice. "J . . . Just back off now, B . . . B . . . Bull. You leave those l . . . ladies alone."

"Why shore thing, Mr. Marshal. I done tole you already I was jest funnin'. Now you quit pointing that thing at me an' we'll talk about this, okay?" said Jackson in a patronizing tone.

The marshal lowered the shotgun at Jackson's request, relieved that the situation was apparently now well in hand. Had he been more experienced, he would not have relaxed so soon, nor would he have allowed the miner to walk up within arm's reach. Furthermore, he would have realized that rather than the situation being under control, things were about to get worse. In fact, if he had any idea of what was about to happen next, he would have let loose with both barrels in the miner's belly.

As it was, he only started to realize he had made an error, perhaps a fatal one, when Jackson abruptly lunged forward and ripped the gun from his grasp. In a follow-up motion, Jackson struck the lawman's head with the gun so hard that the butt-stock shattered, and a load of buckshot discharged in the air. Bates fell down flat on his face, with the right side of his skull caved in. He made only a slight gurgling sound as the life drained from him.

Wasting no time over his victim, Jackson faced the stunned

crowd. "Y'all seen it. It was self-defense. He come at me with that scattergun. I didn't have no choice, right?"

He then dropped the shotgun and started again toward Rosa and Consuela, who stood in horrified disbelief at seeing yet another man killed in front of them in one day. The difference was that this was a clear case of cold-blooded murder.

Jackson halted when a new voice cut through the street. "*Leave my girls alone, or you'll face the wrath of Almighty God!*"

Everyone turned to see Reverend Hightower standing in the door of the hotel. He was holding his huge .44 Walker Colt in his right hand. People later remarked that he held the weapon as steady as any gunfighter. And unlike the recently deceased Marshal Bates, the minister showed no signs of fear or hesitation.

"Now see here, preacher-man," said Jackson. "Whadda you mean I'll face God's wrath? I don't believe in no God. Besides that . . . "

"Shut up and listen! You just murdered a man in cold blood. You also insulted and threatened to assault my daughters. You're not fit to live. So if you try to touch those girls again, I'll kill you. Then you will meet God, whether you believe in Him or not, and you won't like what He will say to you."

Then to the people on the street Hightower said, "I'm making a citizen's arrest. A couple of you men tend to the marshal. Somebody else go get another deputy while I hold this man."

"Uh, we ain't got no other lawman, Parson," said one of the onlookers. "Anybody seen Ben Duff?"

"That gunslick's out with that fat banker he babysits," replied another. "The marshal's the only badge-toter we got, and he ain't movin'!"

"Then someone show me where the jail is," said Hightower.

Jackson stood unmoving. "I ain't going nowhere, you stupid old fool, 'cause you ain't got the sand to pull that trigger. And if you don't pull it, I'm fixing to give you the same thing I gave that town clown."

"Move along," said the preacher.

Jackson ripped out a vicious oath. He paused for breath and

followed up with, "You're just like all them other Bible-thumpers. A bunch of weak-kneed lying hypocrites, full of hot air and no guts."

"Move along," repeated the preacher, unfazed by the bully's insults.

"Hell with you," replied Jackson.

"What did you say?"

"I said you can go straight to hell!"

At Jackson's last words, a change came over the minister's face. It was more than anger, and even more than simple rage. To John Howard, who had pushed his way through the gathering crowd, it looked as if the preacher was struggling internally to control his own rising fury. The minister's better nature appeared to be losing. At that moment, even as fast as he was, Howard was glad that he was not facing Hightower. The older man had a look of certain death about him. Howard wondered if Jackson understood the danger in the man he was facing.

Never taking his eyes off Jackson, Hightower softly uttered a prayer that not even those standing near him heard. "Dear Lord, I know that I shouldn't kill anyone else. Help me to not kill this man, even though he deserves it, and I dearly want to."

For several seconds no one said anything. Then the minister said something else under his breath that no one heard but an astonished John Howard. "I'm going to have to be satisfied with thrashing him." Then, in a louder voice, the preacher said, "John, please make sure that my girls are okay and that none of his friends interfere."

"Whatever you say, Parson," replied Howard. "But are you sure you want to do this?"

"Not exactly. What I really want to do is shoot him. But I'll settle for beating him into the dirt, unless he's afraid to fight me."

Now it was Jackson's turn to be astonished. "You mean you want to fight me? You're plumb crazy, preacher! Hey now, I got it! You want me to come at you so that your gunslick buddy there can shoot me. Well, it ain't gonna work. I ain't gonna whup you. Not with him standin' there."

Hightower handed his Colt to Howard, who accepted it with his left hand and drew his own Smith and Wesson with his right hand. None of Jackson's friends moved. Apparently the stage driver's report of Howard's skill with his guns had been taken seriously.

The pastor then addressed Jackson. "Don't worry about what John might do to you. Worry about what I'm definitely going to do. After I finish with you, you'll think twice before you ever try to harm another living soul."

Jackson finally understood that the clergyman truly intended to fight him. He was supremely confident. He was a foot taller and almost ninety pounds heavier than his opponent, and was also half the minister's age. What was more important, Jackson was reputed to be the best hand-to-hand fighter in the entire territory. In dozens of places, from river boats to mining camps, he had fought too many fights to remember, and had never been beaten. None of his fights had lasted more than a minute or so, except one. Two of his former opponents were dead and five more were crippled. The only person who had ever given the Bull almost as good as he got was Sergeant Donald Reilly of the Second Cavalry. That fight had lasted almost ten minutes in the Yellow Knife Saloon and had ended only after Lieutenant Campbell had walked inside the bar, pulled a revolver, and threatened Reilly with a court-martial if he didn't stop.

At the moment, however, Jackson was a little confused and unsure about his present situation, because the man before him was unlike anyone he had ever encountered. Even though Jackson was totally depraved and profane, he had still been taught as a child to respect a man of the cloth. At the same time, he also had an image of the clergy indelibly imprinted in his mind, that of them being weak and cowardly. But something was wrong, because although his opponent wore clerical garb, there was nothing weak or cowardly about him. In fact, for some reason unknown to him, Jackson suddenly remembered a trip he took to the circus in St. Louis years before. The clergyman standing before him reminded him of the caged African lion that was the star attraction of the show.

"Yeah, that's it," thought Jackson, "a lion."

"Well, are you going to fight me or just stand there fouling the air with your stench?" asked the minister. His voice was cold with contempt. "You've proven yourself to be a bully and a murderer. You accused me of trying to trick you into attacking me so that John could shoot you. That shows that you're also a fool. Are you also a coward? Aren't you man enough to face someone who's not afraid of you?"

Jolted and mentally thrown off-balance by his opponent's taunts, the miner lunged forward. He was so angry that he completely forgot about Howard. He intended to tackle the smaller man and end the fight immediately. His momentum enabled the minister to grasp his shirt front, thrust his foot into Jackson's stomach, and roll backward. Jackson sailed through the air and hit the ground hard before springing to his feet.

Jackson shook his head from side to side in an effort to clear the cobwebs. "Fancy trick, little man. I ain't never seen that particular move done no better. But I reckon that's all you got, so I'm gonna beat you to death once I get my hands on you."

Closing with Hightower, he unleashed a series of punches with both hands. They were fast and accurate, with no wasted motion, leading the preacher to understand that Jackson was skilled in boxing as well as rough-and-tumble fighting. Reverend Hightower successfully blocked several punches when Jackson suddenly caught him in the ribs with a hook and then flush on the cheek with a right cross. The impact of the blow to the face was so great that it sounded almost like a gunshot. It knocked the minister several feet backward before he collapsed in a heap. The fight was over.

And it was no surprise to any of the townspeople present. After all, Jackson's ponderous strength was so great that he once knocked out a full-grown bull with one blow, earning him his nickname. Something akin to a shudder ran its way through the crowd. Almost everyone present, including some of Jackson's companions, had secretly been hoping for months that by some miracle, someone would finally beat him. Ah well, at least the preacher had thrown the Bull down before being knocked out.

Nobody other than Sergeant Reilly had even been able to do that, and the older man had fought with courage and skill, winning the admiration of everyone present.

Then something happened, something so unusual that those who heard about it later didn't believe their ears, and some of the eyewitnesses later doubted their memories. However, regardless of anyone's disbelief, the reality was that within mere seconds of being knocked flat, the minister raised himself to one knee, then stood and walked toward Jackson.

Seeing this, the crowd came alive, with conversation growing in volume as more spectators began to fully comprehend what was happening. A man had actually taken Bull Jackson's best punch, and was now coming back for more!

As if things couldn't get any stranger, the man whose jaw should have been dislocated proved that it was not when he said, "Boy, you may be a heathen, but you're a good fighter. I see now that I can't stop you without inflicting permanent damage. You don't deserve a second chance, but I'm going to give you one anyway. I don't want to cripple you. All you have to do is stop now and go with John to the jail."

In response, the surprised brawler cursed and charged again, swinging deadly and fast punching combinations. But this time he just struck air. Instead of blocking, Hightower ducked and then used his own shin to kick the side of his huge assailant's left leg so effectively that he dislocated Jackson's knee.

The Bull stopped cold and bellowed with pain like a wounded grizzly. In spite of his dislocated knee, he still stood upright. He only stood for a moment, though. The minister kicked Bull's other leg in exactly the same way, causing the huge brawler to fall to his knees in front of his smaller opponent.

Reverend Hightower now had the killer positioned so that he could use his hands. He did so with simple, yet devastating effectiveness. The clergyman used the outside edge of both hands to strike his opponent's collarbone simultaneously on the left and right sides of the sternum. The sound was like a stick of firewood breaking. Then, grabbing Jackson by his hair, Hightower jerked

Bull's head down as he thrust up his right knee into the brawler's face. Blood and mucous splattered in all directions from the now-beaten giant's battered face. But the good Reverend had not yet finished his sermon. For a benediction, he ducked behind and encircled his right arm around Jackson's neck. In just a couple of heartbeats, the man who had never lost a fight passed out in the middle of the street, bloody and broken.

The buzz from the crowd sounded like hornets disturbed from their nest. Nobody believed what they saw.

"Did you see that? The Bull is out cold. How'd that old man do that?" asked one spectator.

"I dunno," replied another. "I seen it, but I still don't believe it."

"Hey, Reverend, come on in and let me buy you a drink," yelled one of the saloon's patrons. Realizing what he said, the man followed up with, "An' you know I mean coffee or a soda pop."

The crowd laughed in appreciation as Hightower responded, "Thanks for your kind offer. I may take you up on it later. But first, let's get this man to a doctor. He's got some broken bones."

He then walked up to Rosa and Consuela and asked if they were all right. Both nodded their heads in affirmation, although it was obvious by the way both grasped his arm that they were completely overwhelmed by the events of the day. Reverend Hightower assured them that everything was finally over. He then asked some of the men standing by to see that the girls and the old couple got situated in the hotel. Two men who were with their families stepped forward and helped Consuela, Rosa, and the elderly couple inside.

Another man present said, "I'm Eli Thorton. That's my store across the street. You go ahead, Parson. We'll see that the marshal and Jackson get tended to."

Looking over at Howard, the minister nodded. Howard walked over to him and said, "Let's get something to eat now, if you're up to it."

"Something soft," whispered the pastor. "I feel like I've been kicked by a Missouri mule. He could punch, I'll give him that."

"You feel a whole lot better than he does," responded Howard. "When he finally comes to, I'll bet he'll think he really did come face to face with the wrath of God."

CHAPTER EIGHT

Howard and Hightower sat quietly in the hotel dining room as they waited for their steaks to arrive. Howard's came well done and was so large that it almost covered his plate. In contrast, Reverend Hightower's steak was completely rare and was used to cover the side of his face. He looked at Howard, who was preparing to attack the steak with his knife and fork, as he disdainfully considered the lumpy mashed potatoes on his own plate.

"John, my girls will join us in few minutes. My custom is to offer thanks for food before I eat. Shall I ask the Lord to bless your food also?"

"If you want to. He'll probably listen to you better than He does me."

Hightower looked at the gunfighter, but said nothing in response, other than to give thanks. After the blessing, Howard began to eat. Reverend Hightower remained silent for several minutes and stirred his potatoes while Howard consumed the steak.

"Well, John, what did you think about the fight?"

"I have to tell you, Parson, that I've never seen anyone more skilled with their hands and feet. I recognized your Savate kicking techniques. But I'm still not sure how you threw him at the beginning of the fight and put him to sleep at the end. And I'd just about be willing to trade one of my pistols to know how you survived those two punches."

The minister raised an eyebrow. "So, you know about Savate? Not many people in America do. Do you mind telling me how you learned about it?"

Howard considered the man seated across the table from him. It was the character of the clergyman and his actions throughout the day that made Howard break one of his cardinal rules, which was to never reveal any details about himself. Nevertheless, because he felt a kinship with this man, he decided to talk. After all, he owed a debt of gratitude to the man who had defended him with words at the stage station as effectively as he had defended the girls with his hands and feet. He smiled ever so slightly as he thought about this man preaching from the pulpit. He doubted that anyone dozed off during one of his sermons.

"Parson," he answered, "I learned Savate from my father. He had been taught by a French-Canadian trapper he knew. My father also taught me how to shoot, as well as a lot of other things. He was a scholar and gave me a classical education. Now, may I ask you a question? What about your other techniques? I don't think they're part of Savate, and it's a sure bet that you didn't learn them at a seminary."

"As a matter of fact, I did learn them at the seminary. You may not believe me, but I assure you it's the truth. You see, my professor of Greek taught me more than the language. He passed on to me an ancient Greek fighting system called Pankration. It's not very well known, but as you saw today, it can be quite effective, especially when combined with Savate."

"Ah," said Howard, "you're full of surprises. I thought you were just one of those hellfire and brimstone preachers, no offense intended. But now it seems that you're a man of education. Do you really speak Greek?"

"En arche en ho logos, kai ho logos en pros ton theon, kai theos en ho logos," replied the minister. "Shall I translate that for you?"

Howard looked thoughtful for a moment. "No need to. Unless I'm mistaken, you just said 'In the beginning was the Word, and the Word was with God, and the Word was God'."

Reverend Hightower could only stare at his companion. Finally he said, "John, you're the one who is full of surprises. Where in the world did you learn Greek?"

"I really only know a little Greek. My father tried to teach me. I told you he gave me a good education. I recognized some of the words you said and they brought to mind his lessons."

"Your father appears to be a remarkable man. I would enjoy meeting him."

"My father is dead. He and my older brother were murdered by the Union Army during the war."

"I'm truly sorry. Do you want to tell me about it?"

"It's past history. I don't think you would be interested."

"Son, if I had no interest, I wouldn't have asked you. Whether or not you tell me is up to you."

Howard decided to talk. "My dad and my brother were murdered by an arrogant boy general who commanded the Seventh Michigan Brigade. We had a farm in northern Virginia, near Front Royal. My father had insisted that we remain neutral during the war. Even though he supported states' rights, I remember him saying that he would never fire on the Stars and Stripes because he was an American first and a Southerner second. It wasn't easy remaining neutral. Both the Union and Confederate armies tried to recruit him. In any event, we were left alone for the first several years of the war, because it became accepted that my father had forsaken violence and was a man of peace."

"Then on September 23, 1864, Colonel John Mosby attacked a federal wagon train near Front Royal, just a few miles from our farm. It happened to be on my birthday. I had just turned twelve. Colonel Mosby was badly outnumbered and many of his men were captured. The Yankee commander ordered the prisoners to be hanged without a trial. My father heard about it and protested. The Yankee officer executed my father and my brother, as well as several of our neighbors, saying that they were part of Mosby's guerrillas."

Reverend Hightower looked intently at the younger man. "I've heard about that story. Wasn't the Union officer in charge General Custer?"

"That's right. He later claimed that he was only obeying orders from Grant. But even if that were the truth, something I doubt, a soldier should never blindly obey immoral or unlawful orders. And there was more to it. Custer ordered that our farm be confiscated. After my father and brother were murdered, I joined Mosby's

Rangers. I figured that if the Yankees wanted a Howard to ride with Mosby, then they would get their wish. When I joined, no one asked how old I was, because they knew what had happened to my family. I rode with Colonel Mosby until the end of the war. My father and brother's murders caused the deaths of many Yankee soldiers. In fact, Colonel Mosby himself captured and hanged several of Custer's men, just as the Yankees had done."

"What about your mother?"

"She died less than six weeks after my dad and brother were murdered. I don't think she could bear the grief. I didn't know she died until later. I've got no immediate family left."

Reverend Hightower removed the steak from his face. "Now I understand a little better why you feel the way you do toward the Union Army. All I can say is that I'm truly sorry for your loss. I also must admit that if I had been in your place, without God's grace, I would feel the same way you do and probably would have chosen the path you did."

"And what path is that?" asked Howard, in a more belligerent tone than he intended.

"A path of violence that has more than likely brought you into conflict with the law. In fact, I'm so certain of your past that I won't ask you what you've been doing the last ten years, because in spite of your faults, I don't think you would lie."

Howard said nothing at first. Then he said, "Aren't you afraid I'll take offense at your words? Most people seem to think I'm just looking for an excuse to draw down on somebody."

Reverend Hightower started to chuckle, but thought better of it as the pain radiated down his jaw. "No, John. You won't take offense because you know I didn't intend to insult you. Your honor is something that you take very seriously. I'm the same way. Besides, I fear God, not men, including overgrown saloon bullies, or even gunfighters like yourself." Responding to Howard's puzzled expression, he added, "You see, I know a lot about you. Maybe that's because I've learned something about human nature over the last several years. Then again, it could be because I see so much of myself in you, that is, as I was a long time ago."

The minister pushed himself back from the table. "John, would you mind telling how you know Touch the Clouds?"

"It was after the war. Our farm had been confiscated and was destroyed, so I rode west. I stayed a little while with some relatives in Missouri, then went north, just drifting. I ran into some Indians who turned out to be Pawnee. They had surrounded another Indian, a giant of a man, who I later found out was Touch the Clouds. It was the strangest combat I'd ever seen. The Pawnee were on horseback and he was afoot. The Pawnee would charge directly at him, and attempt to strike him with their spears or hatchets. Every time they would try that, he would yank them off their horses, and whack them with his hand. He didn't even use a weapon. He didn't need to."

Reverend Hightower looked interested but confused. Howard decided to answer the unasked question.

"Are you wondering why they fought like that?"

The minister replied, "Yes. It seems strange, although I don't know very much about Indian customs."

"They were trying to count coup," answered Howard.

"I still don't understand. What is counting coup?"

"It's a contest to see who could touch his enemy first," said Howard. "Some people think they learned it from the white man, just as they learned scalping."

"That's interesting. Now, what about your meeting with Touch the Clouds?"

"I was watching the fight from a hill, no more than eighty or ninety yards away, and I had a Winchester .44 rimfire rifle, the same one I later gave Touch the Clouds. After a while the Pawnee got tired of the game because Touch the Clouds kept knocking them senseless. One of them raised his bow to shoot, and when he did, I blew him off his horse. I never did care to watch a bunch of cowards try to gang up on a single fighter, especially one as awesome as that big Indian. The Pawnee turned, and about ten of them started riding at me. I killed four of them and the rest ran like rabbits. It turned out that Touch the Clouds had been wounded. He had two arrows sticking out of the middle of his back. I couldn't see them from where I was at first."

Howard took a drink of coffee before continuing. "After the Pawnee left and I rode up, he finally fainted. I suppose it was because he had lost so much blood. Anyway, I pulled the arrows out, and stopped the bleeding the best I could. Later that day, a couple of the Pawnee came back. I shot them. The next morning, Touch the Clouds came to. Amazingly enough, he spoke English, which he had learned from the 'Black Robes'."

The minister asked, "Weren't the 'Black Robes' some Catholic missionaries who lived with the Sioux? I believe they were Jesuits. I heard they did some fine work."

Howard nodded. "That's right. Anyway, when his people found us, they treated me like I was some kind of hero. I stayed with them almost a year."

The minister had listened intently. "Well, I think it was providential that he recognized you today."

Howard looked at his companion. "I don't know about that."

The clergyman didn't debate the point. Instead he asked, "Would you mind telling me about your plans?"

"I plan to keep riding west, maybe to Montana or Oregon."

"Have you thought about staying here?" asked Reverend Hightower.

"There's not anything or anyone to keep me here," answered Howard.

"Well, what if I offered to teach you how to fight like I do? You said you'd be willing to give up a gun to learn what I did to Jackson. What if I offered to teach you? In just a few months, you could be as good as I am, probably better."

"Aren't you being overly optimistic? It would take years to get as good as you."

The minister shook his head slowly. "In most cases, yes. However, you're strong and smart. And you have had some training in Savate already. And if I may say so, I'm a good teacher." He adjusted the steak on his face and added, "It wouldn't hurt to be as confident empty-handed as you are with a gun. After all, you may run into Sergeant Reilly again one day. The man hates you and is supposed to be formidable with his fists."

"Parson, if things were different, I'd like to learn from you. But I don't want to be beholden to any man, so I'd have to return the favor and teach you how to handle a gun like I do."

"Son, if I taught you, you wouldn't be indebted to me. It would be an honor to teach you. Besides, I doubt you could teach me anything about shooting. I can shoot as well as anyone," responded Hightower levelly. "Don't make the mistake of thinking that a man of peace doesn't know how to fight."

Howard cleared his throat. "I saw the street fight, Parson. After that, I'm not about to question your ability in any type of combat. If you say you can use a gun, I believe you."

"Very well. But why don't you consider staying around a little longer?"

Howard shook his head. "Like I said, I'm riding west. There's nothing here for me."

"Well, if you're certain, then go with God. It has been a pleasure to meet you. I'm glad my girls met you, and I will always remember how you helped protect them. I wish the rest of my family could have met you also."

"Is the rest of your family coming to Gold Valley?" asked Howard.

"Unfortunately, no. My wife and my four sons are dead. I meant I wish they could have met you before they died. One of my boys died a violent death several years ago. My wife and other sons were taken by smallpox earlier this year. My girls and I were spared."

Howard felt his face began to flush. "I'm sorry. I didn't mean to speak out of turn. I guess we both know the pain of losing people we love."

His older companion nodded in agreement. "It's okay, son. You didn't know. But I had almost thirty years of happiness, and nothing can take that from me. And I still have Consuela and Rosa. Besides, my girls and I are going to fulfill my wife's dream."

"What dream was that?"

"She wanted to establish an orphanage. She always loved children, that's why we had so many. She wanted to give hope to children who were alone in the world. I heard that there are at least four or five orphans already in Gold Valley, even though this is a new settlement. So I'm going to provide a home for those children while I preach. I asked you to stay because I could use the help of a man such as yourself."

Howard looked dumfounded. "I'm not suited for work like that."

The preacher shook his head from side to side. "I think you're more suited than you may realize. However, I don't want to try to persuade you into doing something you don't want to do. I learned a long time ago that people have to make their own decisions." He took a sip from his water. "What about other employment then? This is a new town in a new territory. I understand there are more than one thousand people in this town, with more coming in every day. There are plenty of opportunities for someone with your talents. Who knows, you may even meet the right young lady and decide to settle down."

"Parson, I'm not in a position to start any new relationships. It's too late for me."

"Son, you talk like you're an old man like me, and yet you can't be more than twenty-five. You've got a lot of time. If I may say so, you should do yourself a favor and quit feeling sorry for yourself."

Howard felt his face begin to redden. He liked this clergyman but was starting to feel uncomfortable with the direction the conversation was taking. "Perhaps you're right. But it seems that everybody and everything I care about ends up dead. Now, I've got to get an early start tomorrow, so I'll have to excuse myself."

"Okay, John, but consider this. No one is immune to pain and suffering. God never promised any of us an easy time of it on this earth. He just promised to never leave us or forsake us in the tough times, if we follow Him. And He gives us relationships that don't die."

Both men stood up. The minister extended his hand. "As I said, it has been a pleasure to meet you. If you change your mind, my girls and I will still be here in Gold Valley."

Howard shook the offered hand and said, "Take care of yourself and your girls, Parson. I hope we run into each other some time. I won't forget you."

"I won't forget you either. Vaya con Dios, son. Go with God."

*　　*　　*

Rosa couldn't sleep. She glanced over at her sleeping sister and sighed with jealousy. John Howard's sudden presence in her life had not only interrupted her serenity, but now he was disturbing her sleep. While Consuela had bemoaned his departure, Rosa had spent the better part of an hour reciting her ills against him. But now, when she closed her eyes to sleep, she could see only his eyes looking back at her. She admitted that he was good-looking and that he had a way of looking at her that was disconcerting, yet pleasant. It was nothing like she felt when Bull Jackson had leered at her and Consuela. It was different. Howard appeared to openly appreciate her beauty and femininity, but didn't seem vulgar, because in spite of what she had said to him, she felt that he was a gentleman. But he was a still a man of violence, a killer of men. His handsome face and broad shoulders didn't change that. Why did things have to be so complicated?

Finally, she tossed off the sheets and changed back into her dress. Only a warm cup of coffee and a good talk with her father could straighten this out. She walked toward the hotel's dining room with a new resolve to never think *his* name again, when she heard it spoken by her father. She knew he would disapprove of her eavesdropping on his conversation, but she couldn't help herself. She eased toward the doorway to listen.

"I think you have the wrong idea about John Howard," Reverend Hightower told the other man seated with him at the table.

His companion replied in a low voice. "Maybe. I don't know. But just because he's a fast gun doesn't mean we want him hanging around."

"You know as well as I that people are sometimes more than they appear to be," replied Hightower. "John is carrying a lot of pain and grief inside from losing his family. I understand how he feels, and I see a lot of potential in that young man. People can change. I've seen it more than once in my lifetime."

Rosa didn't hear a reply, so she stepped closer to the door and peered inside the room. The man pushed back his chair and, with a glance at her father, began pacing about the otherwise empty room. After several moments of silence, he seemed to have reached a decision. "I'm willing to give him the benefit of the doubt if you can tell me why you have so much faith in him."

The minister became animated as he described Howard's actions at the stage relay station, how he had dealt with not only the Indians, but also Rosa. He also spoke of what the soldiers had told him about Howard's encounter with Sergeant Reilly. Hightower went on to tell of how Howard had stood beside him when he confronted the notorious bully, Bull Jackson.

"So you see," reasoned the minister, "John Howard is the man for the job. You can trust him."

"I trust you," corrected the man. "I hope I can trust him."

CHAPTER NINE

When Howard awoke the next morning, it was to the sound of his sorrel horse snorting. The previous evening he had decided against staying in Gold Valley and rode a mile west of town before bedding down for the night.

"Easy, boy," he said, "I hear them."

Rolling to the side into some bushes, he grabbed his Winchester and surveyed the trail in front of him. Concealed in the shadows as he was, he knew it would be difficult for the riders to spot him. In a barely audible voice he issued a quiet command to the two approaching horsemen, as they drew rein thirty feet from him.

"Keep your hands where I can see them, and don't make any quick moves. What do you want?"

The rider in front cleared his throat as if he were beginning to make a long-winded political speech. He reminded Howard of a snake-oil salesman in Abilene who had been tarred and feathered before being unceremoniously ridden out of town on a rail. This individual looked to be in his late fifties. He had a thin neck which appeared too small to support his large, round face. Thin wisps of pale oily hair stuck out from beneath his pearl gray derby. He wore thick glasses. His small rounded shoulders were a curious contrast to his bulging stomach and hips. His clothing was no doubt expensive, but Howard could not help noticing a dirty ring around his celluloid collar. He carried no visible gun. Howard decided that he liked nothing about this particular person.

When the fat man spoke, it was in a condescending voice that tried to project an air of authority, but fell dismally short of the mark. "I recognize your horse, Mr. Howard," he said, "and there's no need for alarm. We are peaceful. I'm William Pepper. Now . . . "

"Just a minute. I don't care if you're peaceful or not. What do you want?"

Pepper spoke again, "If you'll only allow me a minute, I can explain everything. In fact, this is your lucky day because I'm coming to you with a very attractive business proposition. It is a great opportunity. You would do well to consider my terms, young man, because you're not likely to get a better offer. Now, I'm a very busy and important man, and time is money, so may I continue?"

Howard smiled slightly in amusement at the arrogance of the pompous windbag. Obviously, this unsavory-looking character was used to talking to others as if they were underlings. Howard decided that the unctuous man was right in one respect, however. It was time to get to the bottom line. His curiosity was aroused. At the same time, he decided that any further conversation would be directed toward the second individual.

This man was a direct contrast to Pepper. For one thing, he was younger, appearing to be about forty or forty-five. But age was the least of the differences. Whereas Pepper projected a soft, flabby, and dirty appearance, this man looked like a genuine hardcase. He was dressed in worn but clean clothing, with boots that had recently been polished. He was well set up with broad shoulders and a full, neatly trimmed moustache. He had alert eyes that measured Howard. He gave the impression of quiet strength, and he made a conscious effort to keep his hands in plain view on the pommel of his saddle. Riding in a scabbard below his right leg was an old but well-oiled Henry rifle. The revolver on his hip caught Howard's attention. It looked like the twin of the Smith and Wesson American revolver that he carried himself. Everything about the man indicated that he was a gunman.

Upon further reflection, Howard decided that his initial assessment of the second man was correct. The man was undoubtedly a gunfighter like himself, and he was probably very good. Howard arrived at that conclusion through deductive reasoning, because America in 1876 was a place where most gunmen were dead or retired by the time they were forty. The very fact that this man had reached that age could logically mean only one of two things. He was either lucky or good. Howard decided it was likely the latter.

Howard addressed the gunman, deliberately ignoring Pepper. As he spoke, he stepped out of the bushes. He still held his Winchester against his shoulder with the muzzle down, so that to fire he only had to raise his left arm. He also made sure that he was to the right of the two riders, so that he offered a more difficult target. "Well, sir, it seems that you and Pepper already know my name. I don't know yours and I don't know why you're here. Would you mind telling me about this 'great opportunity' he is talking about?"

The gunman answered in a carefully measured voice. His speech revealed a slight but unmistakable twang of Tennessee, or possibly Kentucky.

"My name is Ben Duff," he said. "I believe what Mr. Pepper has in mind is to offer you a job as town marshal of Gold Valley. The pay is good, about twice what a top hand makes. But if you decide to take the job, you'll earn your money, every cent of it."

So this was the Ben Duff mentioned in Gold Valley the previous day. Howard decided he liked Duff. At the same time, he digested the offer to be a lawman slowly and with no small amount of astonishment. Besides the fact that he had never in his wildest imagination pictured himself as any kind of law officer, something simply didn't fit.

Howard was a good listener, so he knew something about William Pepper from conversations he had overheard in town the previous evening. Pepper was the mayor of Gold Valley and was also the owner of a large ranch, the bank, and was partial owner of a gold mine.

Howard also knew something about Gold Valley. In its short life the town had already taken on an aura of prosperity, and yet it had been plagued with a number of problems. Although there had been no bank robberies, gold shipments had been held up on a regular basis. In fact, the robbery that he had thwarted himself the previous day was the first time in more than four months that the stage had successfully made the run between Gold Valley and Pierre. Also, lawlessness appeared to be rampant. Although it had been in existence less than two years, the town had already gone through eight marshals. Three others had been murdered like Marshal Bates, one had been chased out of town, and the rest had quit. So although there was no doubt that Gold Valley needed a competent lawman, Howard wondered why they were coming to him when Duff appeared quite capable of handling the job.

Howard was direct. "Why don't you take the job, Mr. Duff? Why does the town need me?"

"I'll answer that, young man," said Pepper.

"No, you won't," Howard replied. "I'm talking to Mr. Duff."

"Fair question," said Duff. "The reason is because I work as Mr. Pepper's personal assistant."

"No offense intended, Mr. Duff, but don't you mean you're his bodyguard?"

The older gunfighter leaned back a little in his saddle. "No offense taken, Mr. Howard. To answer your question, yes, a large part of my duties involve protecting Mr. Pepper."

"Still no offense intended, but do you mind me asking how much he pays you?" asked Howard.

"No, I don't mind you asking, but I don't think that it's any of your business, no offense intended."

"None taken. But there's a reason that I'm asking."

Howard shifted his gaze to Pepper. "I'll bet you pay him at least seventy-five or eighty dollars a month. How much does the town marshal make?"

Pepper cleared his throat again. "My boy, I'm not used to people I employ quizzing me on what my other employees make. And furthermore . . . "

"Stop right there," interrupted Howard. "First, I'm not your boy and you don't employ me. Second, unless you start giving me some straight answers, you're not going to employ me. Now, it seems strange to me that this man would not be the marshal. Unless I miss my guess, you're not going to find a better gunhand.

So, if I'm going to consider the job, I'm going to need more information. If you're not willing to provide it, we don't have anything else to talk about."

"Of course, of course," replied Pepper in what was intended to be a conciliatory voice. "We don't need to get off on the wrong foot. Mr. Duff here is paid one hundred dollars a month from my personal funds. As he says, he works for me. Like many important men, I need a bodyguard because I have many enemies and as you guessed, Mr. Duff is the best in his profession. If you become marshal of Gold Valley, I'm prepared to offer you sixty dollars a month. You will also receive fifty cents for each arrest you make and ten cents for any stray dogs or cats you shoot inside the city limits. Now, will you take the job? As I already said, you're not likely to get a better offer."

In response Howard said, "Tell the town council that my fee is one hundred dollars a month, the same as Mr. Duff. If they can't afford that much, you can make up the difference from your personal funds. But understand this; if I decide to take the job, I'll be working for the town, not for you, even if you pay some of my salary. I don't shoot dogs or cats, unless they have rabies. The town council can pay me three months' salary in advance and agree to supply me with one thousand rounds of .44 Henry rimfire ammunition every month. One last thing. I'll need an extra sixty dollars each month so that I can hire two good deputies." He slightly lowered the barrel of his rifle before finishing with, "You would do well to consider my terms, Mr. Pepper, because you're not likely to get a better offer."

CHAPTER TEN

The town council unanimously approved Howard's appointment as town marshal, agreeing to all of his terms after what proved to be a memorable meeting. Howard was not present, preferring to let them discuss the prospect of his employment openly. They met in the private dining room of the hotel. The owner of the hotel, an unusually pretty widow of thirty or so, was a member of the council. She stirred up discussion when she agreed to give Howard three free meals each day, as well as a room.

For some reason, this offer bothered Pepper. He voiced his displeasure in front of the other four members.

"Come now, Angelique," he said. "We've already made him a handsome offer. Why, he'll make more than the Chief of Police in Denver. And even though he will be the marshal, I'm not sure I approve of him being around you all of the time. After all, there may be times when you and he are the only ones present in the diner. How would that look?"

Angelique Mayo looked with distaste at the mayor. It seemed to be obvious to everyone present at the session, except Pepper himself, that she was struggling to be courteous to the obnoxious man, and that it required a major effort on her part.

"Mr. Pepper," she coolly responded, "I've asked you before to address me as Mrs. Mayo. We are not on a first name basis. Secondly, it doesn't really matter whether you approve or not, because who I choose to serve in my hotel and diner is my business, not yours."

"Of course, my dear," replied Pepper. "I'm only thinking of your reputation. After all, you don't have a husband any longer, and I just want to protect you."

The other members of the council exchanged glances, but said nothing. Then Pepper addressed them.

"Don't you other men agree?" he asked.

While the male members sat uncomfortably in their chairs, to a man refusing to look at Mrs. Mayo or Pepper, Angelique said, "Gentlemen, as far as I'm concerned there is no need for further discussion. As I said, I serve whom I please and when I please at my own place of business. You all know that. So now I propose that we vote, and hope that Mr. Howard accepts our offer."

The vote was delayed because at that moment shots rang out in the street, accompanied by the sound of breaking glass. Loud voices filtered into the hotel dining room and grew in intensity as the speakers approached the hotel.

"That'll learn 'em, Kirby," said one of the men. "I betcha they think twict afore they say anything else about Texas or Texicans."

"Yeah, I reckon so," said the one called Kirby. He was a dark, barrel-chested gunman whose accent unmistakably confirmed his Texas origin. "He's lucky I just shot out his windows instead of shooting off his ears."

His three companions laughed raucously in agreement. They drew even with the front door of the hotel and stepped inside.

Spying the men at the table through the open door to the dining room, the one named Kirby uttered an oath about "uppity Yankee counter-jumpers sitting around trying to make medicine when they ought to be in bed." Then, noticing Angelique, he added, "Uh oh. Sorry, ma'am. I didn't know that there was a lady present or I wouldn't a'cussed. We're just looking for a room."

Duff, who had been sitting unnoticed by the front door, stood as the four cowboys stepped through the door. He sized them up as dangerous men, especially Kirby, who he knew to be a gunfighter of the first order. Kirby had ridden with Wes Hardin and the Clements boys. It was said that even Manny Clements and Hardin himself showed respect to Kirby.

Duff spoke to the Texans. "Gentlemen, there's a meeting going on. Why don't you go and get a drink and come back in an hour or so?" He had already slipped off the retaining thong that secured his Smith and Wesson in its holster.

"Uh oh, fellers. Looks like a Yankee lawdog to me. Reckon I might have to teach him some manners," said the youngest of the group. He was a teenager who carried his .44 Colt in a low-slung holster and called himself the "Nueces Kid".

"Shut up, you young idiot," said the one called Kirby. "That ain't no Yankee lawdog. That's Ben Duff. Uh, sorry, Mr. Duff. We didn't mean no harm, just blowing off a little steam. You know how it is. Hope you'll excuse the Kid's big mouth. He don't know you."

Duff nodded his head. "Sure, I understand, Mr. Kirby. Just come back later."

"Sure thing, we'll come back later. Sorry again for cussing, ma'am." Kirby tipped his hat to Angelique and turned to leave.

Two of his companions did likewise. However, the Nueces Kid hesitated. He had been drinking, but was far from being intoxicated. In fact, he was like Doc Holiday in the sense that he actually became even faster and deadlier as he consumed alcohol. Unlike Holiday, he had no reputation and dearly wanted one, even though he had in fact killed more men than the notorious dentist turned gunman. Also, he wanted to impress that fine-looking woman who was at the table. Maybe she was a little older than he was, but considering how good she looked, he didn't care. Finally, he wanted these men he rode with to take him seriously and show him the same deference they showed Preston Kirby.

All of those things caused him to size up the present situation as a golden opportunity. He could show that pretty woman how tough he was, win respect from his partners, and make an instant name for himself, not necessarily in that order. All that stood in his way was this aging pistolero named Duff.

He made his decision then, thinking to himself, "I'll make Duff draw and then kill him or make him back down. He's gotta be pretty good, or Kirby wouldn't say so. But there ain't no way he's as good as me, 'cause I'm just about as fast as Kirby or Hardin."

Then the young man stuck both thumbs in his belt and spoke

to the room at large. "You folks are mighty lucky, 'cause you're fixin' to see a real live gunfight. Duff, I ain't scared of you an' I ain't seen none of your graveyards. If you want me to leave, make me, if you think you're man enough."

Whether the boy expected Duff to draw, talk or back down was never discussed, because just as he finished speaking, he was looking down the muzzle of Duff's Smith and Wesson. Kirby and the other Texans stood perfectly still. Then Kirby slowly raised his hands. The others followed suit. No one in the room, even those who knew Duff, could believe how fast he had drawn his handgun.

"I ain't in this, Ben," said Kirby. He remained motionless, with his hands high and well away from his gun.

"Neither are we," said one of the other Texans.

Duff kept the Kid covered. "All right. Now get him out of here and keep him out. In fact, I'd suggest that all of you ride out of town tonight if you can't make him behave. I don't want to kill a loudmouthed, stupid kid just because he's drunk and trying to show off."

The speed of Duff's draw had caught the Kid flatfooted and speechless. He simply stood there frozen by the cold realization that Duff could have killed him as easily as one could shoot a fish in a barrel. He knew he was very fast himself, but the hard fact was that he had never seen anyone, not even Kirby or Wes Hardin, draw a pistol as fast as Duff had done. So he simply followed his companions out the door without saying a word.

On the way out Kirby paused and said, "Thanks for not killing him, Ben. He ain't a bad sort, really. He just gets mean when he's had too much to drink. I'm afraid he's been itching to kill again after he beat a Mexican pistolero last spring down on the border." He stopped at the door's threshold. "Say, listen here, is it okay if we stay in town if the Kid behaves?"

"Are you giving me your word that you'll keep him out of trouble, Preston?"

"Sure thing, Ben. He'll listen to me, and he's got enough sense not to try me. Now he's got enough sense not to try you."

"Fine, your word's good enough for me. Oh, and how about

not shooting out any more windows? It costs a lot of money to ship glass to here."

Grinning broadly, Kirby said, "Not that I'm admittin' to shootin' out any of them over at the Buffalo Head Saloon, you understand, but I'll guarantee that if any more is shot out, it won't be us doing the shootin'."

With that, the four Texans walked into the street. It was several seconds before anyone inside spoke. They simply looked at Ben Duff, who shifted somewhat uncomfortably at the attention being paid to him.

Finally, Ira Wentworth, one of the town council members, broke the silence. "I for one don't see why we need to hire Mr. Howard. I've been around and have seen the best there is, including Bat Masterson and Hickock. None of them are as fast as Mr. Duff. And Mr. Duff's not only fast, he's got savvy. Did you see how he handled that without any bloodshed? And we know Mr. Duff. All we know about Howard is that he's a fast gun. So why not offer the job to Mr. Duff?"

"Ira," said Pepper, "John Howard asked the same question. My answer to you is the same I gave him and it's the same one I've given before. Mr. Duff works for me. Now I grant you that he is the best at his profession. I even told John Howard that. But because he is the best is precisely why he works as my personal assistant. You all know that a man of my station must have the best protection. That's why I have Mr. Duff and the two Macleod brothers, who are almost as good as he is, on my payroll."

As before, the other town council members exchanged silent glances. However, as before, none of the men said anything until Mrs. Mayo broke the silence.

"Gentlemen," she said, "if we can't have our first choice as marshal, then let's get the next best thing. I move we hire John Howard. Is there a second?"

"Excuse me, Angelique," interposed Duff. "I'm not a member of the council and have no vote, but I can promise you that John Howard is not a second-best choice. He's likely as good as anyone you'll ever see, and will be worth what you pay him."

Ira Wentworth then asked the question on everyone's mind. "I'm not doubting your judgement, Mr. Duff, but I am curious as to how you know how good Mr. Howard is."

"Several things, Mr. Wentworth. First, you all heard what Amos the stage driver said about how Howard handled the attempted robbery. You know that Amos tells things straight. And I talked to Reverend Hightower about what happened. He confirmed Amos' story. Nobody, including me, could have handled it better than Mr. Howard did. Next, I met Mr. Howard and talked to him in person. In my business, you need to be able to size up the competition. Finally, I talked to a young fellow today who just mustered out of the Second Cavalry. He told me about how Mr. Howard backed down Sergeant Donald Reilly, and then did some amazing shooting when the Sioux attacked."

"Donald Reilly backed down?" asked Thomas Bettinger. Bettinger owned of one of two freighting companies in town and had witnessed Reilly's fight with Jackson.

"He did, Mr. Bettinger. Apparently, Mr. Howard told Reilly he would shoot him. Reilly believed him, and lucky for him that he did. Another thing. Howard's a very bright young man. How many men do you know who could have talked a Sioux war chief into calling off an attack and then leaving the country?"

"Thank you, Mr. Duff," said Bettinger. "That answers my question. I guess I'm ready to vote."

The motion to hire John Howard as town marshal was passed without any additional discussion. That order of business completed, Pepper closed the meeting.

After the town council adjourned, Eli Thorton lingered to talk to Mrs. Mayo. After assuring that no one else was within earshot, he said, "Angelique, do you think you should have talked to him like that?"

"Eli, I only wish that you and the other members would talk to him like that. Why do you men let Pepper run this town like it's his own little kingdom? And you know that I'm not the only one who thinks so. Why, your wife told me last night that she feels the same way I do. And we're not the only ones."

"But why did you tell him you're not a first-name basis with him? That had to be embarrassing. Besides, I call you by your first name. So do many others."

Angelique laughed briefly. It was a pleasant, lilting sound that filled the room.

"Eli, I allow you to call me 'Angelique' because you're a gentleman and you always treat me like a lady. The same applies to the other men who call me by my first name. But I don't feel that way about Pepper. I feel like I need a bath whenever he even looks at me."

"I think I understand. But please do me a favor and try to be nice to him. Now you know I'm not asking you to let him court you or even hold your hand. But he is the richest man in town and owns a piece of almost everything. For the sake of business and as a favor to your friends, could you just try to be nice to him?"

The lovely woman sighed slightly. "Okay, I'll try, but it won't be easy."

"Thanks, Angelique," said Thorton, as he turned to leave. "Good night."

"Good night. Give my regards to Kate and the kids." Remembering something, she reached into the pocket of her dress, and extracted a wrapped steak sandwich. "And please give this to Ellen."

"Thanks, Angelique. That little girl of mine sure sets store by your cooking. So does Eli, Jr. He just doesn't care for steak yet. Good night."

"Good night, Eli."

Closing the front door and walking up to her room, Angelique thought of the new man she had agreed to hire. She had heard that he was a gunfighter who was faster and deadlier than anyone, except perhaps Ben Duff. She had seen Howard in the street the day before when poor Marshal Bates had been murdered and Reverend Hightower had beaten Jackson within an inch of his life. Howard had seemed tough and competent. He was also good-looking. His thick brown moustache and broad shoulders reminded her of her late husband, or a perhaps younger version of Ben Duff.

Maybe, she reflected, that was why she had agreed to give him free meals and a room. Then again, it wouldn't hurt business a bit if customers knew that the new marshal would be spending a lot of time at her establishment.

CHAPTER ELEVEN

The inhabitants of Gold Valley got a chance to see how their new marshal handled himself his very first day on the job. If they had any doubts before, they were quickly put to rest.

Like most new western towns, Gold Valley had dirt streets that turned downright muddy after a hard rain. Such was the case in the late morning of Howard's first day as marshal, when a farmer named Reid and his wife rode into town to get supplies. Their wagon splashed mud up on the wooden sidewalk, splattering water and mud on the Nueces Kid and a few other men who were lounging in front of the Buffalo Head Saloon.

Nobody was pleased with the impromptu mud shower. Only one person chose to make a life and death issue of it, however. That person was the Nueces Kid, who was still seething over the events at Mrs. Mayo's hotel the previous evening. He had been simmering and drinking all night and the more he drank, the angrier he became. In his twisted thinking, he imagined that by now the story of how Ben Duff had made him back down was all over town. Now, to add insult to injury, this farmer had gone and splashed mud all over his new clothes. Even though it was clearly an accident, the Kid was looking for the slightest excuse to kill.

"Hey you stupid sod-buster, hold up there!" he shouted. "What's the matter with you, dirt farmer? Don't you know how to drive a wagon?"

Reid pulled the team to a halt when the Kid yelled.

"Hey, fellas, sorry about that. I didn't know that hole was there."

"Being sorry don't cut it, pig farmer. You owe me for a set of clothes and a pair of boots," replied the Kid.

"Look here, mister, I said I was sorry. My missus can wash those clothes for you, and I'll clean your boots if they need it."

"Not good enough, plow boy. You owe me fifty dollars for my outfit. Now hand it over, or I'll take it out of your hide."

"Please, mister. We don't want trouble. We just . . . " The fear in the farmer's voice was palpable.

The Nueces Kid never allowed the farmer to finish his apology. He lunged at him, jerked him from the wagon, and slapped him twice across the face. Pushing him back, he swiftly drew his gun.

"OK, pig farmer, you can fight me or I'll kill you where you stand."

The farmer, overcome with panic, looked desperately around for help. He was new to the west from Indiana, lured by the prospect of rich soil and perhaps gold. He was ill-prepared for frontier life. He was also a man like the recently deceased Marshal Bates, who had never prepared himself to meet trouble, and as a result, had no idea what to do when confronted with it.

After being buffeted the second time by the Kid, Reid finally decided to act. He attempted to tackle the Kid, who merely sidestepped and then struck him along the side of his head with the barrel of his gun, laughing the entire time.

"Leave him be!" screamed Reid's wife. "Why don't some of you men help my husband?" she pleaded.

The Nueces Kid holstered his revolver. "They ain't gonna do nothin'. In this country a man forks his own broncs."

The Kid was now the center of attention and decided he liked the role of the tough guy. "Say, lady," he said, "you wouldn't be too bad looking if you was dolled up in some nice clothes. Not bad looking at all. How about me takin' you home? He won't mind," he said as he motioned toward her unconscious husband.

"You're not taking her anywhere, Kid. Forget it." The speaker was Kirby, who had exited the Buffalo Head Saloon when the Kid pistol-whipped Reid. Kirby's voice was cold.

Something inside the Kid turned over, because in spite of his boasting, he knew he was no match for Kirby, not even under the best of circumstances. He tried to think of a way to save face without challenging the swarthy Texas gunman's orders. He thought he could still look tough if only he had some other target. Then he thought he saw his chance when another man arrived on the scene as Kirby finished speaking. That man was John Howard.

Howard wasted no time. "A couple of you men help pick him up. Ma'am, after they get him loaded, you can drive him to the town doctor. I understand his office is at the end of the next street over."

That taken care of, he turned his attention to the Kid. "Okay, mister, drop your gun-belt. You're under arrest."

"What for? An' who's gonna arrest me? It ain't gonna be you, that's for sure, cause you ain't man enough."

Howard momentarily paused, surveying the scene and assessing those present. That the boy facing him was a gunman was certain. But the black-headed man who had just talked to the Kid was the real problem if he dealt himself in.

"Are you siding him?" Howard asked Kirby. He took his eyes off the Kid for just a moment as he asked the question.

The Nueces Kid seized the chance he thought was presented him. He went for his gun. He was very fast, but he was clearly out of his league. For just as the young killer gripped his gun, Howard drew and fired. For Kirby, who was watching with professional interest, it was a toss-up as to whether Ben Duff or this marshal was faster. Unlike Duff, however, Howard was utterly without mercy. He fired two shots into the Kid so fast that they sounded almost like one. Both bullets hit the Kid in the heart. Before the sound of the shots even began to fade, the Kid fell face down in the mud puddle, and died without muttering a sound, choking on the muddy water. His revolver had not even partially cleared his holster when he died.

Then, for the second time in just a few hours, Kirby found himself on the wrong end of a gun because of the Kid's behavior. He decided he was just about tired of it.

"I ain't part of this, Marshal," he said, as he slightly raised his hands. "That was his play, not mine. So I'd take it right kindly if you quit pointing that six-gun at me. You and me ain't got a fight, unless you want to make one. If you do, holster that smoke-pole an' gimme an even break. Then you an' me can have at it. Howsomever, I'd rather not shoot with a man unless I ain't got no other choice."

Howard carefully considered that. He had heard about the events at Mrs. Mayo's hotel from the town council when he was sworn in earlier that morning. He had also talked with Ben Duff, who told him that even though Kirby rode into town with the Kid, he wasn't a troublemaker, merely a Texan with a wild streak, who wouldn't be pushed around or insulted. Howard also learned that Duff considered Kirby to be a formidable gunman, who was in the same class as Duff and himself. Such information, thought Howard, was good to know. He holstered his gun, but didn't secure it in place.

"All right, Kirby. You and I don't have a problem. We won't have one as long as you obey the law. I think that's fair. What do you think?"

"Suits me. If we fight, I reckon we'd both end up with lead in us, an' most likely we'd both be dead. Ain't no sense in that." He lowered his hands. "One thing you'd best know. Even though I ain't looking for trouble with you, you just bought yourself a peck of it when you gunned that boy. He's got him an uncle who's mean as a rattler and twice as fast. He's hell-on-wheels with any kind of gun. I reckon there ain't hardly nobody better. You best watch yourself."

"Thanks, I will." Then to the crowd that had gathered, Howard said. "For you folks who don't know me, my name is John David Howard. I've been hired as the town marshal. I understand that you've had trouble ever since the town started. I just want you know how things are going to be as long as I'm here. I only know of one way to deal with trouble, and that is to meet it head on." He motioned toward the dead gunfighter in front of him. "So if anyone has any notions of breaking the law, like he did, you know what to expect."

Nobody said anything. However, before noon arrived, the story of the gunfight in front of the Buffalo Head Saloon was all over town. Even though opinions varied about the necessity of killing the Kid, one thing was certain; this new marshal was nobody to fool with. The law had finally come to Gold Valley.

CHAPTER TWELVE

The next few days passed without any noteworthy incidents. It seemed that although the new marshal did not have universal support when he shot down the Nueces Kid, he did command respect, especially from the town's rougher elements. For the first time since the town had started, it was relatively safe for women to walk alone after dark, and children could play in the streets without fear of being hit by a stray bullet.

Howard spent that time familiarizing himself with the town and the people he had been hired to protect. He discovered that the citizens he came into contact with were very careful about what they said and did when he was around. In fact, it seemed that many of them were afraid of him. He found that rather curious, in that he had been hired because of his ability with a gun. He felt that it would be good to get Reverend Hightower's opinion of the situation.

On the evening of his fourth day of work, Howard ran into the preacher and his daughters at Mrs. Mayo's dining room. He noticed that Hightower's daughters looked even better than the last time he had seen them. Perhaps they had started to recover from the shock of the violence that they had seen. Consuela seemed even more cheerful as usual. She gave Howard a big smile when she saw him enter the room and although Howard wasn't certain, he thought she may have fluttered her eye lashes ever so slightly as he approached the table. Her father also smiled when he saw Howard. The marshal even noticed that Rosa appeared happy to see him, or at least wasn't visibly upset by his presence.

"Join us, John," said Reverend Hightower.

"Yes, please do," said Consuela. "Sit here by me. You look very well tonight."

"Consuela!"

The speaker was Rosa and the tone was disapproving, to say the least. She turned a deep shade of crimson. Howard thought that she looked especially nice when she blushed, and it seemed that she blushed frequently when he was around.

"Girls, girls, let's be kind to one another," said Reverend Hightower. "Besides, I don't want John to have to arrest you two for disturbing the peace," he added with a smile.

Howard ordered a cup of coffee and engaged in small talk with the Hightowers. To his surprise, they talked for almost an hour and a half. He was only conscious of the time when Reverend Hightower glanced at his pocket watch.

"It's almost nine o'clock. Why don't you girls go up to the room? I'll be there shortly. I just want to discuss a couple of things with John first."

"Good night, Papa," said Consuela and she kissed him on the cheek. "Good night John, er, Mr. Howard," she added.

Rosa also kissed her father and even said good night to Howard.

As the girls walked up the stairs, Howard and their father overheard them arguing over whether or not Consuela should address the marshal by his first name.

"I just don't understand it," said Hightower, as he shook is head in dismay. "They usually get along famously. Perhaps they're getting tired of the tight quarters in their room. I keep assuring them that we'll only be here a few more days. Our house is almost finished."

Howard decided that it would be best to let the statement about the Hightower girls bickering go by without comment. Besides, he wasn't sure whether Rosa was merely looking after her younger sister, or if she was actually jealous of the notice Consuela paid to him. In any event, Howard admitted to himself that the attention of two such lovely young women was not an unpleasant thing.

"You know," continued the preacher, "they both take after their mother. That is, they look like her, but I'm afraid that Rosa gets her temper from me. Now, let's talk about why you came to see me tonight. What's bothering you, son?"

"You don't miss much do you?" asked Howard.

"Oh, I miss a lot. But as I told you before, I know a lot about you and I think that you have something particular on your mind."

"As a matter of fact, I do have something bothering me that I need your opinion on. It seems that many people in town are giving me a very wide berth. And I don't mean only the troublemakers. Regular folks are the same way. When they speak, they seem to take extra pains to not say anything that will bother me."

"Interesting," mused the parson. "Can you give me a specific example?"

"Certainly. Earlier today I was coming out of the gun shop. As I rounded the corner, I almost ran head-first into an old lady who was walking with a couple of kids. Before I could say anything to apologize, she apologized to me. In fact, she apologized three or four times and shooed the kids away as if they should be afraid of me. What do you make of that?"

The minister looked thoughtfully at his younger friend for several seconds before he replied, "John, she probably was afraid of you." Holding up his hand, he went on, "Now, before you say anything, please hear me out. All these folks know about you it is what they have seen and heard. By now, everyone has heard about your fight with the Sioux, including how you made Sergeant Reilly back down before the battle. They also know about the shooting exhibition you put on at the relay station. And they know how you singlehandedly took down several armed stage robbers. And if that wasn't enough, many of them saw you shoot the Nueces Kid. Now, given those facts, is it any wonder that some folks are afraid of you?"

"Okay, but why aren't they afraid of you? After all, you almost killed one of the most dangerous men in all of the Dakota Territory with your bare hands. Also, it was evident that you could have easily killed him if you wanted to. I don't know of anyone else who could have done that. So what's the difference?"

"There are several big differences. For one thing, I didn't kill Jackson. For another thing, I'm a minister, not a gunfighter. Also, I'm over fifty years old and have two daughters."

"Okay, I think I see what you are saying. Now, what do I do about it?"

"Just give them time, John. Most of them will come around sooner or later. But you can take heart in knowing the town council is solidly behind you. And many other people, probably more than you know, like you. Consuela, for example, thinks there's no one else like you."

"I'm glad at least one of your daughters likes me," said Howard.

The clergyman took a drink of coffee. "Rosa likes you, too. I know you two got off to a bad start, but I strongly suspect that she has revised her opinion of you. She's just reluctant to admit it."

CHAPTER THIRTEEN

The weather turned colder as the days ran into weeks. During this time, Howard found himself spending more and more time with the Hightowers. He eagerly anticipated his regular visits to their new house. He even began to have his evening meals more at their home than he did at Angelique Mayo's hotel diner. As time went by, the tension with Rosa grew less. Of course, her sister Consuela was openly infatuated with him, while her father was becoming Howard's closest friend.

All the while, settlers continued to pour into the Back Hills area. By some estimates, there were between fifteen and twenty thousand people in an area that just a few years before was devoid of whites. The population in the immediate vicinity of Gold Valley had passed the one thousand mark, while other towns in the Dakota Territory were larger still. The tremendous influx of newcomers and his friendship with the Hightowers made Howard reach two important decisions just before Thanksgiving.

The first decision was that he would seek to hire two additional lawmen. He had foreseen that eventuality when he initially told Pepper and then the rest of the town council that he would need money to hire two deputy marshals.

The second decision reached was that he would take up the minister on his offer to train him in hand-to-hand combat. It was true that Howard's father had trained him in Savate, a deadly French fighting system that primarily relied upon powerful kicks to disable an opponent. However, Howard had not practiced in several years, because he had done all of his fighting with firearms. In this, as in almost everything, he was brutally honest with himself, and realized that without his guns, he wouldn't stand a chance against someone as skilled and large as Sergeant Reilly. And while he did make Reilly back down the day they met, it rankled him that the soldier spoke the truth when he said that without Howard's guns, Reilly would beat him.

When Howard sought out the preacher's help, his older friend responded enthusiastically. "John," he said, "by the summer you'll be as good at fighting empty-handed as you are with a gun. I give you my personal promise."

And so it began, and continued over the next several months, with training taking place every day, except Sunday, in a back room of the preacher's newly-built house. Under his mentor's tutelage, Howard found that he hadn't completely forgotten the kicking techniques his father taught him. He was very pleased to learn that with constant practice, he quickly regained his skill and soon began to surpass his original abilities. He was especially gratified to learn the grappling, throwing, and joint-locking holds that were part of the parson's system. The most satisfying part though, without a doubt, was learning from a master of his craft, who seemed anxious to teach his younger apprentice everything he knew. Hightower held back nothing, and Howard eagerly soaked up the considerable information imparted to him, even though it was often quite literally a painful learning experience.

Howard also discovered another fringe benefit from being trained. It seemed that whenever they practiced, both of the preacher's daughters would show up. And they always appeared in tandem. If one was present, the other would soon appear.

Concerning his first decision to hire additional help, Howard sought out advice from Reverend Hightower. They were resting after their second session, and it was one of the few times when Rosa and Consuela were not present.

"Parson," Howard had inquired, "who do you think would be the best men to assist me as marshal?"

"No doubt about it, son, Ben Duff and I are the best choices," replied Hightower with a grin.

"I agree. But Mr. Duff's got a job and you've got a calling. So who do I get?"

"Let's see," pondered Reverend Hightower. After several seconds he snapped his fingers. "I think I know of a couple of men who will fill the bill. One of them is that boy who just mustered out of the army, Ian O'Hara. Remember him? He rode with us on the stage. He's young, but mature for his age. I think he needs a job and I heard that he's a whiz with a rifle."

"Good choice. He was with me when we were attacked by the Lakota. He stood up well and he's a crack shot. Anyone else?"

"That Texas gunfighter named Preston Kirby."

"Preston Kirby? You've got to be joking."

"Why not Kirby? Ben Duff says he's one of the best men with a gun he's ever known, and from what I've seen, he's basically a decent sort of chap. He's just a little rough around the edges."

"Parson, you know I respect your opinion, and I know Kirby's a good gunhand, but that's about the most far-fetched thing I ever heard. Do you know what Kirby thinks about lawmen?"

Hightower's smile returned. "Sure I do. He feels just about the same way you do, and you took the job."

"I took the job for a hundred dollars a month. That's three or four times what a top hand or miner makes. I'm only authorized to pay a deputy thirty a month. Besides, I'm not allowed to pay them in advance."

"I'll tell you what, John. If you offer Kirby thirty a month and he turns you down for more money, I'll make up the difference, as long as the total doesn't exceed fifty dollars a month."

Howard knotted his brows in thought. "No offense, Parson, but how could you afford to pay that much money?"

"There's some things you don't know about me, John. I may not look like it, but I actually have plenty of money. I guess you could say that I'm rich. I see from your face that you again doubt what I'm telling you, but I assure you it's the truth."

A somewhat embarrassed John Howard responded, "Excuse me, Parson, I don't disbelieve you, it's just that you don't seem like you're wealthy."

"Thanks. I try to serve God and not money, but God decided to bless me financially. You see, my late wife was the daughter of a Spanish grandee, whose family had been given extensive land grants on both sides of the Rio Grande. My father-in-law wasn't thrilled about his daughter marrying a gringo, but after the wedding and my call to the ministry, he gave her a sizeable dowry. I took some of that money and gave it to my brother to invest as he saw fit. The good Lord blessed the investments and as a result, I'm able to take care of my girls and fulfill my calling without accepting money from anyone."

Howard digested the information. It seemed that his friend was full of surprises. "I see. Now, may I ask you a question? Are you paying for the new church and orphanage that are being built?"

"Every penny of it, except when I choose to accept donations, and I don't accept donations just because they're offered. I want to be sure that any potential donor is sincerely trying to help in doing the Lord's work, and doesn't have a hidden agenda."

Howard's curiosity was now thoroughly aroused. "Has someone offered you money that you refused?"

"Yes. As a matter of fact, just earlier today, I turned down five hundred dollars."

"You refused five hundred dollars?" asked Howard. Five hundred dollars was a handsome sum of money in that time.

"Absolutely. You see, the person who made the offer told me that he knew that I needed help, and that since almost everyone else in Gold Valley depends on him, he wanted me to know that I could, too. He also told me that he would make time in his busy schedule to be an officer in the church, either a deacon or elder. He said it wasn't really important as long as he had an impressive title, as befits a man of his prominence." Pausing, he added, "As long as I live, I'll probably never get used to the arrogance of some men."

Howard had a strong notion that he knew the identity of the would-be benefactor, but still asked, "Do you mind telling me who this Good Samaritan is?"

"Let's just say that it's a good thing that I don't need a loan from the bank. Especially since I told my daughters in front of him that if I'm not home, they are not to let him in the house unless Ben Duff or you are present."

CHAPTER FOURTEEN

Two days before Thanksgiving, Howard was exiting the gun shop after having the trigger adjusted on his Creedmoor rifle. The rifle was in its case. He was thinking about Thanksgiving dinner with the Hightowers, when unexpectedly a voice boomed in the street, as powerful as a north wind from Canada.

"Howard! John Howard! You ready to die, lawdog? Now's the time!" The speaker was a large clean-shaven man, who wore a sheepskin coat that made him appear even larger. He carried two new .45 Colt revolvers, one on the right side of his hip, and the other canted at an angle on his left front, where it could be accessed in a cross-draw motion. He looked like exactly what he was, a hard-bitten and angry gunman.

Howard shrugged his shoulders and faintly shook his head from side to side. "I don't know you. Why do you want to fight me?"

Nevertheless, he set down his rifle case, and when he did so, he loosened the retaining thong from the hammer of his .44 Smith and Wesson. He noticed that the street quickly emptied itself of people.

"My name's Cole Madison. You gunned down my nephew, my sister's boy. His name was Newton Russell but he called himself the 'Nueces Kid'. He was only seventeen years old."

"Look, Mr. Madison, I'm sorry about your nephew, but he tried to draw on me. I didn't have a choice. You, on the other hand, do have a choice. You can turn around and leave. Nobody has to die today."

The cold autumn air hung like a blanket over the street. The tension from the challenge made things even colder still. John

Howard stared at the gunman who had come to kill him. The gunfighter returned the lawman's steady gaze.

Howard asked another question. "Do you think what happened to your nephew is worth dying for, Mr. Madison?"

"Yeah, 'cause he was kin. So see, I got no choice," Madison retorted. "Anyway, this will be easy, you yellow-livered back-shooter."

Howard ignored the insult, hoping to reason with this man. He hoped to avoid fighting Madison, because he understood very well himself the notion that honor demanded that the death of a family member be avenged. Besides, he had seen too much of death and was growing tired of it.

"You think it's easy, Mr. Madison? You're wrong. Dying is never easy, especially when you're the one who's facing death. And if you keep pushing me, you're the one who's going to die, make no mistake about it. But, you don't have to do this. You can just turn and walk away."

"Can't do that," the older gunfighter replied. He looked like he was ready to draw.

A new voice from the opposite side of the street unexpectedly interrupted their conversation. "You had better think about it Cole, and think hard! You had better not draw against him."

Howard knew that voice. Nevertheless, he turned to look for confirmation. It was as he suspected. The speaker was none other than Ben Duff. Duff had just exited the Gold Valley Hotel and Diner in the company of Angelique Mayo and Reverend Hightower. Howard's surprise at Duff taking his side was even greater than the fact that Duff knew Madison.

At the sight of Duff, Madison was visibly taken aback. "I got no quarrel with you, Ben Duff. But if you're siding this lawdog, I reckon I can fight you too, if it comes to it, after I kill him. I know Newt was no account, but he was the only family I got. He was my dead sister's kid. Besides, Howard shot him in the back!"

Duff nudged Angelique back inside. Reverend Hightower stood fast by the gunman.

Duff then spoke. "That's not true, Cole. Mr. Howard shot

Newt after your nephew started to draw. He didn't shoot him in the back. There were plenty of witnesses, including Preston Kirby. You know that Pres Kirby doesn't lie." Duff paused and took a step forward. "You had better know something else. You know Newt was fast, but his gun never cleared the holster. The marshal was better than your nephew, Cole. He's even better than you."

Madison hesitated. Those few words from Duff shook him like nothing else could, because in the closely-knit fraternity of gunfighters, Duff had a reputation of being not just a deadly shooter, but also a keen judge of men. He was also known as a man who never lied.

Now Madison's mind began racing, like a mustang trying to outrun a prairie fire. What was wrong? Hadn't he been told that he would be facing down an inept town marshal, who had shot his nephew in the back? Now one of the few men Madison respected was telling him that this marshal was a first-rate gunfighter, who had shot Newt after his nephew had started to draw. Even more disturbing was Duff's statement that Howard was even deadlier than Madison himself.

All of that notwithstanding, Cole Madison was not going to be dissuaded by mere words, even from Ben Duff. Madison had been accurately described by Preston Kirby as being as fast and mean, but he was more than that. He had killed eight men in straight-up gun fights and had been shot twice himself. In one of his fights, he had killed two gunmen facing him, and was then shot in the back by a friend of one of his adversaries. Even though Madison was hit squarely with a heavy .56 Spencer slug, he was still able to turn around and slay his ambusher. In the words of the old-timers, he had "rode the river and been over the mountain."

Then Howard's voice cut through the November air like a whip, jarring Madison's thoughts and bringing him back to the cold, hard reality of the present moment. "Listen to me, Mr. Madison. I already told you that you can walk away. We both can. Mr. Duff told you what happened. I don't want to fight you over something your nephew did."

As he finished speaking, he paused, as if to give the older

gunman a chance to consider his options. Then, the old familiar rage began building inside him, threatening to push aside his patience. He had to restrain himself from walking toward Madison to force the confrontation. Nevertheless, he remained where he was. He glanced at Reverend Hightower and thought he saw the clergyman nod his head, as if in approval.

For a few moments after Howard finished speaking, it looked like the other gunfighter might actually walk away. However, when Madison did began walking, it was toward the marshal. Howard stood still, waiting. When the distance narrowed down to twenty-five feet, Madison made his move. He swept down his hand in the fastest draw he had ever made. It was obvious to all onlookers that Madison was very fast. His right hand snaked toward his .45 like a striking rattler, almost too quick for the eye to follow. He was in the process of drawing and cocking the hammer in one smooth, fluid motion, when the first .44 slug from Howard's Smith and Wesson slammed into his stomach. That first shot was followed by two more to the chest.

Madison was numbed by disbelief and shock. This couldn't be happening! He had been beaten to the draw by a lawdog! In spite of Duff's warning, he couldn't believe anyone was fast enough to beat him. Now that it was too late, he learned the bitter truth. But then a feeling of nausea began to well up in his stomach, and quickly spread like poison through his system. He coughed and a thin stream of blood starting trickling out of both corners of his mouth. He coughed again and stumbled forward. Then he completed his draw and finished cocking his revolver as the next bullet hit him squarely in the center of the chest. Still, he refused to go down. Incredibly, he stood and continued to raise his revolver to eye level, knowing he was dying, and determined to take Howard with him. He got off a shot, but his breathing was labored and his vision was blurry. His bullet kicked up dirt beside the marshal. By a sheer act of will he managed to cock the hammer for a second and final shot. He fired without aiming.

Madison's second bullet was more on target, and struck the marshal low on the left side at the hipbone, just above his gun-belt. After the bullet struck bone, it followed along the outside of the pelvis, exiting Howard's lower back.

In desperation, Howard carefully aimed, taking an extra split second to ensure that his next bullet was precisely placed. The bullet struck Madison in the center of his forehead.

Although it was inconceivable, the big gunfighter still stood as Howard cocked his revolver to fire again. However, the seemingly indomitable gunfighter no longer presented a threat. The last shot fired by Howard had penetrated Madison's brain. One heartbeat later, the weight of Madison's revolver suddenly became so great that he could no longer support it. Taking a half step to the side, he dropped his Colt as he tripped over his own feet and fell face down in the street.

Slight tendrils of dust began to rise from where he fell. Bystanders began to slowly filter out of buildings for a better view of the scene in front of them. But Madison was not aware of any of this. He was finally dead.

"I'm sorry, mister," Howard mumbled under his breath. "This didn't have to happen. You could have walked away."

Reverend Hightower and Ben Duff rushed to Howard's side. Reverend Hightower grabbed the lawman's arm. "Are you okay, son? Did you get hit?"

"I'm all right. He almost got me. I guess his bullets went wide." Howard consciously regulated his breathing to calm himself down. Only then did he notice the blood dripping down his left leg. He braced himself for the burning sensation that he knew would begin after the initial shock wore off.

The minister noticed Howard's wound for the first time. "It looks like he did get you." He quickly examined the wound. "Thank God the bullet hit you where it did. As gunshots go, it's minor. It'll be painful, but nothing more."

Hightower pulled a clean handkerchief from his coat pocket. "Hold this against your hip. It'll have to do until we get you to Doctor Parker."

Howard complied with his friend's instruction and said, "Listen, Parson, I want you to know something. I tried to avoid that gunfight. I tried. He could have walked away without it looking like he was afraid to fight."

"I know you tried, son. Remember, Ben and I saw it all. You don't have to explain. Come on now and we'll get you to the doctor. Ben, will you get the undertaker?"

"I'm on my way," said Duff. He added, "You beat him, Mr. Howard, but I've never saw a man take so much lead and still keep fighting. I think God smiled down on you."

Howard looked at the dead gunfighter. "Maybe He did at that," he murmured.

CHAPTER FIFTEEN

The next day when Howard awoke, his hip and left leg were stiff and sore. He was able to walk, but that was about the extent of his mobility. He had been treated the previous day by Doctor Parker, the only physician in Gold Valley. The doctor had agreed with the minister's assessment of Howard's wound, and had assured the marshal that he would recover fully after only a few days. Howard was advised to take things a little easier than normal while he recovered.

He ran into Jeff Hightower when he went to the town jail. The minister was waiting for him inside the office. He was seated behind the desk with his feet propped up. He quickly came to his feet when Howard entered, and shook hands with him.

"I've already got a pot of coffee going on the stove, son. Do you want some?" Without waiting for an answer, he handed a steaming cup to the marshal.

Howard accepted the cup and expressed his thanks. He stiffly eased himself into the vacated chair offered by his friend. He took a sip and grimaced. "Parson, that stuff is strong enough to float a horseshoe."

The minister smiled. "Then I made a good batch. Now that you're wide awake, would you tell me how are you feeling this morning?"

Howard gave his friend a somewhat rueful look. "Well, I think it would be fair to say I feel like I've been shot."

The minister's smiled remained. "You know, I've been thinking about that. If I didn't know better, I would suspect that you got shot deliberately, just so that you could avoid training for the next few days."

Howard smiled wanly in return. "That's not so. Your lessons are easily as painful as this bullet wound."

The minister nodded. "Then they're effective. Seriously though, I want you to lay off training until you're feeling like yourself again. You know, good food may help in your recovery, and that's why I'm here. My daughters asked me to invite you to supper tonight."

"Both of them?"

"Yes, indeed. We eat at around seven o'clock, but you could come . . . "

The invitation was cut short by the sound of running footsteps. A moment later, Ira Wentworth, one of the town council members, came crashing through the door. He wheezed as he struggled to regain his breath. "Marshal, come quick, there's no time to lose!"

Howard set his coffee down on the desk. "What's the matter?"

"We got ourselves a mess, that's for sure and for certain. One of the sporting girls down at the Pink Palace named Lily has got herself a little kid, and she's got a boyfriend named Buford. I don't know Buford's last name. He's usually okay except when he gets drunk. Then he gets mean as all get out. He's drunk now, and he's got the kid in Lily's room! You know him, Parson! Marshal, you got to come right now!"

Howard forced himself to concentrate on the issue at hand, in spite of gnawing pain in his side. "What's the matter, is the child in danger?"

"Yes! Don't you see, Marshal? Buford's got a knife and said he's gonna cut the kid's throat! Come on!"

"You said they're in Lily's room. Where is that?" Howard demanded.

"It's the first room on the right at the top of the stairs. Buford's already cut the kid, but not bad. He says he's going to kill the kid though if he doesn't get to talk to his girlfriend."

"Where's the boy's mother?"

"She's down at the foyer of the Palace with the rest of the girls. No customers are in there right now. Everybody left. Nobody wants to go upstairs as long as Buford's up there."

Howard glanced at the minister. "He said you know Buford. Do you want to go with me?"

"Absolutely. And you'll have other help. Ira, you and John start over to the Pink Palace. I'll meet you there with Ben Duff."

Before Howard could answer, the preacher sprinted out the door, headed for the bank. The marshal and Wentworth followed him outside and turned toward the Pink Palace.

A few minutes later, they arrived in front of the brothel. They were met by Hightower and Ben Duff. Duff had his Henry rifle cradled in his arm.

Reverend Hightower asked, "What do you want us to do, John?"

"Mr. Duff, I'd like you to see if you can get a clear shot at Buford. Don't shoot unless you know that you won't hit the kid. I hope it doesn't come to killing, but for my idea to work, I need to know that Buford's covered the entire time. Mr. Wentworth, is there a back entrance to the Pink Palace?"

"Sure enough is," replied Wentworth. "Lots of its customers are married, an' it's better for business if they aren't seen going in and out."

Howard nodded. "Mr. Wentworth, can Mr. Duff get a clear shot if he goes up the back stairs?"

"I don't know. Wait a minute. There's some barrels in the alley where a man could hunker down and still have a clear shot through that back window of Lily's room. Might be better than going up the stairs."

Howard and Duff exchanged glances. "I'll be in the alley, Mr. Howard. You call the tune," said Duff.

"Okay, the Parson and I will go in the front door. Shoot if you have to Mr. Duff, but I've got an idea that might work without any shooting. Maybe nobody has to die today."

Duff went around to the back and knelt down behind the barrels that Wentworth had described. Howard, Reverend Hightower, and Wentworth went inside the front door.

The women who were employed at the establishment were all gathered in the front lobby. One of them, a tired-looking brunette, was sobbing. Her face was streaked with tears and mascara. She went over to Hightower and grabbed his arms.

"You'll get my little boy out, won't you Reverend Hightower? It's not his fault, he's a good boy."

Reverend Hightower's voice reflected compassion and concern. "Try not to worry. Marshal Howard will handle it. I'll be with him."

The prostitute appeared to notice Howard for the first time. "No! Not him! You gotta promise me you won't let him shoot, Reverend! Lots of folks think he's too trigger-happy. Don't let him shoot or he might hit my boy!"

The minister gently disengaged himself from the distraught woman. "It will be all right, Lily. Marshal Howard's a good lawman, the best in fact. He will only shoot if he has too, and he won't hit your son, I promise you that." He paused and added, "It will be better for you to stay here with the other ladies."

In spite of the seriousness of the situation, several of the Pink Palace girls giggled at the minister's reference to them as "ladies". Ira Wentworth didn't laugh. He was turning a sickly shade of white. Wentworth seemed vastly relieved when the marshal told him he should stay with the women.

When Howard and Reverend Hightower gained the top of the stairs, the marshal saw that the door to the first room to the right of the stairs was partially open. He confirmed that it was Lily's room when he heard a child softly sobbing inside. He removed his hat and handed it to the minister. Then he cautiously peered inside the room through the crack between the door and the wall where it was hinged. What he saw was a dirty, muscular man wearing soiled clothes and a miner's hard hat. He held a little boy at chest level with his right hand and a bloody knife in his left. The boy looked to be about four or five, and was pale and frightened. The boy's right arm was bleeding.

Howard eased back into the hall and removed his Remington derringer from underneath his shirt and stuck it under his belt behind his back. Then he unloaded his .44 Smith and Wesson. "Parson, I need you to go along with whatever I do, however crazy it seems."

"I'm with you, John."

With his .44 in hand, Howard stepped inside the room. The minister followed him. The miner began backing away when they entered, unknowingly positioning himself directly in Ben Duff's gun sights through the rear window. The miner's voice was loud and uncommonly shrill for a man of his size. He appeared to be very drunk or insane, possibly both.

"Now you jest get on out here, Marshal Howard. You too, Preacher Hightower. Lily done tole me that I ain't good enough fer her. She said that I get mean an' crazy when I'm drunk. But I ain't gonna lose her without a fight. See, all's I gotta do is get rid of this kid. The kid's the reason she don't want me around no more, thinks I'll hurt the little brat or somethin'. Well, I'll show her what for!"

"Buford, why don't you let the kid go and you can I can go down to the Buffalo Head Saloon and I'll buy you a drink. What about it?" asked Howard.

"No way, Marshal. You ain't holding any high cards, I am. I done cut this brat once on his arm an' I'm fixin' to cut his throat and you can't do nuthin' about it!"

"Okay, Buford. You're in charge. I see that."

"Yeah, I am in charge for a fact. Don't you ferget it neither, Mister Fancy Lawman."

The drunk hesitated and seemed to be trying to formulate a plan, without much success. Howard decided to help him along.

"Look, Buford. Cutting that kid any more won't help you get things straight with Lily, but I think I know what will help. Why don't you put the knife down on the table in front of you, and then the Parson will go and get Lily and you two can patch things up. How about that?"

"Yeah, right. I may be drunk, but I ain't stupid. If I put down my knife you'll jest shoot me."

"No. I don't want to shoot you. We just don't want you to hurt the kid." Howard looked like he had just made a decision. "I'll tell you what, I'll meet you halfway. Just to show that I'm acting in good faith, if you put your knife on the table and back away, I'll put my gun beside it. Then the Parson will get Lily and you two can talk things out."

The next few moments passed slowly as the drunk considered Howard's offer. Finally, Buford nodded his head. A cunning look crossed his face. "Okay, but I ain't gonna put down my knife first. Seeing as how you're so all-fired anxious to not get the kid hurt, and for us to put down our weapons, how come you don't put your gun on the table first? Then I'll put down my knife."

"I don't like that idea very much, Buford. How do I know you will put down the knife?" Howard's voice reflected just the right amount of apprehension. "What do you think, Parson?"

The minister looked thoughtful. "John, we don't have much choice. There's really nothing else we can do. I think we have to trust Buford to do the right thing."

Howard still looked doubtful, but said, "Okay, Buford, let's get on with it. My hip is killing me. I'll set my .44 down on the table and back away."

"Yeah, yeah, now hurry up Mr. Marshal. An' Preacher Hightower, you stay way back from me. I know all about you an' your tricks. I ain't stupid like Bull was. You ain't gonna get no chance to lay hold of me."

Howard set the .44 down on the table and backed away to his original position. The derringer held behind his back was secure and ready. The drunken man staggered forward unsteadily to the table. His task was more difficult than he had expected because the terror-stricken child started screaming at the top of his lungs and squirming around like a fish on a hook. As Buford reached the table, Howard almost felt like he could read the drunk's mind. He knew that Buford didn't want to give up the knife, but he only had one free hand because he was holding the struggling child. Howard hoped that Buford would opt to put the knife down and pick up the gun. He also hoped Buford wouldn't have enough presence of mind to slide the knife under his belt.

For the first time in years, Howard prayed. He offered a silent prayer for the boy's safety. The answer came quickly as the drunken miner dropped the knife on the table and snatched up the gun.

He then backed away unsteadily. The boy was still ineffectually struggling and crying.

Buford cocked the Smith and Wesson. "Now, Mister Fancy Lawman and Mr. Fancy Preacher. Looks like you two ain't so fancy an' smart after all. Looks like you done gone an' outsmarted yourselves and are fixin' to get yourselves killed. See, I changed my mind. I'm gonna kill the brat all right, but I'm gonna kill you two first!"

Howard knew the .44 was empty, but nonetheless felt a cold chill run through him as the drunk pulled the trigger. After the third hammer-fall, reality began to filter its way through Buford's alcohol-sodden thinking. The boy looked on in such astonishment that he stopped screaming.

"You tricked me! It ain't loaded! It's empty! It's empty!" Buford's screams made the boy's earlier cries seem mild in comparison.

"But this derringer isn't empty, Buford, and Ben Duff's in the alley with a Henry lined up on the back of your head. It's all over. Let the boy go."

"No way, he dies!" Buford began edging toward the knife on the table.

"Do you have a clean shot, Mr. Duff?" yelled Howard.

"I've got him. Just give the word!" Duff shouted back.

Color drained from the drunken miner's face at the sound of Duff's voice. He knew of Duff's reputation and was shocked that Duff had a rifle on him from behind. Drunk though he was, he realized he was trapped.

Reverend Hightower then said, "Buford, I hope you've made your peace with God."

Howard held the derringer steadily at the miner's head. There was death in his eyes. "I'm through waiting. I think I'll kill you right now."

It was never known if it was Howard's words, Duff's, or the preacher's that did the trick. It was enough that the would-be child killer realized that if he tried to inflict any more harm to the boy, he himself would die. Also, drunk or sober, he knew he was inadequate to face Duff, Hightower, or Howard, much less the three of them at once. Bravado was quickly replaced by fear.

"Wait. Wait! Ain't no call to shoot me! I'll let the kid go!" shouted Buford as he released his victim.

The frightened boy made a beeline to Reverend Hightower. The minister picked him up. He took a clean handkerchief from his pocket and commenced to bind the wound on the boy's arm.

At the same time, Buford shakily placed the revolver on the window sill. "Hey, now, I quit, so you can't shoot me. C . . . C'mon now, Reverend, you can't let him shoot me!"

Contempt and rage continued building in Howard, fueled by the thought that as willing as the drunk was to hurt or kill his helpless victim, he was even more unwilling to place himself in harm's way. Howard spoke in a quietly ominous voice. "Yes," he repeated, as if thinking out loud, "I think I'll kill you right now, you cowardly, low-life son-of-a . . . "

"*No, John!*" The minister's voice thundered like he was preaching from the pulpit. "No! Listen to me! He isn't worth it! Don't do it!"

Howard drew two deep breaths. "He doesn't deserve to live, Parson."

"You're right. But I'm thinking about you, not him. Don't do it, son."

"No jury would convict me."

The clergyman stepped toward Howard. The minister made sure the marshal saw the child in his peripheral vision before he asked, "John, would you shoot him in front of this little boy? Don't you think he's seen enough today?"

Howard hesitated. He heavily exhaled his breath and reluctantly eased his finger off the trigger. "All right, Parson. I won't kill him if he doesn't resist arrest. But if he tries for the knife, he's a dead man."

Buford began shaking. His whiskey courage had completely dissipated. "I'll do what you say. Parson, don't let him shoot me!"

"Okay, listen to me," ordered Howard, "Walk toward me with your hands up high. Stay away from that knife on the table if you want to live."

A few moments later, the marshal frisked his prisoner for any concealed weapons while the minister covered him with the derringer handed to him by Howard. They descended down the stairs with their prisoner and his former victim. They were joined at the bottom of the stairs by Wentworth and the employees of the Pink Palace. Ben Duff came in the front door a moment later.

Duff immediately offered congratulations. "Good work, men. Is the boy all right?"

Reverend Hightower answered, "He's fine, Ben." He glanced at Howard. "We're all fine."

The small boy clung tightly to the minister. "You ain't gonna let him hurt me no more, are you?" he whimpered pathetically.

Reverend Hightower gently patted the boy's back. "He'll never hurt you again, I promise."

"But he's strong and mean, and he carries that big knife."

"He's not nearly as strong as Jesus, and Jesus will protect you," replied the minister.

"I ain't never heard tell of nobody named Jesus," said the boy.

"It's all right, son. He knows you, and I work for Him. But let me ask you something. You know me. Do you think I'm strong enough to keep Buford from hurting you?"

The boy's face brightened, "Sure thing." Then his face clouded. "But you can't be with me all the time."

Howard spoke up. "Son, Mr. Duff and I also promise he'll never hurt you. If he tries to even come around you, he'll answer to us."

Reverend Hightower handed the boy to his sobbing mother. The boy tried to put on a brave face.

"Don't cry, Ma. I ain't hurt much, not really, an' he ain't never gonna hurt me again. The preacher said a really strong man named Jesus would protect me. An' the preacher and them two big gunfighters ain't gonna let him hurt me neither."

Several additional onlookers had gathered at the entrance to the Pink Palace, now that Buford was in custody. Seeing that he had an audience, Buford began to sob himself. "The marshal had no call to treat me like that. He was gonna shoot me, shoot me I tell ya'! I ain't no criminal. I jest had a tetch too much to drink, that's all."

The next voice was that of the preacher, not the marshal. "You make me sick at my stomach. Now shut your mouth before I shut it for you."

Buford quit talking but continued sobbing. It was a pathetic sight to see such a large man whimpering like a small child. However, it was obvious that nobody felt any pity for him.

Lily held her son tightly. "Parson, if there's ever anything I can ever do for you, you just tell me."

"You don't owe me anything, Lily. Besides, it was Marshal Howard who rescued your son."

The prostitute turned to face Howard. "I'm beholden to you, Marshal. Same as I told the Reverend, if you ever need anything, anything at all, you just ask." She shuffled her feet and sheepishly said, "Sorry for what I said earlier Marshal Howard, about you being trigger-happy. I was scared and upset. I should'a listened to the Reverend."

"It's okay Lily. You just take care of your son. He's a brave boy." Howard motioned contemptuously toward his prisoner. "And don't worry about Buford. Buford likes living too much. He knows I'll kill him if he bothers your boy again."

Then Howard, the minister and Duff took the prisoner out the door and worked their way through the crowd of onlookers. They escorted Howard's prisoner to the jail and locked him inside one of the two vacant cells. Then they walked from the cell area to the main office.

Howard broke the silence. "Mr. Duff, thanks for your help. And Parson, thank you. I'm glad you were there."

"It was my pleasure, Mr. Howard," replied the other gunfighter.

"Mine also," said the pastor. He added, "John, that was a fine thing you did. You're a good lawman. I'm very proud to be your friend."

Howard looked somewhat embarrassed. "Parson, I'm not sure you should be proud. If you hadn't been there . . . "

Hightower held up his hand. "Please excuse me for interrupting, but you don't need to say anything else. Regardless of how you felt then, or feel now, you did the right thing. That's what counts. You don't need to explain anything."

Howard nodded his head. A few seconds later he felt compelled to ask a question. "Parson, I'm curious about something you said in the Pink Palace. Aren't you preachers supposed to be full of Christian charity?"

"Why do you ask, son? Are you wondering about what I said to Buford, about offering to shut his mouth for him?"

"Yes."

"Normally we are charitable, or at least we should be. But charity begins at home. You see, I know something about this situation that you don't. I didn't tell you because there wasn't time. Also, I suspected that you might have shot Buford outright if you knew in advance."

"Knew what?"

"That little boy is Buford's son."

CHAPTER SIXTEEN

The next evening, Howard decided to start recruitment for his police force. He began looking for Preston Kirby. As he suspected, he found the Texas pistolero playing poker in the Buffalo Head Saloon. He noticed that conversation ceased when he approached the table.

"Mr. Kirby," he asked, "could I talk to you about something?"

"I reckon that depends on what it's about."

Howard smiled to himself, thinking that was just about he same response he would have made. "I'll tell you what, let me buy you a drink and explain what I've got in mind, and if you don't like it, walk away. I'll give you five dollars just for hearing me out. It shouldn't take more than five minutes. Even if you're not interested, you'll earn a dollar a minute."

Kirby gave the marshal a puzzled look. "Lemme see if I got this straight. You're willing to buy me a drink and give me five dollars just for listening to you for five minutes?"

"That's right. What about it?"

Kirby stood up and glanced at his pocket-watch. "Gents, I'll be back in about five minutes. Looks like I ain't flat broke after all."

They walked to a corner table where they would have a little privacy. John Howard and Kirby both reached for the chair that faced the entrance. They compromised when Howard pulled another chair around at an angle, so that both of them had their back to the wall and could view the front door while they talked. Both kept their hands above the table.

Howard started the ball rolling. "Kirby, I'll get right to it. Do you need a job here in Gold Valley?"

The puzzled look returned to the Texan's face. "Depends on what the job is. I had me a good job on the Longstreet spread. Old Man Longstreet was a mighty fine boss, more like a pa to me than a boss, but I'm sorta tired of punchin' cows. I ain't a counter-jumper and have just about decided I ain't much good at mining. I don't much care for being underground."

Howard nodded in agreement. "I know what you mean. I know you're a good man with a gun and I need a couple of deputies. The pay is thirty dollars a month. Are you interested?"

Kirby's sudden laughter rang out so loud that half of the saloon's customers turned to look at the two gunfighters. "You know something, Marshal, I seen a lot of things in my life, including one of them fancy stage plays the last time I was in Denver. There was some feller there who told jokes. He was good, but not nearly so funny as you, nossir. Why do you reckon I'd wanna be a sure-enough lawdog in a Yankee town?"

"Perhaps for the same reason I took the job; the money."

"You do beat all, Marshal, what with your fancy talk an' all. You can do all the perhapsing you want, but how come you think these Yankees would hire me, anyhow?"

"Probably because they hired me. Look, Kirby, I know you could handle the job because some good people recommended you. I told them I didn't think you'd do it, but thought I'd ask because I'd like to have you working with me."

Kirby's facial expression shifted slightly as he mentally noted that Howard said "working with me" instead of "working for me." He took a sip of whiskey. "You mind tellin' me who it was that recommended me?"

"Ben Duff for one and Reverend Hightower for another. In fact, the Parson said that if it was a question of money, he would pay you another twenty dollars a month out of his own pocket."

Kirby tilted back his hat. "Now let me get this straight. This Preacher Hightower, the one what whipped Bull Jackson no less, he said he wanted me to do this job?"

"That's right, and he and Ben Duff weren't the only ones I

talked to. Hiram Longstreet was also in favor of hiring you. He said you were the best foreman he ever had and was the fastest man with a gun he had ever seen."

"Mighty kind of Old Man Longstreet. And this preacher said he'd pay me twenty a month out of his own pocket?"

"That's right."

"Then I reckon the Bull must've really rung his bell, even harder than anybody thought. I heard that preacher was one of the good ones. Where would an honest preacher get an extra twenty a month? They don't even make that much, usually."

"Kirby, I asked him the same thing. I'm satisfied with his answer. If you want to hear it, you can go ask him."

"Naw," replied the Texan. "Ain't no need to if you say so. Besides, him having money ain't no stranger than him being able to do what he done to the Bull. I swear, he's about the blamedest preacher I ever run into."

"That he is. Now, what about helping me out? I need a good man siding me."

"Why you reckon you need help? You kilt Cole Madison, an' he was good. Fact is, he was better'n good, he was one of the best. I reckon there ain't more'n two or three men alive that could have out-shot him. I woulda hated to have to tackle Cole my ownself."

"He was a tough man," agreed Howard. "There aren't many like him around." Howard adjusted his position. The wound in his hip was beginning to bother him. "Well, what about it? Will you take the job?"

Kirby still didn't look convinced. "I dunno. I still don't see as how you need much help."

"Look Kirby, anyone can use help sometimes, especially in a town growing as fast as this one. Besides, I think you and me, and maybe a third man like us, would make a police force as good as any. I think we could protect the folks who need it. And I think we could do it better than most lawmen. You know the ones I'm talking about, the Yankee lawdogs who think it's a crime to have a southern accent or to be a cowhand in town just trying to have a little fun."

Kirby turned the glass in front of him, causing the whiskey to swirl. "I dunno. The whole notion kinda seems strange. Just the sound of it—Preston Kirby, Yankee Lawdog. Yessir, it do sound strange for a fact." He chuckled at the thought. "But you know, it sort of tickles me. And I'll tell you straight, I could use some cash money. See, I got me a wife back in Texas. Cuter 'n a button. Best-lookin' gal in the whole state, I reckon. Sweetest, too. She's how come I don't go near the Pink Palace. I been tryin' to get some money so I could send for her." He shifted in his chair. "Hmm . . . let's say maybe I was interested. What would I have to do?"

"Basically help me keep the peace."

Kirby folded his hands on the table and stared for several seconds at the buffalo head mounted on the wall over the bar. "See, it's like this. I normally ain't got no use for the law. I ain't real educated and can't talk fancy like you and Ben Duff. I can't even hardly read and write. And I don't cotton to people messing in my business like Yankee lawmen do to southern boys."

Howard nodded in agreement. "I don't like Yankee lawmen bothering us, either. But like I said, if you take this job, you won't be harassing anyone. In fact, you'll be working with another former Confederate soldier, namely me. All you'll have to do is just keep order and protect anybody who needs it, like when the Nueces Kid pistol-whipped that farmer and insulted his wife. I heard what you said to him when I got there. I'm confident that you would have stopped him if I didn't."

"That was different. If that farmer had been by hisself, I most likely wouldn't have done nothing. The Kid may have been a troublemaker, but he was right about forking your own broncs. I just can't abide by women, kids, and old folks being bothered."

"Kirby," said Howard as he laid fifty-five dollars on the table, "here's the five I owe you for hearing me out, plus another fifty for your first month's salary. I'm willing to take a chance if you are. What about it?"

Kirby stared at the money. "I won't wear no tin star."

"I don't wear one either," replied Howard as he patted his

shirt pocket. "Mine stays in here, unless I need to take it out. You can do the same thing."

Kirby considered the buffalo head some more. "Ain't you being kinda free with the town's money and the parson's money, what with paying me in advance? How do you know I won't just take that cash money and ride for Deadwood or even Yankton?"

"Because I know your type of man. You ride for the brand. You wouldn't take money unless you earned it," said Howard. "Besides, Reverend Hightower and the town wouldn't be out the money, I would. I'm not authorized to pay in advance."

"You do beat all, Marshal. You surely do beat all," said Kirby as he pocketed the cash.

CHAPTER SEVENTEEN

The next day, Howard decided to augment his tiny police force by another man. For his next deputy, he chose to take Reverend Hightower's advice again and sought out Ian O'Hara, late of the Second Cavalry. He found O'Hara lounging on the street near the Hightowers' house. The house was located at the edge of town. And O'Hara wasn't alone. It seemed that several young men also found a reason to gather there.

When Howard approached, he was greeted by a more open and friendly response than he was used to. True, he could still sense some tension in the air, yet at the same time, the men present didn't seem to be too skittish around him. At least, they didn't stop talking upon his arrival, and no one begged his pardon.

"Trooper O'Hara, might I have a word with you?" asked the marshal.

"Sure. Except I ain't 'Trooper' O'Hara anymore. I'm just plain old Ian O'Hara, looking for adventure and romance, or maybe just two bits so I can eat supper tonight," grinned the redhead.

"I can't help you with the romance part, but I expect you got that handled. That's why you and these other young bucks are hanging around this particular house. But I might be able to help with the other."

"Marshal, if you're talking about buying me supper, I'm all ears," replied the ex-cavalryman.

"So are the rest of us, Marshal Howard," piped up another man.

"Is that so?" mused Howard. "I'll tell you what. I count an even half dozen men here. I'll buy supper for anyone who can hit a target I pick, one out of two times. And there's no risk involved.

You don't have to put up any money to shoot for supper. Any takers?"

Everyone present agreed readily, because after all, hadn't the marshal said it didn't cost anything to compete? After Howard named the target, however, all but O'Hara dropped out. This was because Howard designated the head of a shovel that was propped up on its handle against a small boulder, some two hundred yards distant, down the road leading away from town.

"Ain't no reason to waste a shot at that thing," grumbled one of the former contestants. "It'd be pure luck to hit somethin' that little-bitty so far away."

"Yeah," replied another. "I don't reckon a man would have much chance of hitting that rock it's propped up against, much less the shovel."

"Well, I'm hungry, and I got me some cartridges, which I might add, I can't eat," said O'Hara. "One thing, Marshal Howard. I reckon I'd like to stroll down to that shovel and look around a little before I shoot it."

"Go ahead. But if you're concerned about anyone being hit by a ricochet, don't worry. Kirby and I already scouted the area. Nobody's near it right now, except Kirby, and he's hunkered down by that clump of boulders beyond the target. If you shoot, you won't hurt anyone."

"Good. And you say I've got two shots to hit it?"

"Yes, if you need them."

Now a flurry of betting began among the onlookers. It seemed that none were as hard up for cash as O'Hara, because they all had money to wager on whether or not he could hit the shovel. The dilemma they faced was that no one would bet that O'Hara could hit the target. This was quickly solved by Howard himself, who gave even odds that O'Hara's bullet would find its mark.

Now the gamblers hesitated, being nervous at the prospect of betting against the marshal. However, when Howard told them that he would give them two-to-one odds, greed overcame hesitation. After the men pooled their wagers together, there was almost twenty dollars at stake, just about the amount a man would earn working a month in the mines. Howard himself was risking almost forty dollars, having given the two-to-one odds.

O'Hara looked at the lawman. "You don't believe in putting any pressure on a feller, do you, Marshal?"

"There's no pressure on you, O'Hara. I'm the one who will be out forty dollars if you miss, not you."

O'Hara shook his head sideways in disagreement. "I reckon I don't see it that way. See, I really ain't got no money. I lost it all in a poker game over at the saloon. I couldn't afford to pay you back, and I don't like owing anybody."

"O'Hara, if you miss, you won't owe me a thing. I'll pay the money and no hard feelings. Besides, I think you can hit that shovel. What do you think?"

For a reply, O'Hara reached down and picked up some dirt. He let it sift slowly out of his fingers. The brown particles of soil fell almost straight down, with only a slight motion to the side. O'Hara then proned himself out on the ground, laying his hat to the side. He made one adjustment on the rear sight of his .45-70 Springfield rifle and squeezed off a shot. An instant later, the shovel clanged against the side of the rock, and slid partly to the ground.

The observers spontaneously applauded, even though they were out some cash. Apparently, they felt it was worth the price they had wagered to see the marksmanship displayed by O'Hara.

Howard's next words caused another round of applause. "I'll tell you what, gentlemen," he said. "If you can ante up two bits or so for O'Hara's supper, we'll call it even."

"Sure enough, Marshal. Here's thirty cents. That'll buy him the biggest steak in Miz Mayo's diner." The speaker was a miner who had the most money riding on the outcome, a five-dollar gold piece. "It's mighty good of you to not take our money. Still and all, you won it fair and square."

Howard disagreed. "Not really. I'll let you in on a secret. I've seen O'Hara shoot. He knocked an Indian off his pony farther away than that shovel. Now I know a man's a bigger target than the head of a shovel, but O'Hara did it from horseback while he was being shot at himself. A rifleman who can pull that off shouldn't have much difficulty winning the bet we made today."

All attention was suddenly focused on the front door of the Hightower residence. Rosa stepped out. She was carrying a Springfield rifle similar to O'Hara's, except it was in .50-70 caliber. She appeared not to notice that everyone was staring at her. She did notice John Howard.

"Why were you shooting, John?" She asked.

The use of his first name was duly noted by a surprised and slightly flustered John Howard.

"I wasn't shooting, Rosa. This young man was," replied Howard, motioning toward O'Hara.

"What was he shooting at?" she inquired.

"That shovel by the boulder down the road. If you look hard, you can see the shovel still leaning against the rock."

"Why did he shoot it?"

"I asked him to. I told him I would buy him his supper if he could hit it. What I really had in mind though, was to see if a shot he made at an Indian was more due to skill than luck. He just proved it was skill." Howard then turned to O'Hara. "Since you're as good as I thought you are, would you like to work with Preston Kirby and me, keeping the peace in Gold Valley?"

O'Hara grinned from ear to ear. "Does a bear sleep in the woods? Of course, I'll do it."

"Good. Let's meet later today at the town jail to discuss your duties." Pulling an envelope from his pocket he added, "Your first month's salary is in there. There's thirty dollars. Gold Valley pays its lawmen in advance."

O'Hara considered the money handed to him. "One thing, Marshal, before I take the money. I'm a right fair hand with a rifle, if I do say so myself, but I ain't no great shakes with a pistol. Don't get me wrong, I can hit what I shoot at every time, 'bout easy as I can with a rifle. But what I mean is that I ain't fast like you, Ben Duff, or Preston Kirby. Truth is, I don't even own a short gun, just this Springfield and my new Winchester '73. You still want to hire me?"

"Sure. Good judgement and accuracy are more important than speed. Besides, if I had a choice, I'd rather use a rifle myself, most of the time."

Then all attention turned back to Rosa. She had leaned the big Springfield rifle against the house by the front door, stepped briefly inside, and reappeared holding a cushion. While the men, Howard included, looked on in wonder, she folded the cushion in half, and then placed it on the porch rail and laid the forearm of the Springfield on it. Then she knelt down while she positioned the buttstock against her shoulder.

"Careful now, Miss Rosa, if you're really planning on shooting. Women and guns don't mix, no ma'am, not at all. 'Specially with a big gun like one of them Springfield rifles. They got some kick to 'em." The speaker was the miner who had given the money for O'Hara's supper.

Rosa smiled sweetly. "Then perhaps everyone had better stay out of the way."

She carefully sighted and squeezed off the shot. The shovel, struck by the heavy bullet, fell the rest of the way to the ground. Everyone present, including Howard, could only stare in wide-eyed amazement.

She smiled at Howard and then turned to the miner who had warned her about the Springfield's recoil. "What do you know? You're right, it does have a heavy kick." She continued to smile at Howard. "Well, John. It looks like you owe me supper now, as well. I'll let you know when I want to collect. Perhaps we can talk about it later this evening when my papa and sister return."

CHAPTER EIGHTEEN

Later that evening, Howard returned to the Hightower residence and saw all three family members sitting on the front porch. There was also a fourth person there, whose presence caused the lawman to wonder about his eyesight. Were his eyes going bad, as he heard had happened to Hickock? On a closer look, he determined that his eyesight was all right, and that Ben Duff was, in fact, also present. Everyone seemed very comfortable. Was Consuela holding Duff by the arm? It was hard to tell in the dim light. When Duff saw the marshal, he stood, tipped his hat to the girls, and shook hands with their father.

He met Howard on the way out and was courteous as always. "Good evening, Mr. Howard. I was just leaving. I hope you have a pleasant visit."

Howard nodded in return. "Good evening, Mr. Duff."

Howard noticed that he experienced a twinge of jealousy when he saw Duff. It was irrational, yet nonetheless there. Perhaps he resented the obvious good feelings that the Hightowers had toward the older gunman. That puzzled him, because they had only been in Gold Valley a few months. Rapidly sorting out his feelings as he approached the house, he admitted to himself that he especially didn't like Rosa talking to Duff. After all, although Duff was more than twice her age, he was a handsome man with smooth manners.

Upon further reflection, Howard decided to not fret over the situation any longer, because he was developing a strong hunch that Rosa truly liked him, which was why he had accepted her earlier invitation. Furthermore, he knew that Duff was supposed to be courting Angelique Mayo, and that he had the reputation of being a gentleman. Lastly, Howard knew with certain conviction that Rosa's father would not let anyone take advantage of either of his daughters. Anyone, even a gunfighter of Duff's reputation, would be foolish beyond all measure to incur the anger of Reverend Hightower with his daughters' well-being at issue.

When he gained the steps of the porch, Consuela could barely contain herself. She jumped out of her chair, and with the agility of a young deer, skipped to meet him, her hands extended. Grabbing both of his hands, she escorted him to the porch. "Papa, Rosa, look who's coming to pay us a visit!"

"Hmm," replied her father, "it looks like it might be Marshal Howard, Consuela. Am I right?"

Consuela took her father's bantering in stride. "Yes, I do believe it is." With a mischievous grin, she added, "but perhaps I should search him for identification just to make sure."

Howard was grateful for the shadows that were falling, because he felt his face begin to redden. He thought he saw the minister and Rosa blush also, or was it just his imagination? Consuela seemed to be the only one who was having a good time.

"You'll not search anyone, my child," said her father in a stern voice. "Fun is fun, but do you want to give John the wrong impression?"

"I'm sorry, Papa," replied a subdued Consuela. "But we all know I was only joking."

Hightower looked at his daughter with open affection. He never could stay upset for long with either of his girls. "Of course you were only joking. Now, why don't you and I go inside and check on supper? You will be joining us for supper, John?"

"With pleasure," answered Howard.

"Papa, I want to stay outside," complained Consuela.

"I know you do. But we don't want the steaks to burn. You know your old papa can't even boil water, much less cook and prepare food."

"But why can't Rosa finish cooking supper? It's not fair. Why should she get to stay with John?"

Her father didn't reply. Instead, he gently took her hand in his own. Then he extended his right hand to Howard and shook hands with him. "Consuela and I will be inside. Supper should be ready in about twenty minutes." He then ushered his younger daughter through the front door.

With the porch to themselves, Howard gazed for several seconds at Rosa. She blushed again. There was no doubt the second time. "I'm sorry that my little sister was making such a fuss over you." She emphasized the word *little*.

"I'm not sorry," said Howard. "She's a beautiful girl. But, I also know she's a good girl who was just engaging in some harmless flirting."

Rosa frowned deeply. "But she's only a child." She softened her expression and added, "Still, I agree with you. She is a good girl, and she is beautiful. She looks like our mama."

"And she looks like you, only not so beautiful."

The cloud that had descended on Rosa's face completely evaporated, and was replaced by a shy smile. Her hands began to tremble, and she nervously twisted them. Howard, however, did not notice, because his eyes were full of her lovely face.

After several seconds, she murmured, "Thank you. I've wondered if you had even noticed me." She slowly allowed her brown eyes to meet his penetrating gaze.

Howard blurted out his next words without thinking. "I would be blind not to notice one of the most beautiful women I've ever met. I haven't stopped thinking about you since the first time I met you. Sometimes, when I think of you, I regret that I am not more than I am."

Rosa took a step closer to him, and the scent of her made him lightheaded. She looked deeply into his eyes as she asked, "How can you say that? You are quite a man. Everyone knows that."

Howard involuntarily shook his head from side to side. "Rosa, you don't know much about me. Remember those things you said when we first met? You were closer to the truth than I care to admit."

She disagreed. "No, that's not so. I only said those things because I was embarrassed and frightened. But I was wrong. Papa had a long talk with me that very night. And we've talked about you many times since then. Papa convinced me how wrong I was."

Howard kept gazing at the beautiful girl before him. "Rosa, in the last ten years since the war ended, I've done a lot of things that I'm not proud of. In the dime novels, they sometimes write about gunfighters who are really European royalty or heirs to great fortunes in the east. But that doesn't apply to me. I'm just a drifting saddle bum with no home, no family, and no country." He grinned nervously. "I suppose if I were a poet, I would say that I am a man alone."

"But you are not alone. You have my father and my sister . . . and me." Her blush returned and her voice trailed away.

Howard was more confused now than when he had discovered that she could shoot. That she might be romantically interested in him both pleased and confounded him beyond all of his widest expectations. He took a step toward her that brought them face to face. His arms slowly encircled her waist, and she gently raised her lips to meet his as they held one another in the fading light.

In spite of the chill in the night air, Howard felt warmth flood over him as they kissed. For the first time in over a decade, Howard felt at peace with himself. In the embrace of this girl, he felt anger and bitterness melt away, more quickly than snow in the sunshine. He was not sure of what was happening to him. Nothing he had ever experienced had prepared him for these emotions.

The moment was broken by the creak of the door and the sound of Reverend Hightower clearing his throat. "You two had better get inside before Consuela finds you like that. Besides, supper is ready."

CHAPTER NINETEEN

Beginning that evening when Howard and Rosa first kissed, the gunman started to see the world in a different light. He no longer felt like he was alone. He was less cynical, less aggressive, and more patient. In short, he was becoming a better man.

Of course, there were many people, like those with mining interests, who were glad to have Howard as the town marshal, regardless of any shortcomings he might possess. The Gold Valley Mine and First Strike Mine were the main reason the town of Gold Valley came into existence. While not nearly so large or profitable as the larger Homestake Mine near Deadwood, the mine owners still employed a sizeable number of miners and other workers. Consequently, the town also had more than its fair share of thieves, grifters, prostitutes, crooked gamblers, and claim jumpers.

Fortunately for the people of Gold Valley, having lawmen with well-deserved reputations as gunfighters helped to maintain the peace. Even Ian O'Hara was an asset, because although he was not considered a gunfighter like Howard and Kirby, most people knew he was a dead shot with a rifle or pistol. The young ex-trooper had another valuable asset, his personality. He was known for being affable and friendly, willing to give the other fellow the benefit of the doubt. Preston Kirby was also easygoing, although he was known to be a dangerous gunman. John Howard was considered another matter when he first arrived in Gold Valley. Few would have described him as being friendly and affable. The marshal was regarded, even by his growing number of supporters, as being totally devoid of mercy.

However, another side of Howard had started to emerge, the side seen by Reverend Hightower from the first time they met.

This positive side of Howard's personality was coming more to the forefront mainly as a result of his association with the Hightowers and particularly his romantic involvement with Rosa. Consequently, more and more of the people of Gold Valley were beginning to think that maybe, just maybe, there was more to this new marshal than just a quick temper and fast gun.

The developing change in Howard was soon demonstrated through the unfolding of certain events. He was shown to possess more than just courage and fast reflexes. He was also shown to have a high level of astuteness, a quick wit, finely honed intelligence, and yes, even mercy. This served to win Howard grudging respect from those people who initially thought he was too eager to kill.

One such event occurred on a Saturday night at the Buffalo Head Saloon, a few days before Christmas. Several cowhands had joined the miners for a Friday night filled with drinking, gambling, and carousing. The cowboys were employed at one of three ranches that had started nearby. Like almost all patrons of the saloon, these men were armed.

All of them reckoned themselves to be men of consequence who should be given a wide berth, especially after having tasted of the free-flowing liquor that sold for a nickel a shot. However, there was one young boy present who fancied himself as an unusually dangerous pistol-fighter.

This would-be gunman bore the same name as a real gunfighter, Dave Mather. Nobody knew if the boy's real name was actually Dave Mather, or if he had adopted the name so that he might be mistaken for the genuine article, Mysterious Dave Mather. After all, Mysterious Dave, as his nickname implied, was an enigmatic gunman who was regarded as a deadly shootist, but about whom little else was known. It wouldn't be the first time or the last time that an unknown person had tried to cash in on the fame of a known gunfighter by attempting to assume their identity.

The source of the young man's name aside, it was evident that he had something in common with another gunfighter, the recently-deceased Nueces Kid. He resembled the Kid both in terms of age and external appearance. However, all similarities ended there. The Kid, it must be remembered, while a braggart and bully, was nevertheless a bonafide gunfighter, who could back up his tough talk with a fast draw and accurate shooting. That the Kid was a dead gunfighter was simply due to the fact that he had drawn down on a faster and more ruthless gunman in the person of John Howard. The Kid was also someone who could handle his liquor. This particular cowboy, calling himself Dave Mather, could not.

Mather's mistake started after he drew into a full house to take the table stakes of the poker game he was playing. There was more than fifty dollars that he raked into his hat. Normally, had he not been under the influence of John Barleycorn, he would have realized that he had more than two months' wages in his possession, and that it would behoove him to take care of it. But he was young, drunk and reckless, and wanted to impress everyone present.

"Hey everybody," he exclaimed, "anybody's who's a friend of mine gets a free drink on me!"

The boy instantly discovered that everyone in the place was his friend, because all at once everyone jammed their way to the bar. The were even joined by several men who were loafing outside the saloon. That was okay, because a bleached-blonde, teenaged saloon girl named Kathy appeared out of nowhere, and was Mather's new best friend. Had Mather been sober, he wouldn't have looked twice at the girl, because her looks were already being ravaged by her lifestyle. The culprits were venereal disease and the alcohol that she fortified herself with every night in order to help her face the prospect of being pawed by drunken, sweaty miners and cowboys.

However, Mather was far from sober, and didn't realize his mistake until after all of his money was gone. What's more, as soon as his money disappeared, so did all of his new-found drinking buddies, and, although it was hard for him to believe, even his new girlfriend deserted him.

"Hey, c'mon back here," he slurred, as she walked away to another customer.

"Sorry, honey," she responded, "looks like you're flat broke again. Come back an' see me when you've got fifty dollars to spend just on me."

"Hey, you ain't worth more'n fifty cents, and I done spent that much on you. Get on back here."

The girl responded by telling young mister Mather where to go, complete with an obscene hand gesture. The words, the gesture and the ensuing laughter of the other customers all combined to cause Mather to snap. He staggered out of his chair and screamed, "Get back over here you dirty whore, or I'll shoot them fancy earrings off you!"

"Watch it, cowboy." The speaker was Sean Finnegan, who as his name implied, was as Irish as Paddy's pig. Finnegan was a natty dresser who sported a bowler hat like Bat Masterson. He dressed well because he had been a poor boy in the old country, and now was a successful businessman, namely the proud proprietor of the Buffalo Head Saloon. He had seen to it that he was present in his establishment more often than not after the incident in which Kirby had shot out windows following an insult by one of his bartenders. He felt relieved that this boy was no Preston Kirby.

"Settle down, bucko," he repeated, "and I'll stand you for a free drink. Just remember, no gunplay is allowed in my saloon."

Mather turned to glare at the dapper Irishman. "Yeah, is that so? You reckon you can talk to me like that cause if I do anything y'all jest call that big bad killer of a marshal, huh? Well, boys, bring him on, an' that Texas gunslick that's his deppity. I ain't afeared of either of 'em! I'd shoot 'em soon as look at 'em! Bring 'em on! They ain't nuthin' but a couple . . . "

Mather's voice trailed off as he began to notice that quiet was rapidly engulfing the room. The piano player stopped, and no one spoke. However, several men looked toward a back corner table in the shadows. A wave of panic suddenly swept over Mather, to the extent that he almost wet his pants like a two-year old, when he saw that both Howard and Kirby were sitting at the table. Both lawmen stood as one.

"Here we go," said Kirby. His voice was low and calm. "Reckon this here's when I start earning my money. You want me to take him, John?"

"Wait a second," replied Howard. "I promised someone that I'm not going to shoot unless I absolutely have to." He carefully scrutinized Mather.

"Take a close look at him, Preston. We may not have to kill him. Do you see what I mean?"

The Texas gunfighter's eyes narrowed as he saw what Howard was talking about. "Okay, maybe you're right. How do we play it?"

"You get him to talking. I'll get closer to him and disarm him. What do you think?"

"Let's do it. Hey, an' try not to get betwixt me an' him, just in case." Then to Mather, Kirby said, "Look partner, let's talk about this here thing. Ain't no reason for anybody to start shooting. Somebody might get hurt if we do."

"Huh?" Mather was now confused as well as drunk. "Ain't you Preston Kirby?"

"Sure enough. That's the name my pa give me."

Mather became even more confused. "An' you ain't gonna fight me?"

"Look son, I don't want to fight you. Ain't got no call to. Why don't you just take that free drink an' forget about fightin'?"

While Kirby held Mather's attention, Howard eased closer and closer to the drunken youth. When he had closed the distance to about six feet, Mather suddenly noticed him, and went for his gun. Nobody except Howard and Kirby saw what happened next because they were all too busy diving for cover. Nobody felt they needed to see what would happen, though. In the minds of everyone present, except for the two law officers, the outcome was a foregone conclusion. There was hardly a soul present who would have given a plugged nickel for Mather's chances of living to the ripe old age of twenty.

Therefore, no one was surprised at the two loud noises that followed. What was surprising was that they were not gunshots. They were the sounds of Howard's fist striking Mather's temple and Mather's body hitting the floor. Mather was knocked out cold, but was alive. In fact, he would be none the worse for wear, except for a headache the size of Kansas when he would finally wake up the next day.

Howard took Mather's gun from the holster, frisked him for any other weapons, and faced the saloon. "Can anyone give us a hand carrying him outside?"

A thoroughly relieved Sean Finnegan answered, "Sure, Marshal. Rufe, why don't you and Meagher tote him out. It'll be worth a drink apiece."

While the still-unconscious drunk was being dragged outside, Finnegan said, "Thanks for not shooting him. Blood's mighty tough to get up." He hesitated before asking a follow-up question. "Begging your pardon, Marshal Howard, but can I ask you a question?"

"You don't have to beg my pardon, and neither does anyone else, unless they're looking for trouble," replied Howard in an irritated tone. In a slightly less harsh voice he followed with, "What do you want to know, why Kirby or I didn't shoot him?"

"Well, yes, now that you mention it, why didn't you?"

"Do you want to tell him, Preston?" Howard asked.

"Okay. You see, Mr. Finnegan, that there boy wasn't no real hairy-legged pistol-fighter. He was just a little drunk kid trying to be a big man."

"How did you know that?"

"Easy. See, the boy hadn't loosened the thong from his hammer. If he had tried to draw, especially as drunk as he was, it would have taken him from now till the Fourth of July to clear leather. And there was something else."

Now everyone was listening. "What was that?" asked the saloon-keeper.

"You want to tell him, John?"

Howard nodded at his deputy. "Okay. The other thing was that he's carrying a .36 caliber Colt Navy revolver. It's a fine weapon, but like all cap and ball pistols, there has to be percussion caps on the cylinder nipples for the gun to shoot. His pistol wasn't capped. Maybe he was drunk when he loaded it, I don't know. In any event, it was very easy to see that with the light behind him. He couldn't have shot that gun if he wanted to."

The bartender nodded but still had one more question. "But what if he had another gun and tried to use it?"

The two law officers exchanged brief glances. It was Kirby who answered the question.

"Then I reckon them fellers wouldn't be toting him outside. They'd be headed to the undertaker, instead."

CHAPTER TWENTY

Howard was invited to spend the Christmas holiday with the Hightowers. He consented, of course, and for the first time since the deaths of his family, the melancholy he had experienced at that time of year was actually replaced with anticipation and happiness.

He and his deputies were having an easy week, allowing him to spend time with Rosa and her family. Everyone in Gold Valley seemed to be, if not on their best behavior, at least not as intent on engaging in the unbridled pursuit of mayhem and destruction.

Howard wanted to get something special for the Hightowers, especially Rosa, but had no idea of what to get her and Consuela. He sought advice from Angelique Mayo. He got the chance to speak with her during one afternoon when she was going over her hotel books in her office.

She looked up with a lovely smile when he knocked on the door of her office. "Come in, John. I don't see much of you lately. How have you been?"

"I'm fine, Mrs. Mayo, in fact better than fine. But I need some advice. Do you have a minute?"

"Of course, John, on the condition that you call me 'Angelique'. That's what my friends call me."

"Okay, Angelique. I just don't want to seem discourteous or appear too forward."

"John, I would never mistake you for being discourteous or too forward. Besides, I suspect that you feel about Rosa Hightower the same way I do about Ben Duff."

Howard was somewhat surprised that Angelique had confided in him like she did. While it was rumored that the beautiful hotel owner and Duff were courting, it had never been confirmed.

Her candor served to make Howard feel more at ease around her, so much so that he felt safe in saying, "Then Ben Duff is a lucky man. Rosa is the reason I'm here. I want to get her and Consuela something special for Christmas, but don't have any idea what to buy them."

"For Consuela, anything from you would work. But you're always safe in getting her a pretty parasol. I happen to know that she likes green. Further, I know that Mr. Thorton has received a shipment of new parasols that came straight from Chicago. If you would like, you and I can stroll over there today or tomorrow, and I'll show them to you."

"I would be much appreciative. Now what about Rosa?"

She knitted her eyebrows together and considered the question. Suddenly, she snapped her fingers and motioned to Howard. "I think I know of the perfect gift. Shut the door and come over to the desk. I want to show you something."

Howard closed the door and complied with his landlady's request. When he drew near, she stood up and pulled out a gold cross from under the top of her dress. It was secured by a gold chain around her neck, and had four diamonds embedded in it, one at each of the four ends the cross.

Howard was impressed. "That's magnificent. But it looks like it's one-of-a-kind. Besides, I think I might have to rob a bank or mine payroll to pay for it."

Angelique laughed. Her laughter was as pleasing to the ear as her appearance was to the eyes. "You silly goose, I'm not offering you this one. It was given to me by Ben. But look here."

With that, she extracted a small cedar box from the top of her desk. She opened it to reveal some inexpensive costume jewelry. Then, with a conspiratorial wink, she pulled out the felt-lined base of the box, to reveal a false bottom. In the bottom of the case was the mate to the cross and chain that she wore. She handed it to Howard so he could examine it.

"I think that your Rosa would love that particular piece of jewelry." She finished with, "And now, in the words of our town marshal, 'What do you think,' John?"

Howard could only stare. "I can't accept that, Angelique. Like I said, I can't afford it, unless I rob Pepper's bank."

"Perhaps it would serve that dirty old toad right if someone did hold up his bank." She laughed with Howard at her own joke. "Just kidding, John, about robbing the bank. But in all seriousness, I think you can afford this."

"I'm hesitant to ask, but how much is it?" inquired Howard.

"It's free. Now wait just a moment before you say anything. Consider this is a gift from me to you. I would be pleased for you to give it to Rosa. The only price involved is that you can't tell anyone where you got it."

Howard was dumbfounded. "This makes no sense. That has to be worth at least one hundred dollars, maybe more. Why would you give me something that valuable?"

"Simply because I want to. But think of it this way. Since you've been here, my business has tripled or quadrupled, both in the hotel and the diner. People feel absolutely safe with you here. Having you around these past few months has probably made me more money than the price of this cross and chain."

"But how did you get two pieces like that? Did Ben Duff give you both of them?"

"Actually, no. The one in the jewelry box is one that I picked up in Chicago when I went there on business last year. You see, before I left Gold Valley to visit Chicago, Eli Thorton asked me to pick up one from the jeweler who made it. Eli and his family were going to make the trip with me, but had to cancel when his wife got sick. When I got there, I thought it was such a beautiful work of art that I asked the jeweler to also make one for me. He did. I didn't tell anyone because it was none of anyone's business. I brought the one Eli purchased to him. Imagine my surprise when Ben gave that very cross and necklace to me last Christmas. Unbeknownst to me, it turned out that Ben had Eli order it especially for me. Naturally, Eli didn't share that information with me when he asked me pick it up for him."

Now it was Howard's turn to laugh. "So Ben Duff had a one-of-a-kind piece of jewelry made for you that wasn't really one-of-a-kind. You had an identical one made later. What did he say when you told him?"

"Good Heavens, I never told him! And you can't either. That's the price, your silence. I can't use two, and I would die before I would disappoint Ben. I've been wanting to see that the right person gets this one. I think Rosa Hightower is that person."

Howard could only look at Angelique in quiet admiration. "You are quite a lady. I'll say it again, Ben Duff is very lucky to have someone like you." He tapped his fingers on the edge of the desk. "I accept your gift. Rosa will love it. May I tell her the story behind it?"

"That's entirely up to you. I would only ask that if you do, you swear her to secrecy. Better yet, don't tell her. As I said, I wouldn't hurt Ben's feelings for anything. You're in love yourself. You should know what I mean."

She walked around the desk and handed the cross and chain to Howard, who placed it in his pocket. He felt a surge of deep affection for this cheerful and lovely woman. In gratitude for the gift, he spontaneously hugged her.

Unfortunately, neither of them noticed that when Howard had closed the door earlier, he had unknowingly left it partially ajar, just enough for someone about to enter the room to look inside first. Had they looked in the direction of the doorway when they embraced, they would have seen Ben Duff standing there, silently staring at the two of them with a look of total dismay and consternation on his face.

CHAPTER TWENTY-ONE

Howard arrived at the Hightower residence around noon on Christmas Day. He came bearing gifts that would have appeared incongruous to someone not familiar with him. For Rosa, of course, he had the exquisite gold and diamond cross that had been passed on to him from Angelique Mayo. He gave Consuela a fancy parasol that had been picked out by Angelique. However, he also brought Rosa and Consuela matching .41 caliber Remington double barreled derringers. They were identical to his own hideout gun, except that they were nickel-plated and had genuine ivory grips.

He realized that the .41 lacked long range stopping power, but felt that it was very effective up close. Also, at only a scant eleven ounces in weight, and less than five inches in length, he knew that the tiny pistols were small enough to be comfortably carried in either a purse or dress pocket. He also believed that a two-shot pistol on one's person was far more effective than a more powerful six-shot revolver that was out of reach.

Even though he knew that most western men respected women and would not bother them, he remembered very vividly the first day they arrived in Gold Valley, when the girls were accosted. He was determined to take no chances where the safety of Rosa and Consuela was concerned.

He gave a leather-bound Bible to Reverend Hightower, because he had seen the one used by his friend. It was dog-eared from use, and was so worn that it was about to fall apart.

When he arrived at the front door, Consuela was there to greet him, as always. She kissed him on both cheeks and taking him by the hand, escorted him to the parlor. "You're early. Papa and Rosa had to run an errand," she said. "They should be home in a few minutes."

Being alone with the seductive girl made Howard uncomfortable, to say the least. "Perhaps I should wait outside, Consuela."

"Nonsense. You are perfectly safe with me. I won't bite you," she said with her most engaging smile. "Here, let me take your coat."

As Howard slid his coat off, there was a moment when his arms were immobilized. It was at this precise moment that Consuela decided to assist him. She stood in front of him and, in a thinly-veiled effort to take the coat, she wrapped both of her arms around him. She pressed herself against him. She inhaled sharply but didn't say a word.

Howard was caught completely off-guard. The Hightower women seemed to have that effect on him. "Consuela, I think it's best that you let me do this myself. You're just a child, and don't know what you're doing."

"What's the matter," she gently taunted, "are you afraid of me?" Her face was only a few scant inches from his. "Or are you afraid of yourself, and think that you would like to kiss me?"

Pressing herself more tightly against him, she murmured, "You said I'm just a child. I say I'm a woman. What do I feel like, a child or a woman?"

Howard refused to answer as he tried to extricate himself. He was keenly conscious of the intense beauty of this girl, and was very much aware of her considerable feminine charm. At the same time, he knew that he was in love with her sister. He had no intention of being unfaithful to Rosa, and the longer he and Consuela stayed in that position, the more his resolve began to fade as the temptation to kiss her grew.

He succeeded in pulling his arms out and gently pushed her away. "Consuela, you're a beautiful young woman and can take your pick of suitors, only not me. You and I will always be close friends, and I do care for you, but not as I love Rosa. Think of me as your big brother."

Consuela looked at him as he spoke, and the beginning of a small tear took shape in her left eye. Her lips trembled slightly as she murmured, "I don't want to think of you as a brother, but as my beau. I don't care about the difference in our ages. Why do you love Rosa and not me? Everyone else seems to think I'm pretty. Why don't you?"

"You are far more than just pretty, you're very beautiful. But I'm in love with your sister." Howard took her hand in his. "Who knows why these things happen as they do? Your father is the philosopher; I'm not. Perhaps he could tell you why. But I have told you the truth. We both know that for us to become involved would be wrong. We can't do that, can we?"

Consuela wiped her eyes. She was naturally ebullient and happy, and couldn't stay melancholy for long. "No, we cannot, even if we want to." Consuela's next words brought to Howard's mind the meeting he had a few days earlier with Angelique. "Rosa is so lucky to have someone like you."

Unknown to either of them, there was another similarity between that present encounter and the one with Angelique, because in both instances, there were unseen observers. Whereas at the hotel it was Ben Duff, that Christmas day it was both Reverend Hightower and Rosa. Unlike the meeting at the hotel, where Duff remained silent and unobserved, this time the presence of Reverend Hightower and Rosa was announced with a Christmas greeting by the minister.

At the words of her father, Consuela spun around. In addition to sharing exceptional beauty with her older sister, she also shared another trait. When she blushed, she looked even more vibrant and lovely.

"How much did you hear?" she asked in an uncharacteristically high-pitched voice.

"Enough, Consuela," said Rosa.

Consuela had a defiant look on her face. "I guess I should say that I'm sorry, but I can't help how I feel. I wish he loved me."

Rosa looked at her younger sister with warmth and understanding, something that surprised and pleased Consuela. "He does love you, Consuela, just as he said. Just not like he loves me."

Reverend Hightower looked at the three of them and addressed

Consuela. "You will have someone of your own one day, little one. You will have someone who loves you as deeply as John loves Rosa. But stay my little girl for just a while longer, please."

"Papa, I will always be your little girl, as will Rosa." Then, with a hint of mischief in her voice, Consuela added, "I'll behave myself around John, for all of our sakes, but if Rosa ever fails to treat him right, he knows who he can turn to."

CHAPTER TWENTY-TWO

One morning, a month after Christmas, a lone rider walked his horse down the main street of Gold Valley. There was more traffic than might be expected on the street because the weather had turned unseasonably warm for that time of year. The rider's name was Michael Briscoe, and his first order of business was to visit the local general store. He assumed that the worn-out Confederate greatcoat and hat that he wore might draw unwelcome attention to himself in a Yankee town. Like the other members of the outlaw gang he rode with, he knew the value of maintaining a low profile and always seeking anonymity. However, Briscoe's caution exceeded normal limits, even for a bank robber, and bordered on acute paranoia.

After changing clothes in the store's dressing room, he sauntered across the street to the bank. Walking inside, he stood in front of the open counter, across from which a customer could conduct a legitimate transaction or make a larger withdrawal at the point of a gun.

Quickly scanning the bank's interior, Briscoe made a mental note of several things. There was a large iron safe behind the tellers' cage that appeared to be impervious to anything except several sticks of blasting powder. However, if things worked according to plan, there would be no need to blow up anything, because the youthful-looking outlaw noticed that the door to the safe was ajar. In his mind, this meant that the owner of the bank was overconfident and probably paid insufficient attention to security details.

A moment later, he was forced to reassess his judgment of the bank's security. This was because he saw two guards sitting quietly in the corner, where they could watch the customers. One of them was nondescript, except for the fact that he wore a 1858 Remington revolver in a shoulder holster that was visible under his open coat. This seemed rather unusual to the young robber, not only because shoulder holsters were rarely seen at that time and place, but also because most gunfighters that he was familiar with had made the transition from cap and ball to cartridge revolvers. He had even heard that Bill Longley had finally swapped his old Dance .44 revolver for a more modern Colt .45.

The second guard was larger, and was holding a larger gun. It was a ten gauge double-barreled shotgun. Fortunately for Michael, he himself appeared to be an ordinary, if somewhat young, range hand, and not a hard-bitten bank robber and killer who had participated in several successful holdups in Kansas and Missouri. The guards merely glanced at him and then looked away.

After looking at the guards, he temporarily dismissed them from his thoughts. He knew that once the gang had the information about them, they would either devise a plan to disarm or kill them outright after beginning the robbery. The guards' future welfare, and that of anyone else who might be inside at the time of the holdup, was no concern of his.

Considering the potential of success in robbing this particular establishment, the gang's leader himself had reminded Michael and the rest of his men of one big factor in their favor, the element of surprise. This bank, like others in Dakota, had never been robbed before. In fact, as Michael stood there, a fat man who appeared to be the bank president came out of an interior office. The man was in the process of boasting to a customer about the bank's security— that if any outlaws like the James gang dared to show their faces in Gold Valley, they would get an even worse reception than they had received in Northfield, Minnesota a few months earlier.

"Man, bad news sure travels far," Michael thought ruefully. The debacle in Minnesota was only a few months old, and yet news of it had already reached this town deep in the Dakotas, several hundred miles west of Northfield. He was glad it was the James gang that had been shot to pieces, and not the men he rode with. At the same time, he did feel sympathy for Frank and Jesse, because he shared their sentiments toward Yankee-owned banks and railroads. He also secretly envied them, and hoped that the gang of outlaws he rode with might someday receive the notoriety of the famous brothers from Missouri. He was especially bothered because the four bank robberies his own gang had made had been attributed to the James boys.

As his thoughts returned to the present, he selected a teller to conduct business with. The choice was easy because there were only two tellers, a man and a middle-aged spinster. He chose the spinster, a mousey-looking woman with reddish hair that was rapidly turning gray, who wore a drab gray dress.

Briscoe smiled to himself as he prepared to engage in a performance that would have made a professional actor like Eddie Foy proud. It was a role he had performed several times in the past. Unlike a professional thespian, however, his goal was not to seek applause, but rather to seek information. He had honed his skills to a considerable degree, and was aided by his innate cleverness and youthful good looks. That was why he was always given the job of scouting ahead, before the rest of the gang hit the bank.

Approaching the teller with a smile, he said hello and slid a twenty-dollar gold piece under the cage. Accepting the coin, the clerk asked how he wanted his change.

"Bills, I guess. And make it singles. I like a thick wad of money. Makes me feel rich. I hope to really be rich one day."

"I know what you mean," she said. "I like carrying a lot of bills myself, when I have them, that is."

He gave her a boyish grin and said, "Thanks, ma'am. Only man I know with a great big wad of money is my boss. He runs about eight thousand head of cows down in Texas and is thinking about moving some of his herd up here, now that the Sioux are pretty much beat."

The elderly lady smiled back. "Well, it would be a good idea. We've already got three ranches in the area. Mr. Pepper, he's the president of the bank, well, he owns one of the ranches."

Briscoe continued to smile. "Really? That'll impress my boss.

See, he'll probably figure that a feller with gumption enough to run cows would be smart enough to run a bank where his money would be safe. I bet you never had any problems at this bank, have you?"

"No sir, young man, not a bit," she primly replied. Then, encouraged by his smile, she lowered her voice to slightly above a whisper, and drew closer to the counter. "Do you see those men by the door? They're guards. And do you know that we have a town marshal who's faster than Wild Bill Hickock and is meaner than Doc Holiday? Nobody knows much about him except that he's killed several men in gun battles."

"No kidding?"

"That's right, young man. And he has a deputy who may be as good as he is. And that's not all. Mr. Pepper, he's the bank president, well, he has a bodyguard who's just as fast as the marshal, maybe even faster. Of course, Mr. Duff, he's Mr. Pepper's bodyguard, well, he stays with Mr. Pepper all of the time, so Mr. Duff isn't here when Mr. Pepper eats lunch. But we always have those two guards by the door. So your money is safe here."

Briscoe looked thoughtful. "Ma'am, that Duff feller you mentioned . . . could that be Ben Duff?"

"Why, yes it is. Do you know Mr. Duff?"

"No ma'am, never met him. But I've heard of him. Some say he's killed twenty men."

"I don't know about that. But I wouldn't be surprised. Oh, he's a very nice man and quite handsome, but so is our marshal, and he killed another gunfighter in the street his first day on the job. I guess you just never can tell . . . you know what they say about judging a book by its cover. Of course I'm sure that doesn't apply to, well, a nice young man like yourself."

Briscoe had to restrain himself from laughing outright at the unintended irony of the elderly woman's statement, as he envisioned her being shot to pieces in the upcoming bank robbery.

However, to the teller he said, "Ain't it the truth." He added, "You know, ma'am, my boss will be hitting town tomorrow. Now he's got him this habit of wanting to talk to folks he's doing business with at a meal. You know how it is with some of these bigwigs."

The teller responded sympathetically, "Oh yes, I know just what you mean. Mr. Pepper, well, he's the same way."

Briscoe pushed back his hat and scratched his head. "My boss has got himself this other funny habit. He always eats at exactly noon. Do you reckon your bank president would be willing to meet him for lunch tomorrow to talk about setting up an account here?"

"Of course, that's no problem at all. In fact, Mr. Pepper, well, he always eats lunch himself from noon until about 1:30 or 2:00. Do you want me to set an appointment?"

Briscoe smiled. "Yes ma'am. My boss will be here at noon tomorrow. His name is Jenkins."

"Well, I'll be sure to tell Mr. Pepper that Mr. Jenkins will be here at 12:00 tomorrow."

Briscoe tipped his hat as he turned to leave. "Thank you, ma'am. You've been a big help."

Walking to the hitching post outside, Briscoe pulled out his pocket watch. It was almost 10:00 A.M. He shoved the watch back in his pocket, mounted his steeldust mare and began riding down the street. He was very grateful to the talkative clerk. Once the rest of the gang had his report, there should be no problem at all. That the job might result in another bloodbath like Northfield never occurred to him. Like many criminals, he overestimated his own gang's abilities and underestimated the abilities of everyone else, particularly law enforcement officers. Besides, he thought that his gang would not make the same mistake that the James gang did. Thanks to the clerk, he thought he knew everything he needed to know. They would hit the bank that very same day in about two hours, a little after 12:00 noon, when Duff would be away. They would hit hard and fast, and be gone before the marshal even knew that there was trouble. Normally they might have planned some sort of diversion at the time of the robbery, but since no banks had ever been robbed in Dakota, they would have enough of the element of surprise without one.

The route out of town took him past the city marshal's office. Out of habit, Briscoe looked casually toward the office, thinking,

"I wonder who's the town clown that old bat was talking about. Faster than Hickock? Ain't likely. I'd of heard of him if he was so good."

He saw no one as he rode past the marshal's office. Glancing across the street, he briefly noticed a broad-shouldered man reclining back in a chair against the wall. Briscoe thought he looked like a gunman, although he could not have put into words why he thought so. Could he be the gunslick marshal mentioned by the teller? Probably not. No badge was visible and the man wore a gray Confederate hat, causing Briscoe to think out loud, "Yep, he's a gunnie, for certain. But he ain't no lawdog, an' if he is, he ain't worth much, 'cause he ain't paying no attention to nothing."

Briscoe was right in judging the man to be a gunfighter. He was wrong in thinking he was not a lawman, and that he wasn't paying attention. John Howard had watched him since he first exited Thorton's General Store.

What the young killer also failed to notice was that the marshal had earlier spoken briefly to a young redheaded man about Briscoe's own age. After the conversation, the redhead had discreetly climbed to the top of Thorton's General Store, and there hunkered down behind a big .45-70 Springfield rifle. Briscoe also failed to notice that another man, this one squarely-built and black-headed, had casually walked into the alley beside the bank. He carried a ten-gauge Greener shotgun unseen beneath his long coat.

After Briscoe had left town, John Howard walked inside the bank. He went immediately to the tellers' cage. He talked to them for less than two minutes. He then walked straight into Pepper's office. Stepping inside, he glanced to the side and saw Ben Duff sitting in a chair with his back against the wall. Howard nodded toward Duff and spoke to Pepper. "It looks like we may have a problem in a little while. We need to talk."

Pepper looked at the marshal with his usual condescension. "Young man, don't you know not to enter my office without knocking?"

Howard was in no mood to engage in needless conversation with the dirty banker. He was abrupt and to the point. "Unless I'm wrong, there's going to be a robbery attempt within the next couple of hours, probably between noon and 1:30. Are you interested in protecting your bank or not?"

Pepper shot a quizzical glance at Duff. Duff asked, "Why do you say that, Mr. Howard?"

"There was a young cowboy who just left here. He wasn't more than eighteen or so. I watched him ride into town. The first thing he did was to go into Thorton's store and buy a brown coat to replace the one he had on. The one he had looked like an old Confederate greatcoat. I wondered at first why he would do that. Then the thought occurred to me that he was trying too hard to not be noticed. I watched him go into the bank. He only stayed a few minutes and then rode out of town. So I came over and talked to the tellers. Miss Bradford waited on him. She said he got change for a twenty-dollar gold piece. He said he wanted his boss to meet Pepper for lunch tomorrow at noon, but I suspect he was really trying to find out about the bank's security, and the time of day you wouldn't be here. I think they're going to try it today, when Pepper and you are supposed to be at lunch."

Pepper questioned Duff, "Does that seem like a reason for alarm, Mr. Duff? After all, we've never had an attempted bank robbery in Gold Valley, or anywhere in Dakota, for that matter."

"It may very well be that Mr. Howard is right. Those circumstances by themselves don't mean anything, but taken together, they are suspicious. Anyway, it can't hurt to take precautions. I would close the safe and lock it. Keep just a few dollars out. I'll alert the guards. I also think that I'll replace Miss Bradford as the teller. Mr. Howard, what have you done?"

"I've got O'Hara with his Springfield across the street on top of Thorton's General Store. Preston Kirby is in the alley between the bank and the gun shop. He's got a ten-gauge Greener express gun loaded with buckshot. I'm going outside and see if I can spot the gang members when they come into town. Most likely, they'll drift in one or two at a time."

Duff nodded in agreement. "I think you're right. Be sure to also watch down the street. I expect that they will probably have men at opposite ends of the street."

Howard agreed. "Good idea. You might want to have Pepper deputize a few of his men, like the Macleod brothers. That way they can act in case the robbers try some sort of diversion to draw attention away from the bank. I think O'Hara, Kirby, and I should concentrate on the bank itself. Mr. Duff, if you replace Miss Bradford like you suggested, I think we'll have everything covered."

Pepper looked owlishly at the marshal. "You seem to know a lot about bank robberies, Marshal," he commented.

"Yes, I do, just about as much as Mr. Duff does," replied Howard dryly, as he walked out the door.

CHAPTER TWENTY-THREE

The robbery attempt came a few minutes after twelve o'clock. Two men wearing dusters and low-crowned hats sauntered their horses to the front of the gun shop. From the shadows, Kirby watched them dismount. His eyes glinted in anticipation. He was no murderer, but had killed before, with every shooting being face-to-face with other gunmen. In fact, he could have carried nine notches on his revolver, if he were so inclined. Then again, notching your pistols was generally a tinhorn's trick, and Kirby was anything but that.

Two more men got off their horses at the far end of the street, in front of the Yellow Knife Saloon. The young outlaw Michael Briscoe rode up in front of the bank. He was accompanied by the gang leader and one other man. They had hoped to use the same tactics that had worked many times in the past, to move quietly inside the bank, and then to hit fast and hard, never hesitating to kill if necessary to gain compliance. Surprise and intimidation were vital to their success. The leader of the outlaws had learned that lesson well when he rode with Bloody Bill Anderson. The difficulty this time was that the opposition was not surprised, was equally well-armed, and was prepared.

Dismounting their horses, they strolled casually inside. As soon as they entered the building, they drew their guns. Briscoe felt gripped by uncertainty as they entered because the old lady had been replaced by a man who had a dangerous look about him. Briscoe had only a moment to reflect on the sudden turn of events.

The gang's leader, an unkempt man of indeterminable age, shouted a command, "Hands up and hands steady!"

They were the last words he would ever utter. His order was

drowned out by the sharp report of Ben Duff's .44. The bullet entered the robber's right eye and blew out the back of his skull, showering Briscoe with blood and bone fragments. Briscoe dropped his gun and lost his nerve.

The third outlaw inside the bank ducked behind a table and turned it over, hoping to use it for a barricade. He fired an unaimed shot over the top. Doing so, of course, required that he expose his hand while he fired. When he did, the second shot from Duff's gun struck the outlaw's revolver, clipped off the robber's thumb, and cut a bloody furrow across the top of his arm. The wounded outlaw's screams of agony curdled the blood of Briscoe, who was doubly glad he had opted to surrender rather than fight.

In contrast to Briscoe, the two outlaws outside by the gun shop drew their guns, in preparation for shooting their way out of town. They had no intention of sticking around to see what fate had befallen their companions inside. Apparently, they were proponents of the old adage that taught that there was no honor among thieves. However, their plans for a rapid departure from town were cut short by a voice from the alley.

"Hold it!" The accent was unmistakably Texan.

They two would-be robbers stopped. They recognized the menace behind the voice.

Kirby spoke again in a conversational tone. "You boys got a ten-gauge covering you. At this range it ought to cut you in half. You want to shuck them guns or you want to die?"

One of the outlaws decided on the spot that a life of crime wasn't all it was cracked up to be. The prospect of jail wasn't nearly so unpleasant as the alternative.

"Don't shoot mister. We quit."

"Okay. Now real easy-like, put them six-shooters on the ground. Don't drop 'em. Lay 'em down."

Both of the robbers complied wordlessly.

"Now, you gents just keep your hands up and walk toward me."

"We can't see you mister," complained one robber.

"Just walk toward the alley, real slow."

After both thieves were in the middle of the alley's entrance, Kirby gave another order. "Now, just sit yourselves down. Uh uh. Keep them hands up. Don't do nothing stupid. We'll just sit tight till some more folks get here. Don't make me shoot you boys."

The robbers were sitting down when the shorter of the two stumbled. He caught himself against the side of the building with his left hand.

"Don't try me, boy!" warned Kirby. He was too old a hand at this type of thing to take a chance or let his guard down.

His warning was to no avail. The robber jerked up his right hand with a pistol in it. He never had a chance to use it. A load of buckshot caught him squarely in the middle of the chest. He didn't live long enough to even consider how foolish he was to try to tackle a gunfighter of Kirby's caliber.

The second robber wasn't about to make the same mistake. "I ain't fightin'! I ain't got no hideout gun like him! Don't shoot!" His voice was full of desperation.

In contrast, Kirby's voice was still calm. "Don't fret yourself none, son. You ain't gonna die if you don't do something stupid like your partner. Just sit yourself down like I done told you."

Other action was simultaneously taking place in front of Thorton's store. Howard faced down the two outlaws at the other end of the street, his Winchester at the ready. "Don't move!"

"I'll get the one on the right if you get the other one," yelled O'Hara from the top of the store.

The robbers were caught flatfooted, right in the middle of a crossfire, if they chose to make a fight of it. They had already heard the shots from inside the bank and the alley, and realized they were in a bad position.

"Don't shoot. We quit!" yelled the older of the two.

Howard answered in a voice loud enough for O'Hara to hear every word. "Okay, dismount one at a time. You on the roan, get down first. If either of you tries anything, you both die. My friend on top of the building across the street has a .45-70. He never misses."

"We quit mister, don't shoot!" begged the man on the roan as he slowly dismounted. "We ain't gonna fight." To the robber who was still mounted, he pleaded, "Charlie, don't you try nuthin', boy, you hear? They'll kill us both if you do, sure as daylight!"

After both outlaws were down, Howard ordered them to lay flat on the street, with their arms spread away from them. Then he disarmed both men and frisked them for other weapons while O'Hara covered him from the rooftop.

Inside the bank, the outlaw behind the table decided to give up. He had lain for just a few seconds behind what he thought was a safe barricade when a heavy ten-gauge shotgun slug plowed its way through the oak tabletop and sprayed a shower of splinters in the hapless thief's face. After having his right thumb shot off by Duff, and his eyes temporarily blinded by the splinters, he thought that it would be better to be a jailbird, albeit a crippled and possibly blind one, than a dead bank robber.

"Don't shoot me no more! I quit!"

"Slide your gun out," commanded Ben Duff.

That accomplished, he gave further instructions. "Now raise up. Move slow."

The robber stood unsteadily, whimpering the whole time, "You gotta get me a sawbones. I ain't got no thumb and I got splinters in my eyes. You gotta help me!"

"You're alive," said Duff without sympathy. "That's more than you deserve."

CHAPTER TWENTY-FOUR

News of the attempted holdup didn't make its way into the eastern newspapers, even though two robbers had been killed, the same number as had died in the calamity the James gang had faced in Northfield the previous year. There were two reasons why it did not. The first was because the robbery had not been attempted by a group of famous outlaws. The second reason was that although Gold Valley had an ever-increasing population, there was still no local newspaper or telegraph.

After the aborted attempt to rob the Gold Valley Bank, a time of relative peace and quiet descended on Gold Valley, because the unseasonably warm weather ended when a winter storm howled in from the north and covered the high plains country with snow and sub-zero temperatures. That helped ensure a more tranquil state of affairs. It seemed that people were so intent on just trying to stay warm, that they were less inclined to commit criminal acts.

The freezing weather enabled John Howard to settle down to a routine. He was able to spend some time every day with the Hightowers. He constantly trained with Reverend Hightower and usually ate supper with the family. It was during this time that his love for Rosa grew to the point that he decided to ask her to marry him. However, he was plagued by some nagging doubts. He felt he wasn't good enough for her, and he remembered that every time he cared about anyone, he ended up losing that person. He also began to worry that his past might catch up with him. Finally, he shoved his doubts aside and resolved that he would ask her.

They were sitting in the parlor of the Hightower's home after supper the evening he mustered up the courage to tell her that he wanted her to be his wife. Reverend Hightower and Consuela were cleaning the dishes. When he finally got the words out, Rosa beamed a radiant smile and kissed him.

"Of course I'll marry you, John. I love you also, and always will. The sooner we get married the better I'll like it."

For a few minutes, they sat there, he with his arm around her and her leaning against his shoulder. He gently pushed back a strand of hair that had fallen across her forehead and said, "Rosa, I want us to be married, but we can't just yet. I've got some things I have to get straightened out first. But I do promise you that I'll love you forever, and we will be married soon."

She gazed up at him. "We have time, my love. We'll always have time. When you are ready, just ask me. You already know my answer."

*   *   *

Howard left the Hightowers' house that night in freezing weather. He never noticed the cold, however, because for him, life was as warm as the glowing embers on a fire.

Only a few things about his job situation bothered him and prevented his thoughts from dwelling entirely on Rosa. One incident was minor—a disagreement with the town council over carrying guns inside the corporate limits of Gold Valley. Another thing was a far more serious matter. There was a growing problem with robbers and cattle rustlers in the area around Gold Valley. Three ranches had been established in the vicinity. One was owned by William Pepper, and the other two owned by Texas cattlemen who had driven thousands of cattle north to the newly-opened Black Hills territory.

All of these cattle ranchers, Pepper included, hired men skilled not only in handling a rope and branding iron, but also firearms. That was understandable, for while most of the Sioux had only recently been forced from the Black Hills by the never-ending tide of white settlers, there were still numerous bands of Indians roaming Dakota and Montana. Their bands numbered from two or three warriors up to thirty or forty. Fortunately for the white men, there were no longer bands of several hundred warriors in the territory, like the one commanded the previous autumn by Touch the Clouds. The warriors, dispossessed of their lands by a government that had broken its own treaties, were branded as "renegades" by that same government. They were rightfully resentful and bitter. They were also superb and dangerous fighters who would kill any white they came across.

Dozens of white renegades also inhabited the Black Hills. These white outlaws operated in groups that could include as many as twenty men, or more. Some of them tried their hand at robbing stages and miners, while others found the allure of free cattle to be more stimulating. There seemed to be a least one of the latter outfits operating near Gold Valley, because all three ranchers noticed more and more missing cattle.

One of the ranchers, a hard-eyed old Texan named Hiram Longstreet, sought out Howard one day while the marshal and Rosa were eating in Angelique Mayo's diner. Longstreet was a man who normally wouldn't have wasted his time with any lawman, preferring to handle his own problems in his own way. But in the case of Howard, he made an exception. He liked Howard. Even more, he actually respected the marshal, and Hiram Longstreet didn't respect many men, especially those who carried a badge in a Yankee town.

Longstreet tipped his hat to Rosa when he approached the table. "Beg pardon, Miss Rosa, for interrupting your supper." Then to Howard he said, "Might I have a word with you, John?"

Howard put his fork down and stood up. "Of course, Mr. Longstreet. Do you care to join us?"

"Thanks, don't mind if I do." Longstreet sat down and asked the waitress for a cup of coffee.

The elderly rancher removed his hat and said, "I got me a problem, son. Somebody's stealing my cows. And they ain't taking just a couple, like them sod-busters and miners do. I don't mind that so much. But I'm talking about fifty or sixty head at one fell swoop. An' I ain't the only one. Kilcoyne and that Yankee banker Pepper are losing cows, too."

Howard considered the rancher's problem briefly before answering. "Do you have any idea who's taking your cattle and where they are?"

"Nary a clue, that's why I come to you. See, I normally don't have much to do with the law. Most of 'em down home are in the hip-pocket of carpet-baggers and scallywags. But you and Pres Kirby ain't like that. An' you boys got savvy. An' I gotta be honest and say I can't seem to throw a loop over this here situation. So that's why I'm here talkin' to you."

"I'll try to help you, Mr. Longstreet, although I don't think I have any authority outside the town limits. Some of the town council aren't too happy with me right now either, and likely won't like the idea of me working outside the town."

"I heard about your trouble with them from Pres, last time he visited the ranch. Seems like some of them got their back up because you wouldn't enforce a deadline."

Rosa asked, "What's a deadline?"

Howard answered, "It's a boundary that restricts freedom. In Kansas, there's a city marshal named Earp who got the town council to designate a certain point that cowboys coming off the trail can't go past. Later he also made it a line no one can carry a gun past. Apparently, the idea has gained some support in other towns, as well. That's what the town council wanted here, a place where everyone would have to surrender their guns when they come into town."

"How come you refused to enforce the deadline?" questioned Longstreet.

"Because I don't think it would work. In my opinion, an armed society is a polite society. I think that people are more likely to respect the rights of others when the others can defend their rights. And it was interesting that the head of the town council, William Pepper, wanted to exempt some of his own men like Ben Duff and the Macleod brothers from the requirement. He seemed anxious enough to take the means of personal defense away from everyone else, as long as he was still protected himself. He even had the gall to say that a different standard should apply to him because of his position."

Longstreet grinned. "What did that conniving skunk think when you told 'em you wouldn't enforce it?"

Howard smiled at his friend and Rosa. "He told me that I would follow his orders as long as I worked for him and the town council. I told him they could fire me any time they wanted to. Then Angelique Mayo took the floor. She first reminded Pepper that I worked for the town, not him. Then she said that the deadline was restrictive and unfair, and that they should listen to my opinion. It took some persuasion on her part, but she finally managed to convince two of the other five members to vote with her. I think she might have shamed them into it by telling them that if they were going to be community leaders, they should start thinking more for themselves instead of always kowtowing to Pepper."

The rancher laughed. "I bet that went over real good. Well, at least we got somebody with smarts and guts helping to run this town. Yessir, that Missus Mayo is a special lady—good looks and good sense. Quite a combination. Kinda seems a shame though, when a woman's got more gumption than a bunch of men."

That remark prompted a response from Rosa. She spoke in a demure voice that had only a hint of irony in it. "Mr. Longstreet, you might be surprised what a woman could do. We're not really all that helpless. Why, some of us can even shoot guns and think on our own."

Longstreet's face colored slightly. He and everyone else had heard about Rosa's shooting display the day Howard had hired Ian O'Hara. He conceded, "Yes'm, come to think about it, I expect you're right. In point of fact, if you'll allow me to say so, Miss Rosa, I don't never recall seein' nobody prettier than you, even Missus Mayo, an' I sure wouldn't want to shoot against you for money!" He looked at Howard and back at Rosa. "An' I'll tell you something else, if I was fifty years younger and single, I'd sure have tried to give John a run for his money with you."

Rosa gave a broad smile, revealing even white teeth. "Why, thank you, sir. That's a very gallant thing to say. You're very kind." Rosa unconsciously squeezed Howard's arm as she finished speaking. "I do like to shoot, but am glad I have someone who makes it unnecessary for me to have to handle a gun to protect myself."

Longstreet chuckled. "I reckon you've been roped and branded, John, for sure and for certain." Longstreet had his hat on his lap. He noticed some dirt on the brim and flicked it off. "So John, you reckon there's anything you can do about this rustling trouble?"

"Give me a little time, Mr. Longstreet. I'll see if I can come up with something. I'll also talk to the town council. They're mostly good people, with one exception. They're all just afraid to buck Pepper, except for Angelique. But I'll talk to them anyway. All they can do is fire me."

Longstreet answered, "Look here, John, if they ever did fire you, you can come to work for me. If Pepper can have Ben Duff and those gun-slinging Macleod brothers as 'personal assistants', I reckon I could hire me one myself, especially if he was as good as you."

"What about Pres Kirby and Ian O'Hara?"

"Sure, I'd give both those lads jobs if they got fired on account of you helping me. Fact is, Pres took a herd up the trail to Kansas for me back in '71 and he come up from Texas with me last year. He knows he can come back any time. He still drops by from time to time to see me. I wisht he hadn't got tired of punchin' cows. Best ramrod I ever had." Longstreet got up from the table. "Thanks for hearing me out John. I'll be seeing you later." He tipped his hat to Rosa. "Good evening, Miss Rosa."

After the rancher left, Rosa said, "I like him John. They say he's a hard old man, but I think he's nice. I hope I didn't embarrass him."

"I like him, too. As we say down south, he's rougher than a cob. But he's a gentleman and a real man in every way. He's past seventy but still works every day from sunup to sundown. You know that Pres rides out to see him sometimes. He told me that the last time he was there, some of the hands were trying to break a horse, a blue roan with a mean streak a yard wide, as Pres described it. No one could ride him. In fact, nobody would try to ride him more than once; the horse was that rough. Finally, Mr. Longstreet got on board."

"Did he break the horse?"

"No. He kept getting thrown off. After the fourth time he hit the dirt, Pres told him he was going to be hurt, because he was so long-in-the-tooth and feeble. Mr. Longstreet said he would show him who was too old and feeble, and that he was going to keep going until the horse got tired of bucking him off. He said he could wear down the horse before the roan wore him down. So Pres told the hands at the corral that he would deputize the whole lot of them, and that their job was to keep Hiram off that horse. Longstreet asked why he was deputizing a dozen men to handle one long-in-the-tooth and feeble old man. Pres told him it was only because there weren't any more available, but if need be, he could round up every man on the ranch, and even get more from town."

After laughing with Rosa over the story, Howard became pensive, and sat silently as he considered his course of action. After a couple of minutes, Rosa tapped him lightly on the arm. "Are you going to stare at your coffee all evening, John?"

"Sorry. I was just thinking about who could be behind stealing those cows. My gut instinct is that Pepper is behind it."

Rosa disagreed. "I think he's an absolutely hideous man, but he's lost livestock himself. Why would he steal his own cattle?"

"That's what's got me buffaloed," admitted Howard. "I'm probably way off base suspecting him. It's just that I wouldn't believe him if he said the sun came up in the east and set in the west."

"Why don't you talk to Papa and Ben Duff? They might be able to help."

"Ben Duff works for Pepper. Why would he bite the hand that feeds him?"

"It was just a thought, dear. Sometimes people are more than they appear to be. But you should talk it over with Papa."

CHAPTER TWENTY-FIVE

After Howard and Rosa finished their meal, he walked her home. At the front door, Howard kissed her and turned to leave. Rosa went inside. However, she was inside only a few seconds when she returned with her father and sister. Reverend Hightower walked surprisingly slow. The girls looked pale and drawn. Rosa called to Howard, who returned to the porch. Howard had never seen Reverend Hightower look so distraught.

"Parson, you look like death warmed over. What's wrong?"

"I guess you haven't heard. I just came from Bull Jackson's house. He's dead. He committed suicide. I'm afraid it's my fault." Hightower looked old and tired.

Howard was completely taken aback. "I can't believe he would kill himself. I certainly don't see how you could be responsible."

The minister sat on the porch swing. Rosa and Consuela sat on either side of him. Each held his hand. They rocked back and forth for several seconds before anyone spoke.

"John, it was my fault, or at least partially so," explained the minister. "You know what I did to him the day we arrived in town."

"Of course. But you didn't do anything wrong. In fact, you held back. You could have killed him. If I had been in your place, I would have shot him."

The minister slowly nodded his head. "I'm not saying I was wrong for whipping him. But did you know that he was permanently crippled and couldn't work any more after that?"

Howard shook his head from side to side. "I didn't know that. I thought that you told me that kneecaps could be set back in place."

"His knees weren't the main problem. It was his collarbone. It didn't heal properly and he lost use of his right arm. After awhile the mine cut his wages because he couldn't do as much work."

"Then how could he pay his bills? I thought he must be working because I heard he was not only paying his bills, but in fact, was doing very well. Some people said he must have found some gold himself, because he bought himself a house. It wasn't very big, but was better than that shack he used to live in. How could he do that if he wasn't working?"

Rosa answered for her father. "Papa gave Jackson's wife the money. He started sending them twenty-five dollars a month after Jackson couldn't work any longer. Papa told her it was compensation from the mine. That wasn't a lie," she quickly added. "We own forty-five percent of the First Strike Mine. Papa wanted to help provide for Jackson's wife and three children."

"Parson," Howard said, "Pres Kirby said you were the 'blamedest' preacher he'd ever heard of. I agreed. And now I think I understand even more. Did Jackson find out about the money?"

"He did earlier today. He was going down to the Pink Palace and overheard one of the girls say that the money had really come from me, not from the mine. You see, not many people know we own a large share of the mine."

"How would a girl at the Pink Palace find that out?"

"I suspect one of the other shareholders of the mine told her. I was trying to convince the other owners that the mining company should offer some type of compensation to injured workers, not just to Jackson. I told the other shareholder that I was paying Jackson's family until his arm healed. I'm afraid that he told one the Pink Palace girls."

"Was that other shareholder Ira Wentworth?" queried Howard.

"Yes it was, although it doesn't matter now. I'm just sorry I mentioned it to Ira in the first place. You see, I'm convinced that's why Jackson killed himself, because I was paying his family the money. His wife told me that he came home drunk and asked her about it. Then apparently one of his children told him that I had been over to the house sometimes. What the child didn't say was that I always had at least one of my daughters with me. I don't know if it would have mattered anyway because Bull was drunk. He slapped his wife and accused her of having an affair with me. His wife told me that he just couldn't understand an act of charity, especially from the only man who ever beat him in a fight. The last thing he said was that after he was dead, his wife wouldn't have to sneak around any longer to see me. He also said to tell me that I could buy female companionship at the Pink Palace for a lot less than twenty-five dollars a month."

Howard drew a slow breath. "But Parson, I don't see how that's your fault. You've always said that men are responsible for their own actions. It wasn't your fault that Jackson attacked Rosa and Consuela. You didn't make him keep fighting after you threw him down the first time. You didn't make Wentworth cheat on his wife and tell a prostitute what you had done. You didn't make Jackson try to find the solution to his problems in the bottom of a whiskey bottle and in a whore house. And you didn't make him kill himself. It seems like he reaped what he sowed."

Consuela, who had been quiet to that point, spoke up. "John's right, Papa. You're kind and decent and serve the Lord. Nobody could fault you."

Howard agreed. "Consuela's right. You're a man of God, Parson, one of the few real ones I've ever seen. Blaming yourself doesn't change that."

Further conversation was prevented by two gunshots that sounded like they came from the next street. Howard looked in the direction of the noise. "Sounds like it might be trouble. I'd better check it out."

Rosa kissed him again. "Go ahead, dear. Consuela and I will stay with Papa."

Howard sprinted toward the sound. When he arrived near the area where the shots came from, he saw something several yards ahead that caused him to melt into the shadows with his gun drawn. He saw three men in the center of the street, all with drawn handguns, their attention focused away from his direction.

The one on the far left yelled, "Maybe them shots didn't hit you O'Hara, but sooner or later we'll get close enough and find you so they will. You can't keep hidin' like a scairt rabbit. An' you ain't got them gunslicks you work with to protect you now, have you boy? Reckon we're fixin' to show you what happens when you cheat people."

Howard crouched behind a hitching post. "Good evening, gentlemen. This is John Howard." Howard's voice was low and conversational, but still carried in the clear night air.

All three men froze for a long moment. To say that they were taken by surprise was an understatement. Eventually, the one who had been speaking found his voice. He was a tough-looking cowhand who carried his revolver in a cross-draw holster. It looked liked one of the new Colts, although Howard was too far away to be certain.

Upon recognizing Howard's voice, the man carefully holstered his handgun. "Ain't looking for trouble with you, Marshal Howard. We want that redheaded woodpecker who's your deppity."

Howard kept his tone calm and even. "But if you have a problem with my friend, you've got a problem with me." Then, although he couldn't see his deputy, in a louder tone he asked, "Are you okay, Ian?"

From a distance of at least one hundred yards down the street, O'Hara replied, "Good to hear you, John. Yeah, I'm okay. I was afraid I was going to have to shoot these fellers if they kept up with this foolishness." O'Hara still remained concealed.

Howard himself didn't move. "You gentlemen stay where you are. You on the left . . . no, don't turn around. You're fine the way you are. What's the problem with Deputy O'Hara?"

The men in the street still didn't move. When one of the cowboys answered, his voice was uncertain. "Uh, sure Marshal. I'll tell you what's wrong. It's like this, we was playing poker at the Lucky Lady Saloon and this card sharp in there gypped us. Then that deppity of yours threw us out when we tried to get our money back. We reckon your man's working with that fancy gambler. He can't get away with lettin' that gambler cheat us and then throwin' us out. Uh, you want us to unbuckle our gun belts?"

"No, of course not. Keep them. You can even draw your guns as far as I'm concerned. I would dislike shooting an unarmed man, so go ahead and draw, if you think it's a good idea."

"We ain't wantin' to fight you, Marshal."

"That's entirely up to you. But it wouldn't be much of a contest. We've got cover and you don't. What's more, the three of you make nice silhouettes in the middle of the street under those street lamps." Howard raised his voice again. "If we start shooting, my guess is that I'll get two of you and O'Hara will get the third. What about it, Ian?"

O'Hara yelled back. "Not a chance. I bet I can get two before you do. Reckon we'll just have to dig the bullets out to see after it's over." O'Hara was young but smart. He followed Howard's lead perfectly.

Howard chuckled softly before speaking. "Mr. O'Hara's betting me that he can get two of you before I do. If he's got his single-shot Springfield, I think I'll win. On the other hand, if he's got his Winchester, I think he might win. What do you gentlemen think?"

The man who had fired his gun answered. "Now hold on a minute. Just hold on. This ain't exactly fair. We can't even see you two, an' you got us in a crossfire. Reckon we'll just have to wait to settle things with him."

"Waiting isn't an option." The marshal dropped his conversational tone and replaced it with one steeped in sarcasm. "So you three big, bad men are willing to gang up on one man, but aren't willing to face odds not in your favor. Is that the way it is? Well, guess what? We're going to end this thing right now, not later." To the cowboy who had been doing the shooting, he said, "Since you're so anxious to fight him, then you can do it, right now, one at a time."

Now the spokesman for the cowboys was more uncertain. "You mean you ain't gonna side him?"

"He doesn't need anybody to side him in a fair fight. He could even handle two of you at once. But three to one is long odds. It's a stupid gamble, and O'Hara is no fool. So, he'll take you on one at a time. Now it's decision time. Are you going to back up your big mouth or back down?"

The cowboy was gaining some confidence, now that Howard himself wasn't going to participate. The man admitted to himself that he wouldn't have a chance trying to match someone like Howard, Ben Duff, or Preston Kirby. But O'Hara was another story. After all, the young deputy marshal didn't even carry a handgun, just a rifle.

"Okay, Marshal. Just me and the kid, man to man, here in the street."

"Just a minute. What's your name and how old are you?" asked Howard.

Now one of the other cowboys in the street spoke up. "How come you want to know his name and how old he is?"

"I want to know what to put on his grave marker. You two, you can drop your gun-belts now and move a couple of feet to the side."

The leader of the three spoke again as his companions complied with Howard's order. "My name's Fairfield an' I'm thirty-three. An' I done killed me a man before this."

"Fine, Fairfield, now I know how to mark your grave." To O'Hara, the marshal shouted, "Are you ready, Ian?"

The redhead stepped out in the street. He could barely be seen in the dark, because the street lamps near him were not lit. He held his Springfield rifle muzzle down at a forty-five degree angle. "Any time. Okay, Fairfield, you say when."

None of the men in the middle of the street moved. Then Fairfield said, "Now just hold on there. I can't hit him that far away. I already tried. I can't even hardly see him. He's gotta fight me with a pistol up close. That's how it's gotta be done."

Howard answered, "Wrong again. You picked the fight, so he picks the weapons and terms of combat. Draw and shoot, or back down and walk away. If you walk, keep going. Leave Gold Valley and never come back. I'll shoot you on sight if I see you again."

The would-be duelist began to have second thoughts. He suddenly remembered that he had heard something about O'Hara's uncanny skill with a rifle. Besides, he knew that he himself couldn't hit a dimly lit target so far away with only a handgun. He was also aware of something Howard reminded him of, that he was under bright street lamps.

O'Hara started walking forward, just like Cole Madison had done to Howard. O'Hara's rifle was still pointing down, although the buttstock was cradled in his shoulder. When the distance narrowed to seventy yards, Fairfield could stand the pressure no longer. He drew his gun and fired. He had heard that Bill Hickock had killed Dave Tutt that far away with only one shot from Hickock's .36 Navy Colt. What he failed to understand was that he was not Hickock, and O'Hara was not Tutt.

The slug fired from the cowboy's revolver was never recovered, unlike the heavy five hundred grain bullet from O'Hara's rifle. The Springfield's bullet tore through the middle of Fairfield's chest, leaving a gaping hole where it exited. It was recovered a few days later by a youngster who noticed it embedded in the side of a building down the street.

Fairfield fell to the dusty street. His companions stood by wordlessly. Due to the surprising shock of seeing their friend killed, they failed to notice that O'Hara stopped, ejected the empty cartridge case, and placed a new round in the chamber of his rifle.

Howard broke the silence. His voice was no longer harsh. "Nobody else has to die. Do you two want to leave or get what your friend got?"

One of the remaining cowboys spoke. "Can I turn around?"

"Go ahead, just be slow doing it."

When the cowhand faced Howard, the lawman saw that he was not much older than O'Hara. The cowboy spoke again. "We'd like to leave town, Marshal. Reckon you and Mr. O'Hara would let us?"

"Of course, but don't come back."

Then to O'Hara the young cowhand said, "Sorry about what we said, Mr. O'Hara. We don't want no more trouble with you. Uh, Marshal, can we pick up our gun-belts?"

"Of course. And on your way out of town, stop by the undertaker's office with your friend. His office is at the end of the street behind O'Hara, by Doctor Parker's office. You two can pay for burying him, and notifying his next of kin."

The cowboys carried their dead comrade away as onlookers started filtering into the street. O'Hara walked up to Howard and muttered, "I was hoping we could talk them out of it. That's why I didn't kill him at first. Nobody was on the street and I was behind cover. Now that it's over, I'm getting sick at my stomach. Does it ever get easier?"

Howard laid his hand on his friend's shoulder. "Never. But if it ever does, then it's time to hang up your guns."

CHAPTER TWENTY-SIX

The following day, Howard saddled his sorrel for a ride north of town to Longstreet's ranch. He asked Ian O'Hara to go with him. Howard told Preston Kirby where they were going, and assured him that they would be gone no longer than two or three days. He also told Angelique Mayo. She said she would inform the town council.

The two lawmen stopped by the Hightower's house on the way out of town. Rosa and Consuela were cleaning the windows of the house when they rode up. Howard dismounted and kissed Rosa. She returned his kiss but blushed. He asked her what was wrong.

"It's broad daylight, John, and Ian is watching." Rosa spoke in voice barely louder than a whisper. "What will he think?"

Howard grinned. "He probably thinks that we love each other. He's a very bright lad and has a keen grasp of the obvious."

Apparently Rosa had not spoke as softly as she intended because O'Hara said, "It's okay by me Miz Rosa. He's your man. If I had me somebody that loved me like you do him, I reckon I'd never worry about anybody seeing her kiss me."

Consuela added, "If I had a man like him, he could kiss me any time at any place."

Rosa's blush gradually faded. She and Howard walked to the porch. O'Hara remained on his horse. He looked in admiration at Consuela. He thought his longing gaze was unnoticed. It was not.

"What are looking at, Mr. O'Hara?" asked Consuela.

Now it was O'Hara's turn to blush. "Beg pardon, ma'am. I wasn't trying to be rude. You just look so . . . "

O'Hara's words were cut off by the creaking sound of the door as it opened and Reverend Hightower walked out. He shook hands with Howard and greeted O'Hara.

"Papa," said Consuela, "I think Mr. O'Hara was about to pay me a compliment when you came out."

Hightower looked at the young deputy with a stern expression. Howard wondered if was because his friend was still wrestling with the guilt feelings that had developed over Jackson's suicide. However, such was not the case. Even though the clergyman had a rough time of things the previous night, he had successfully resolved his feelings of guilt. He was already back to his old self, ready to preach the Word and minister to anyone who needed help. In the case of Deputy Marshal Ian O'Hara, however, he didn't appear to be willing to give help. Even his daughters and Howard didn't know that his hard expression was a feigned look. Their lack of knowledge was shared by a very flustered Ian O'Hara.

"Well, out with it, boy," said the minister. "What were you going to say?"

Ian looked at John Howard. Howard shrugged. His expression told Ian he was on his own.

O'Hara looked at the preacher and then at Consuela. He drew a deep breath and blurted out, "I was fixin' to say that I think Consuela is just about the purtiest girl I ever laid eyes on and I'd like to come callin' some time or go riding with her or just sit and talk or whatever she wanted to do, if that's okay with you, Parson."

The look on the minister's face was replaced by a bland expression. "It's okay with me son, but you need to ask Consuela. It's up to her."

O'Hara's face was as red as his hair when he asked, "Well, Consuela, you reckon I could come callin'?"

Consuela seemed to carefully consider her answer. After what seemed an eternity to O'Hara, she finally smiled and answered, "Of course, you may come calling, Ian. I would like that. You may come calling any time."

"Any time her sister or I'm at home," amended her father.

Everyone talked for a few more minutes, before the two lawmen mounted and said goodbye. O'Hara looked liked he was so happy he could hardly contain himself. The meeting with Consuela had apparently taken his mind completely off the events of the previous evening.

It required the better part of an hour before Howard and O'Hara came into view of the main headquarters of Longstreet's ranch. They rode to the ranch house and spied Longstreet through the front window.

The rancher motioned for them to come inside. "Glad to see you boys. Coffee's on. Want some?"

The two lawmen hitched their horses and followed Longstreet into the house. It was spacious and surprisingly clean and tidy, considering that Longstreet had been a widower for several years and didn't have a maid. They sat at the kitchen table while Longstreet poured their coffee. After he served them, he sat down and they talked while they drank.

After a few minutes, Longstreet asked, "I reckon this ain't just a social visit like Pres makes. You here about them rustlers, John?"

Howard nodded. "I was wondering if you could spare a man to show us where your cattle were when they were rustled. I hope to get an idea from looking over the terrain."

"You don't need one of my hands. I'll show you myself. Fact is, I'd be pleased to take you over to Kilcoyne's place after we finish. Hope you'll excuse me for not offering to take you to Pepper's spread. I can't hardly stand to even be around him. He reminds me of a fat cow tick."

Howard had heard from Preston Kirby that Longstreet was a keen judge of cattle. After the rancher's last comment, he decided that he was also a good judge of men.

Twenty minutes later they were riding toward a low ridge to the west of the ranch. They rode in silence, and an hour later they entered a stand of pine trees. They dismounted and walked to give their horses a breather. After taking only a few steps, Howard felt the hairs bristle on the back of his neck. It was a familiar sensation, one that he often experienced when he felt like he was being watched.

Longstreet and O'Hara apparently didn't feel the same thing, because while they walked, Longstreet took a tobacco pouch from his shirt pocket and began to build a cigarette. When he had it completed, he offered the pouch to Howard and O'Hara. The lawmen thanked him but declined the offer. Howard didn't smoke and was intent on verifying whether or not his feeling of uneasiness was justified.

A faint movement among another stand of trees across the meadow suddenly confirmed his suspicions. He looked through his field glasses and as he did so, his eyes widened ever so slightly. Standing among the trees some two hundred yards distant was a wolf. It was a large beast that appeared to weigh at least one hundred and twenty-five pounds. Howard then noticed two partially grown cubs playing near the big wolf. Contrary to Howard's initial guess, the animals had not spotted them, because the direction of the wind was wrong.

While Howard watched the wolves, Longstreet asked him what he was looking at. For a reply, Howard handed the older man his field glasses.

Longstreet cursed when he saw the wolves. "You reckon we could get closer to them things so I could get a shot at them?"

"I doubt it. Besides, I thought we were looking for rustled cattle."

Longstreet shot a quick look at the marshal. "We are. But those wolves kill cows. I'm aiming to shoot them if we can get closer." Then a thought occurred to the rancher. "Say, I just remembered. You're some shakes with a rifle, as good as you are with a pistol. Reckon you could hit 'em from here? I'll give you ten dollars a pelt."

"I could, but I won't."

"How come?"

Howard took the field glasses back. "Those wolves aren't bothering us. Besides, I like wolves."

"But look here, John, them wolves kill my cows. They cost me money."

Howard nodded. "I'll grant you that. But I'm not hired to kill wolves. I think the big one is the mother. If I shot it, the cubs would probably die."

"That's the idea."

"No. If you want them dead, you've got to do it yourself." Howard waved his hand as the rancher started to protest. "Mr. Longstreet, I'm not questioning your right to shoot them. I just won't be a party to it myself. Besides, a gun shot would alert anyone for miles around of our presence. If we're close to where your cattle were stolen, that's the last thing we want to do."

Longstreet moved the cigarette to the other side of his mouth. "Deputy O'Hara, I reckon you could hit them critters about as easy as John. You want to earn some quick money?"

"I could always use some quick money, but I reckon I got to float my stick the same as John. I was a pretty fair soldier and aim to be a good lawman, but I ain't no wolfer. Besides, I reckon John was right when he said a rifle shot would let anybody hereabouts know we're here."

The rancher finally nodded in reluctant agreement. "Reckon you boys are right. Okay, we won't bother 'em for now."

After four hours of riding, the three men covered all of the places where Longstreet had lost his cattle. At the last location, they spotted several tracks that appeared to lead off to the northwest. After studying the tracks at length, Howard admitted to himself that he was no closer to solving the crime than he was at the start of the day.

Longstreet saw his consternation. "Got you bamboozled, ain't it?" There was no rancor or recrimination in the question, just a statement of the obvious.

Howard agreed. "It does for a fact. I wish I could read tracks like some friends of mine. Some of them could follow a snake's trail over a flat rock."

"Reckon you could get in touch with your friends? I'd pay 'em fair wages."

Howard shook his head. "They wouldn't work for you. You see, this used to be their country until a few years ago. The friends I'm talking about are Sioux Indians."

Longstreet replied, "Makes no never mind to me. I'll pay any man an honest wage for an honest day's work."

"But it would matter to them. They look at us the same way

we look at the carpet-baggers who came to the South after the war."

O'Hara had been silent for several minutes. Now he spoke up. "Don't reckon you need nobody but me. I can track about as good as any Indian, if I do say so myself."

"I didn't know you were a tracker, Ian," said Howard. "Why didn't you tell me?"

"On account of you never asked. But I reckon I can read sign about as good as I shoot a gun. You know, tracks is funny. They all got a story. Now you take these here tracks. You can see where about forty or fifty head of cattle walked. An' you can see where the four, no, make it five gents was driving 'em. Feller ridin' drag tried to brush away the tracks. Didn't do too good a job." Pleased with himself, Ian went on. "Feller on the left side got hisself the makin's of a problem. His horse has got him a loose shoe."

They followed the tracks for another two miles or so. They were gaining in elevation as they gradually skirted the side of the ridge. O'Hara dismounted again and studied the ground. He put his finger up to his lips. "Looks like they're down in that draw up ahead. We got to be real careful. We're mighty close."

Howard looked closely at the tracks. They seemed to be converging, but told him little else. Then he noticed how the terrain ahead shifted downward for a few hundred yards, until it suddenly formed the draw O'Hara must have been referring to. He thought that if the rustlers were smart, they would have a couple of guards out, probably on the finger of the ridge east of the draw.

O'Hara seemed to read his thoughts. "You know, if I was taking another man's cows, I'd be sure to post a couple of men up high so they could see anybody coming up."

Longstreet echoed that sentiment. "Something else. I reckon I'd have some more men, too, where I was taking them cows. There's still plenty of Sioux hereabouts."

They picketed their horses in the brush. Then they walked on foot for about three hundred more yards, staying off the trail. Unmistakable sounds began to filter through the pines. There were cattle up ahead.

The men froze when they heard the sounds. Howard spoke softly. "Good job, Ian. No doubt about it, Mr. Longstreet. Ian has found your cattle."

Longstreet could hardly contain his elation. "You're good, Deputy O'Hara, mighty good. What are we gonna do now, John?"

"I think we need to have someone get closer and see if he can determine how many men are up there. Ian, are you good at sneaking up on someone?"

O'Hara nodded. "I'll be back in a few minutes. Better stay put till I get back."

As he finished speaking, the ex-trooper melted into the foliage. He scarcely made a sound when he left or when he returned thirty minutes later with his report. "They got a man on that ridge for a fact. I seen the sun shine off something up there. There's at least twenty men in that draw. They got close to five hundred head, and that don't count the cows I couldn't see in the brush. But I give 'em this, they ain't slackers. Why, they got 'em a right nice cabin built and a barn of sorts."

"Did you recognize any of them?" asked Howard.

"Can't say as I did. Then again, I was so interested keeping 'em from seeing me that I stayed far back in the bushes so I didn't get too close. How do you want to play this out, John?"

"I think you and Mr. Longstreet should ride back to his ranch. You leave him there and head back into town. Pres probably needs to stay there to keep an eye on things, but you can get the Parson and a few others, and come on back. Stop by the ranch and get as many men as Mr. Longstreet can spare."

O'Hara disagreed. "I reckon I ought to be the one to stay here, John. I'm better in the woods than you are. I don't think they'll be able to spot me."

Howard mulled over his friend's statement. "I think you're right. Are you sure you'll be okay?"

O'Hara flashed a big grin. "I campaigned against the Sioux and Cheyenne for the last three years, ever since I was fifteen. I don't expect those hombres down there are half as smart as the

Indians I've fought. It won't take a whole lot to keep 'em from finding me. Besides, I got some courting to do with Consuela. I ain't about to let anything louse that up."

CHAPTER TWENTY-SEVEN

The lawman and rancher made good time getting away from the area, but in their haste, they failed to recognize that they had been spotted by some rustlers who were concealed further back along the trail. They had been able to slip by them un-noticed on the way in because they had been traveling more slowly, and subsequently more silently.

Although Howard would not have recognized the rustlers, they knew him very well, having been given a detailed description of him by their employer. They were also well aware of his phenomenal shooting skills, so they were not anxious to face him in a fight. That meant that they would attempt an ambush.

The smell of pine permeated the air. Howard allowed himself to enjoy the fragrance of the aroma. He thought to himself that there was little to compare with the wonder of nature, other than the love of Rosa. All in all, life was finally good.

"Take care, gunfighter. Pretty soon, you may fancy yourself as a philosopher. You might even start attending the Parson's Sunday services on a regular basis," he cautioned himself.

Further contemplation by Howard was prevented by a softly uttered expletive from Longstreet. The rancher added, "Looks like them wolves is shadowing us. See 'em over there to the right by those bushes? What do you reckon them critters is up to?"

"Probably they're just curious." Howard suddenly reined his horse to a stop. The wolves had disappeared without warning into the thick bushes. "Mr. Longstreet, I think something spooked those wolves. We had better . . . "

The violent eruption of gunfire drowned out whatever the lawman was going to say. Six hidden riflemen opened fire at the same time. The hastily-planned ambush worked. The dry-gulchers took their victims completely by surprise and had enough firepower to do the job. Their only mistake was in opening fire from too far a distance. They also failed to remember that when shooting downhill, a rifleman should hold low.

Nevertheless, at the crash of gunfire, Longstreet toppled from his saddle. A .50 caliber slug from a Sharps rifle hit him at the base of his neck. He was rendered instantly unconscious and felt no pain because the heavy slug severed his spinal cord. He died before he fell from his saddle to the ground.

Howard was stuck twice, once high in the back just to the right of his spine, and once through the upper part of his lungs. He barely managed to stay in the saddle as he slumped forward. He tried desperately to hold on as his big sorrel galloped at full speed through the trees and undergrowth. Several hundred yards down the trail, Howard grew increasingly dizzy from the loss of blood. He fell from his saddle and struck his head on a rock. Although the blow to the head was relatively minor compared to the impact of the bullets, it was still enough to make him lose consciousness.

He briefly came to several minutes later. At first he didn't know where he was or how he got there. Then the fiery pain in his back jolted him into reality, even if only temporarily. He tried to move. As pain and nausea enveloped him, he decided it would be better to merely try to stay awake. He was unable to do so, however, and passed out again. It seemed that as he drifted in and out of consciousness, dreams and reality became so enmeshed with one another that he could not distinguish the difference between the two. The only constant was the excruciating pain that he felt. He consoled himself with the thought that at least he was still alive to feel the pain.

He thought that he heard voices but wasn't sure. Then he vaguely saw two men. At first, Howard thought that a couple of Sioux warriors had found him, because although these men were indistinct, they appeared to possess aquiline features. Further, in his pain-induced state, Howard thought he could feel rather than hear their voices, but he wasn't sure. They spoke with an accent unfamiliar to Howard; or perhaps it was really the absence of any accent. He felt himself being carried, although he wasn't sure how. Then again, he couldn't be sure of what was real and what was merely a hallucination.

The man nearest to him spoke. Was there a hint of agitation or frustration in his voice? "Why do we protect this one?"

"He needs help," was his companion's laconic reply.

Howard thought that they might not be Indians after all, because of their speech. Then again, in his current condition he wasn't sure what an Indian, or anyone for that matter, would sound like. A horse abruptly snorted in front of Howard. He squinted his eyes for a better look and saw several horsemen riding straight at him and his strange benefactors. His mind screamed a warning, but the words would not come. But there was no need to warn his companions. None of the approaching men even looked their way. He couldn't understand why the riders couldn't see him and the men with him. Yet the outlaws just rode by him and his guardians, close enough so that he could hear their voices. They were engaged in a heated argument. He could distinguish some of the words.

"Sure you hit the marshal. We all seen it. So where is he? Old Man Longstreet is graveyard dead. Howard was hit hard, too. There's a heap of blood on the trail, but he flat out vanished. He couldn't just disappear, but he did. We can't even find that big red hoss he rides. This don't make no sense."

Another voice chimed in. "Look, he can't have got too far. Sonny and Possum Jim seen him fall right around here. We gotta find him and make sure he's finished. You know what the boss said."

"Yeah, I know what he said, but it don't make no never mind. If Howard ain't here, he ain't here. It's that simple."

Then the voices of the ambushers faded as Howard and his two mysterious guardians moved further down the trail. Mercifully, Howard lost consciousness again, which lessened the searing pain that consumed him.

CHAPTER TWENTY-EIGHT

When Howard came to again, it was to the plaintive cry of a lone prairie wolf that shattered the silence of the night. He opened his eyes and saw that he was on a makeshift pallet inside Reverend Hightower's church. He thought that it was unusual that a lobo would venture so close to town. He never remembered how or when he got to the church.

Reverend Hightower spoke to the wounded marshal, "Welcome back, son. I was afraid we'd lost you. How do you feel?"

"Like I've been shot. Is Ian okay? They shot Mr. Longstreet. Did he make it? Did you talk to those two men who brought me here?"

"I didn't see anyone except you, John. I don't know about Ian or Hiram. Your horse came up with you draped over the saddle. I'm thankful I was still here praying and studying, or I would have missed you."

He wiped Howard's fevered brow with a damp cloth. The wolf howled again.

"You know, John," mused Reverend Hightower, "if I were still in Texas, I would be wondering if that wolf had four legs or two legs."

"Huh?"

The minister continued, "With the moon being full like it is, I'd be inclined to suspect the two-legged variety. In Texas, they call a full moon a 'Comanche moon' because that's when the Comanches prefer to raid the settlements. But I'm afraid that tomorrow morning when the sun comes up, the day will bring something worse—a gunman's dawn. The men who did this to you are just as ruthless as any Comanche, and they're better armed."

"So they're looking for me, then?"

"Oh yes. A dozen of Pepper's men have been scouring the town for you for the last several hours. They trailed your horse to town. They're spreading this crazy story that you're behind the rustling. They even claim that you murdered Hiram Longstreet earlier today when he confronted you."

The information overloaded the wounded lawman. He didn't know what question to ask next.

Reverend Hightower spoke again. "I probably told you too much. I gave you some laudanum to ease the pain. It'll also help you to sleep. Try not to worry. I know you didn't do anything they're accusing you of. You'll be safe with me until we can get you to Doctor Parker."

"Thanks, but how do you know they won't get me?"

"Because they'll have to go through me to get to you, and that won't be easy. Almost ten years ago I lost one of my sons to a bunch of killers. I'll not stand idly by and let it happen again."

Howard nodded off. When he awoke he tried to adjust the bandage around his torso where it itched, but was too weak to move his arms. He never remembered the bandage being applied.

He involuntarily yawned and saw Reverend Hightower by his side.

Howard formed his next words with difficulty. "Parson, I've got to tell you something while I'm still able. If I get out of this thing alive, I want to marry Rosa. Would that be all right with you?"

"Of course. I'll even perform the ceremony. But we need to talk about several things first."

Further conversation was prevented by voices coming from outside the church. Howard fought a losing battle to stay awake. He thought he heard Reverend Hightower tell him to stay in bed, although he wasn't sure. In fact, years later, Howard would still be uncertain if he accurately remembered anything that happened that particular night.

Shortly after Reverend Hightower left the room, Howard awoke with a start. He thought he saw the same two men who had helped him on the trail. He wondered why he had not seen or heard them come in the front door when Reverend Hightower departed, and the rear door was bolted shut from the inside.

"It is almost over," said the one nearest to him.

"Yes," replied the other. "Now we wait."

Just then, a series of shots rang out in the street. Howard felt himself gripped by a nameless fear, unlike anything he'd known since the death of his family. He wished he could bring his thoughts into focus, but was unable to do so. He dozed off again, in spite of himself.

When he awoke, he was in a stupor, as he was before when he nodded off. He didn't know if he had been asleep for a minute, an hour, or a day. He saw that his two enigmatic companions were still present. Then he saw a familiar face. It was Jeff Hightower. The minister was talking with the other two men. Reverend Hightower said something that Howard could not hear.

The man nearest Howard's pallet answered in a barely audible tone. "Yes, it is time."

Howard struggled to speak, but was unable. In fact, he didn't know whether he was awake or still asleep. All he knew was that he had a thousand questions. For some inexplicable reason, the sense of dread that had overwhelmed him earlier was no longer present. The opiate, perhaps? He closed his eyes and as he did, Reverend Hightower and the other two men walked away. Howard never saw them again.

CHAPTER TWENTY-NINE

A few minutes earlier, Reverend Hightower had walked out into the night. In the street in front of the church he was met by a group of a dozen or so men. All were carrying guns and torches. The man in front had a new Colt .45 in his right hand. Reverend Hightower recognized him as being one of Pepper's bodyguards. The man had a small, frail body, a ferret-shaped face, and quick, nervous movements. Like Cole Madison, he was one of that rare breed of gunfighter who carried two guns, and could use both with equal effectiveness. He went by the name of Sonny Chandler. He was one of those who had participated in the ambush of Howard and Longstreet.

Chandler pointed his revolver at the minister. "We've come to search this church for John Howard. You hiding him inside?"

Reverend Hightower looked at the gunman with cold contempt. "So, it takes all of you to search for one wounded man? You ought to be very proud of yourselves. I wonder which one of you shot him in the back?"

Two of the men in front looked at each other, then at Chandler. They appeared to be brothers.

The older one, Philip Macleod, answered the minister. He didn't ask how the preacher knew that Howard had been shot in the back. "Me an' my brother never back-shot nobody, Parson. I expect we neither one got much use for any low-life scum who would do such a thing. We just want to find Howard. Sonny here claims Howard shot Hiram Longstreet outside town an' got away. He rounded up me an' my brother an' some other fellers to help find him."

"All of you should leave this place." The preacher had no fear in his voice, something that made a huge impression on the men he was facing. "The deputy marshals should be around soon, and besides, I understand that more than a few folks are talking about forming a vigilante committee. If they do, they'll hang anyone suspected of shooting the marshal. You Macleod boys should go back to Arkansas, if you're innocent."

"Me and my brother ain't innocent, not by a long shot, but we kinda fancy ourselves to have some kinda standards. Like I done tole you, we never shot Howard or anybody else in the back. We just want to look inside the church for him."

"No." The one word statement had a sense of finality.

The ferret-faced gunman could stand no more talk. "I had about enough of this!" railed Chandler. "You two Macleods are supposed to be tough. Are you gonna let some old Bible-thumper buffalo you? An' what about the rest of you? We're holding guns, not him."

Then to the minister he said, "We ain't wasting any more time. We looked everywhere for that marshal. We think you got him hid in the church. You turn him over right now, or something real bad might happen to them two fine-looking daughters you got."

Hightower started walking toward the gunmen. "If you try to harm one hair on their heads, may God have mercy on you."

Philip Macleod spoke rapidly, with a surprisingly pleading voice. "Hold on, Reverend. Stop right there. I mean it! We don't wanna shoot you, but if you come any closer we will, 'cause we ain't gonna try to fist-fight you. An' if we shoot, we ain't gonna miss."

Glancing with contempt at Chandler, Macleod hastily added, "An' don't you fret none about your girls. Ben Duff's with 'em. Ain't nobody stupid enough to try to hurt 'em, especially with him around. They're just insurance till we get Howard."

The preacher visibly relaxed. He stopped and stood ten feet away from Chandler.

"See," said Chandler scornfully, "he ain't so tough. You all been acting like he's a one-man army or somethin'. But he ain't nuthin'. He don't want to be shot no more than the next man. Now see here old man, your time's run out. We think you're hiding Howard in there. If you don't stand aside and let us look, we'll shoot you. An' don't think that this is gonna turn out like some dime novel or one of them fairy tale Bible stories, where the good guys win. You sure as hell ain't gonna win nothing. Nossir, you ain't got no way out. Give us Howard or we'll kill you. You got one minute to make up your mind."

Andrew Macleod looked at Chandler. So far he had been silent. "Hold on, Sonny. Nobody said nuthin' 'bout shooting down an unarmed man, 'specially a man like this here preacher. Me an' my brother sold our guns to Pepper, sure enough, but that's all we sold. We ain't murderers."

Several of the other men in the gang agreed with the Macleods. This angered Chandler.

Chandler looked contemptuously at the Macleods. "So you Arkansas hillbillies are all of a sudden gettin' a conscience? I reckon it's too late for that. It don't matter none that you wasn't with us back on the trail when we shot Howard, 'cause you already taken the money for this job. You can't back out." Chandler cocked his gun. He pointed it at the minister. "I ain't foolin' no more with you. You gonna move aside or get shot?"

Reverend Hightower stood like a stone wall. His face was utterly devoid of fear. It was a picture of quiet strength. He said, "You should all leave. You might murder me, but that won't get you John Howard. It will just buy your own death."

Andrew Macleod looked at his brother, then at Chandler. "He ain't talkin' an' he ain't letting us inside. Let's go."

The other men stood by waiting. Then most began to holster their guns, turn and walk to their horses.

Chandler seemed to have difficulty making up his mind. "Maybe you're right."

He let down the hammer of his revolver and started to turn. Then without warning, he cursed, spun around, and shot the minister in the left leg. The Macleods and the others looked on in stunned disbelief.

"I warned you this ain't gonna have no happy ending, you old Bible-thumper!" Chandler's voice had an insane ring to it. "Now let's see how one of you self-righteous hypocrites dies!" His last words were punctuated by a second shot, this one to the preacher's other leg.

Still, the minister stood. Then he began taking short, wooden steps toward the astonished gunmen. Chandler fired three shots into the center of the minister's chest. The older man faltered, but continued to advance, coming within one-arm's reach of the crazed killer. He reached out with both hands and seized Chandler's lapels. Chandler fired the last round from his right-hand gun between the minister's eyes, screaming wildly the entire time. He drew his left-hand gun as Reverend Hightower fell forward against him. The minister kept his iron grip, forcing the gunman to his knees, just as he himself fell.

Chandler was in such a state of panic that he seemed to forget about the loaded gun he had just drawn as he screamed, "Get him off me! Get him off me!"

But there no need for his insane babbling, because Reverend Hightower relaxed his hold, and collapsed to the ground. The scene had a surreal quality about it. Everyone was noticeably shaken. The other gunmen continued to stare in shocked disbelief. They had holstered their guns. Then, simultaneously, the Macleod brothers drew their revolvers, and held them down at their sides.

"Phil, did you see that? Shot to doll rags like that, an' still trying to fight, still trying to grab hold of Chandler," said a clearly shaken Andrew Macleod.

"Never seen nothin' like it." Philip Macleod looked at Chandler with revulsion. "Sonny, you ought not have done that. That was raw, mighty raw. Ain't much man in you, is there?" He turned his attention back to his brother. "Andy, I reckon we made a mistake riding for this here outfit. Bodyguarding an' fightin' for wages is one thing. This is somethin' else. Reckon we don't need money that bad."

His brother nodded in agreement. "Yeah, I expect you're right." He imperceptibly eased the muzzle of his gun toward Chandler.

He echoed his brother's words. "Sonny, you ought not to have done that." He glanced at his brother. "Phil, whadda you want to do?"

Philip Macleod looked at the dead clergyman and decided there had been enough killing for one night. "Reckon we ought to ride, little brother."

Chandler was confused. He sensed that the Arkansas gunfighters and the others didn't approve of what he had done, although he wasn't sure why they should care. He thought that because they worked for the same employer, they were men like himself, who were devoid of any type of ethics, and were only concerned with their own personal gratification. He was wrong. Furthermore, both the Macleods and the other gunfighters had decided they were not going to be hanged for something that Chandler had done. Already several people were gathering, drawn by the gunshots.

Chandler was still befuddled. He didn't understand why everyone was backing away from him and the dead preacher. Although he had fast reflexes, he was slow-witted and didn't realize that the rest of the group were trying to distance themselves from him and the cold-blooded murder he had just committed. As for the others in the gang, they were hoping that the onlookers had seen that Chandler was the one who pulled the trigger, not them. At the same time, they were trying to discreetly blend into the crowd.

Unknown to the demented killer, the ever-increasing throng of angry citizens was not his biggest concern, it was Ben Duff. The older gunfighter worked his way through the crowd to where Reverend Hightower's lifeless body was sprawled out.

Duff looked at the dead minister, and as he did, all color drained from his face. "Who did this?" The question hung in the air and demanded a response.

Philip Macleod answered for himself and his brother. He spoke to both Duff and the crowd. "It weren't us, Ben. It was that little weasel Chandler."

"Hold on there!" Chandler shouted. "Who you callin' a weasel? An' what if I did shoot him? He's hiding Howard. Besides . . . "

"Enough!" commanded Duff. "You Macleods can ride. So can the rest of you, except Chandler. Chandler, drop your guns."

"Huh? You trying to give me orders? I ain't gonna do it."

But there was fear mixed with confusion in the voice of the nervous killer. Chandler was fast and had killed several men, but he was a sure-thing killer. He wanted no part of what Ben Duff could give him. Even though he still held a loaded gun, his sense of self-preservation told him that he was facing certain death in Duff. Although he never would admit it to anyone, he doubted he could beat Duff even with a drawn gun. Furthermore, even if he were lucky enough to get lead into the older gunman, he knew with certainty that he would die himself.

Chandler addressed Duff a second time, his voice a curious mixture of shame and bravado. "An' you can't shoot me, Duff. See?" He dropped his left-hand gun into its holster. "My guns are both holstered. Look, all you people are witnesses. I ain't gonna draw against you, Duff. You can't make me."

Chandler started walking toward his horse. Then he turned around and smirked. "Ain't so smart after all, are you, Duff? I done killed that old man an' there ain't nuthin' you can do about it. I'm fixin' to just ride on out of here. To stop me you'll have to shoot me in the back in front of witnesses. You got too much gunman's pride to do that."

Duff drew his revolver and held it squarely in the middle of the back of the departing killer. "Don't try to leave, Chandler. I won't tell you again."

"You're wastin' your breath. You ain't no lawdog. You can't arrest me. I'm riding. Think though maybe I'll stop by and see them Hightower gals on my way out, since you left 'em alone." Chandler swung one leg over the saddle of his horse. "See you in hell, Duff."

"Wrong answer." The thunderous report from Duff's .44 reverberated through the night as he finished speaking.

The heavy lead slug caught Chandler in the center of the back. It was that sudden, that unexpected, and that final. Chandler dropped to the dirt. The dying gunman had been right about one thing. It wouldn't have mattered if he had tried to face Duff with a loaded gun in his hand. There was no way he could come close to Duff's speed and accuracy. In less than a minute he would be dead, only fifty feet from the man he murdered, and never considering that Reverend Hightower's last words had proven prophetic. The pastor's murder had truly caused his own death.

As the last of Chandler's life's blood drained from him, he was cautiously approached by Ben Duff. Duff's revolver was cocked and ready. Duff was joined by Philip Macleod.

Chandler used the last of his remaining strength to turn his head toward Duff. He was too weak to move any other part of his body. His final words were gasped out in little more than a hoarse whisper and were heard only by Duff and Macleod.

After the dying gunfighter's last words, Macleod looked at Duff. Macleod's voice reflected the consternation he felt. "Whadda you think about what he said, Ben? You reckon he was trying at the last minute to do one decent thing?"

"I don't know. Phil, I want you to do me a favor. I want you to write down what he said just before he died. Then I would like for you and your brother to go to Deadwood and wait a few days until I send for you."

Macleod still looked confused. "Uh, sure thing, Ben. If that's what you want. But don't worry none about gunnin' him. That ratty little killer deserved to die. Tell you the truth, me and my brother was sorely tempted to shoot him after what he done. I know Andy was fixin' to when you come up."

Duff patted the younger man on the shoulder and walked over to the dead clergyman.

In the ensuing commotion, the other gunmen had holstered their guns and walked toward their horses. Andrew Macleod walked over to Duff and gestured toward Reverend Hightower's corpse. "He was a man, that one. Uh, you still lettin' us ride, Ben?"

Duff nodded his head.

The Macleods mounted. They were last seen riding toward Deadwood. Nobody tried to stop them. The other gunmen scattered like a covey of quail, each man hoping that nobody recognized him.

As for Duff, he walked over to the dead preacher. In the darkness, none of the onlookers could see him clearly as he knelt beside Reverend Hightower's body. If they had, they would have been surprised to see him place something in the coat pocket of the deceased minister. They would have been even more surprised to see the tears that flowed freely down his face.

CHAPTER THIRTY

Preston Kirby had just arrived at the jail when he received word of the preacher's murder. He heard that Pepper's men were involved, so when he saw Ben Duff walking toward the jail, he had reason to be wary. In fact, when Kirby saw Duff, he quietly slipped into the alley and waited until the older gunman passed. Only then did he reveal his presence with a warning.

"Hold on there, Duff." Kirby's order was accented by the sound of a gun hammer being thumbed back. "That noise you just heard was me cocking the right barrel of this sawed-off ten gauge. Reckon I won't need the other barrel. You even twitch a muscle, an' I'm fixin' to splatter your guts all over the street."

Duff slowly raised both hands. He answered in a strained voice, "Kirby, I know what you're thinking, but you've got to give me a chance to explain. There's no time to waste. I assure you that within five minutes I can answer all of your questions. If my explanations don't suit you, go ahead and use that Greener."

Kirby was impressed with Duff's nerve, but didn't let his guard down. The Texan wouldn't back down from anyone in a fair fight, even someone like Duff. However, he was convinced that Duff was probably involved in the ambush of Howard and murder of the minister. Therefore, given those circumstances, he had no intention of giving someone as deadly as the older gunfighter an even break. He ordered Duff to keep his hands away from his gun, and to walk into the jail.

"I'll drop my gun-belt first, Kirby, if that will suit you. Then I'll walk ahead. You can set the terms, but you've got to hear me out before you do anything rash."

"Okay. Shuck that gun-belt and go on in the jail. An' you best not have no hideout gun."

Once inside, Duff wasted no words. "Reverend Hightower was gunned down a few minutes ago in front of the church. Sonny Chandler murdered him. I killed Chandler when he tried to leave. There were several hired guns looking for John Howard. It seems that Hiram Longstreet, the rancher, was murdered outside of town when Howard was wounded. The gunmen thought Howard was in the church. Reverend Hightower wouldn't let them inside to look. That's when Chandler murdered him. Howard's in the church right now. I've got Eli Thorton and four other men who can be trusted guarding John, in case the men hunting him come back. I've sent another man for Doctor Parker. I'm on my way to the Hightower's house. I left the Hightower girls there."

Kirby's reply was laced with suspicion. "I heard most of that the crew looking for John was working for Pepper, same as you. How come you wanna help him?"

"You might not believe this, Kirby, but you and I are on the same side. I've got to leave Gold Valley for a few days. There are some things I have to do. You've got to ride for Fort Pierre. Don't wait until sunrise. Leave now. When you get there, I want you to send a telegram to Yankton. The contents of the message I want you to send are on this paper in my shirt pocket. Let me pull it out with my left hand and put it on the table. After you read it, you'll know everything you need to."

"I ain't much of a hand reading. What does the note say?"

Duff cursed bitterly. "Listen, man! You can read well enough to get the gist of it." He placed a folded piece of paper on the table and backed way, his hands raised. "Now read it!"

Kirby frowned as he squinted at the note. Then his eyes opened wide in amazement as he laboriously deciphered the contents. "This here's about the blamedest thing I ever heard of. How do I know it's the truth?"

"Think about it a minute and you'll know it's true." Duff looked directly at the lawman, and then purposely lowered his hands. "I'm taking my gun back now. Are you going to shoot me, or ride for Fort Pierre?"

Kirby made his decision. He lowered the shotgun. "Reckon you ought to get yourself heeled again. I'm riding for the fort." He stuck out his hand. "Good luck."

Kirby looked once at Duff as he left the office. Duff was strapping on his Smith and Wesson. Kirby went to the livery and got his horse, a tough, mouse-colored little mustang called a "grulla" in the Texas border country. He also picked out another horse, one that had recently belonged to Cole Madison. It had more or less become the property of the town of Gold Valley after Howard had killed Madison a few months before. Kirby knew that he could make the ride to Fort Pierre faster if he took two mounts and switched riding them after one became tired.

As Kirby left town, Duff went to Angelique Mayo's hotel. He banged loudly on her door. There was no time for formalities. When she met him, she was dressed in a robe that had a Smith and Wesson .32 revolver in the robe's pocket. Her right hand was on the tiny gun. When she saw her visitor was Duff, she took the gun out and laid it on the seat of a chair by the door.

As with Kirby, Duff wasted no time. A scant five minutes later, Angelique was dressed and moving out the door.

Less than thirty minutes later, the only doctor in town was examining Howard's wounds. The physician was assisted by his wife, a trained nurse. As Duff had said, Eli Thorton and several other townspeople stood by while Howard's wounds were tended to. All were armed. During the examination, Howard briefly came to. While he was conscious, he spoke to Thorton and the other men. In spite of the opiate he had been given, Howard was able to stay coherent long enough to ask about Reverend Hightower. He also told the listeners the approximate location where Longstreet had been shot and where O'Hara was watching the rustlers and stolen cattle. He passed out again. Shortly after Howard finished speaking, another party of over thirty armed men rode out of town toward Longstreet's ranch.

Thorton cuffed his hat back. "Is he going to live, Doc?"

Doctor Parker looked from the wounded marshal to the storekeeper. The doctor's face was set in hard lines from worry. He was an experienced and capable physician who moved west with his wife and children after the Black Hills opened to white settlers. He had tended too many gunshots in the Civil War to give an overly-optimistic answer.

"I don't know. He's young and strong. Also, the bullets missed his spine and there's no apparent infection. Those things are in his favor. On the other hand, he's lost a lot of blood. If I had a way to get new blood into him, he would fare much better. I've done everything I can do. The rest is up to him."

"It's also up to God." Heads turned to the front door of the church to identify the speaker. It was Rosa Hightower in the company of Angelique Mayo. "When will he be well enough to move, Doctor?"

The physician scratched his head. "I honestly don't know, Miss Hightower. My best advice would be to leave him right where he is for a few days. Then we can move him over to my office."

Rosa disagreed. "That won't be necessary, Doctor Parker. He can be moved to our house. My papa and sister can help me take care of him."

No one answered. Doctor Parker faintly nodded at his wife. She moved to Rosa's side and held her hand.

"Sit down, dear." Mrs. Parker was a compassionate and considerate woman who had discovered over the years that she had a unique talent for comforting others in times of pain and grief. She and her husband were supporters of Howard and were friends of the Hightowers, and so she summoned all of her ability to tell Rosa as gently as she could about her father's death.

Her intentions were good and honorable, but ineffective. Rosa fainted.

CHAPTER THIRTY-ONE

When John Howard finally awoke, he felt a warm breeze on his face. He opened his eyes and looked around. He saw white lace curtains gently moving in front of the open window of his room. From the angle of the sun, he assumed it was probably some time in the afternoon. He had no idea where he was or how long he had been there. He even wondered for a brief moment if he had really been shot, because he felt no pain. He rolled to his side. That simple movement erased any doubts he held. The pain he experienced was enough to make him yell out.

Rosa was sitting by his bed. "Lie still, now, my love," she advised.

The sight of her leaning over him had tremendous therapeutic value. Her voice comforted him like nothing else could. She smiled and lightly kissed him on the forehead. Looking around he also saw Consuela in the room. Upon seeing him awake, she skipped over and also kissed him.

"I knew he would be all right, Rosa. I just knew he would be." Consuela's voice reflected both happiness and relief.

"You were right, Consuela. John, how do you feel?"

"Your father asked me the same thing last night. I feel like I've been shot. Speaking of the Parson, where is he?"

Both girls clutched his hands. They looked at one another and then at Howard. "Our papa is in Heaven," Rosa answered softly. "He was killed the night you were shot."

Howard felt a depth of sadness unknown to him since the death of this own father and brother. "We lost him? How? Why?"

Rosa sat on the bed beside him. "He was shot down by a gunman named Chandler. He was one of the gang that came looking for you at the church."

Howard looked stonily at the ceiling. "Then Chandler's a dead man when I get out of this bed." He tried to sit up. The pain forced him to stay down.

"Calm yourself, dear. Chandler's already paid for Papa's murder. He was shot himself that same night trying to escape."

Howard relaxed. "Good for Pres Kirby."

"Mr. Kirby didn't kill Chandler. Ben Duff did."

Howard was perplexed. "Ben Duff killed him? That's strange. Both he and Chandler are in Pepper's hip pocket."

The Hightower girls exchanged quick glances but didn't reply at first. Then Consuela said, "Just because Mr. Duff works for that dirty old man doesn't mean he's in his hip pocket. Mr. Duff is a friend of the family. He's a good man."

Howard was too weak to argue. Besides, if Duff had killed the murderer of his friend, then he was to be commended.

"When is your father's funeral? We have to make arrangements."

Rosa and Consuela looked at each other again as Rosa said, "Papa was buried two days ago. You've been asleep for three days." She leaned over and kissed him again. "Now you should rest and not talk any more until the doctor gets here. Consuela, would you go fetch the doctor and tell him John is awake?"

When Consuela left, Howard remembered something his friend had told him that night at the church. He said to Rosa, "I don't understand something your father told me the last time I saw him. Perhaps it was the laudanum he gave me. He said he had lost one son to gunmen and wouldn't lose another. What was he talking about?"

"He meant that he thought of you like a son."

"I know that. But what did he mean about losing a son to gunmen? I thought your brothers and mother died of smallpox."

Rosa sighed. Her lovely face was temporarily marred by a frown, as she considered the question. "We rarely talk about my oldest brother. He was called Benito, after my Uncle Benjamin. He was much older than Consuela and me. I remember him as being strong and handsome, but with a chip on his shoulder. You see, he didn't look like the rest of us, who favored our mother. He looked like Papa, with blond hair, blue eyes, and a fair complexion. He was never well-liked because he looked like an Anglo, not a Mexican. I'm afraid he grew to despise Papa because of his looks. My brother went to Papa when he was twenty-one and demanded his inheritance. He left home."

"Did he ever return?" asked Howard.

"He did not. He went north to Texas and became a leader of bandits that preyed upon Mexicans. Later he killed the son of a powerful Mexican rancher who had insulted him. The fight was fair, but it didn't matter. The rancher sent six of his toughest vaqueros after Benito. All were pistoleros. They say my brother killed four of them before he was cut down. He lived for two days in intense pain before he died."

"Did he ever make peace with your father?"

"No, although Papa and Mama both made it to his bedside while he was dying. With his last breath, he cursed Papa. It almost destroyed Papa. He said he should have done something, anything, but . . . " Whatever Rosa was going to say was stifled by her quiet sobbing, as she buried her face against Howard's shoulder.

They stayed that way for several minutes. When Rosa regained control of her emotions, she wiped her eyes and raised up. "Now you know, my love. It happened almost ten years ago, but Papa carried that burden for the rest of his life."

Howard could only imagine the mental anguish her father had endured. He tried to comfort the woman he loved. "Your father was a good man, Rosa. I've never met any better. He was not to blame for the path your brother took. Your father taught me that each man must make his own choices and live with the consequences. And I know that he helped me more than you could imagine."

The door opened. Consuela had returned. She came to the side of Howard's bed and squeezed his hand. "Doctor Parker will be here in a few minutes, John. In the meantime, there's someone who wants to see you."

She went back to the door and led Ian O'Hara inside. O'Hara

grinned and started to shake Howard's hand vigorously. He stopped when Howard groaned from the movement.

"I told all of 'em, John. I sure enough told 'em, an' I was right! I knew you was too mean an' ornery to die from a couple of little ole bullets."

"I came close, Ian. What happened out there after we left?"

The redheaded deputy sat down in one of the chairs. "It was the durnedest thing. A little while before the posse got there, one man came riding up so fast you'd thought ole Beelzebub hisself was after him. Best I could figure, he brought a warning, on account of that everybody lit a shuck just a few minutes later. The way I figured, them yahoos knew that the posse was comin' from Gold Valley."

"How did you reach that conclusion?"

"Easy enough, I reckon. When they vamoosed, they headed northwest, toward Deadwood, away from Gold Valley. Say John, you look pretty much done in. Doc Parker's on his way. Why don't I leave you alone till he gets here?" He stood up and started for the door.

"Fine, Ian. Just one more thing before you go. Where's Pres Kirby?"

O'Hara paused at the bedroom door. "Don't reckon anybody knows. Some folks say he rode out the night poor Reverend . . . " He stopped and gave a sheepish look to Rosa. "Sorry, Miss Rosa."

Rosa smiled sadly. "It's okay, Ian. John knows about Papa's death. You can talk about it."

At her reassurance, he continued. "That's about all there is to it. Pres is gone. Nobody knows where. Ben Duff ain't been seen around either. An' the Macleod brothers and the rest of them gunnies on Pepper's payroll are gone too."

O'Hara closed the door on his way out. A half hour later, Doctor Parker completed his examination of Howard. "You're going to be fine, John. It will take time and rest, but in a few weeks you should be as good as new. You're very fortunate you had first class medical care at the time of your injuries. Reverend Hightower undoubtedly saved your life." He opened the door. "I'm finished Rosa. You can come back inside."

Howard agreed with the doctor. "Reverend Hightower not only gave me medical care, but he also kept those killers from coming in after me. I just wish I could have done something to keep them from taking his life."

Rosa kissed her fiancé. "They didn't take his life, John. He laid it down for you."

CHAPTER THIRTY-TWO

Howard rested for another week at the Hightower's house. He gradually recovered his strength, to the point where he could move slowly around without the aid of the cane that was supplied by Doctor Parker. He was even able to venture outside. His steps were slow, but he didn't care particularly because he was healing. Nevertheless, Ian O'Hara accompanied him everywhere he went.

While the marshal was convalescing, William Pepper was busier than usual. He summoned a meeting of the town council on the morning of June 25, 1877, one year to the day after the defeat of the Seventh Cavalry at the Little Bighorn. But the purpose was not to reflect on that battle or to discuss the upcoming Independence Day celebration. Pepper had a more sinister agenda. He told the other council members that he had information that directly connected Howard to the cattle rustling. Pepper even said that he had a witness who could prove that Howard murdered Hiram Longstreet.

Over the protests of Angelique Mayo, Pepper called for the council to immediately fire Howard, appoint a new marshal, and convene a grand jury so that Howard could be indicted for the murder of Longstreet and theft of the cattle. He also proposed that the council establish a court and appoint a judge to try the case as soon as possible.

Angelique made no effort to mask her true feelings. "That's got to be the most preposterous thing I've ever heard of! Pepper, you've finally gone too far!" Turning her attention to the rest of the members of the town council, she continued, "You all know John Howard, and you know the gunslingers and riffraff that Pepper employs. Who would you believe? It's no secret that Pepper hates the marshal. Why does he hate him? Because John is all those things that Pepper is not. John Howard is honest and respected. Pepper isn't."

Pepper's flabby jowls quivered slightly as he framed a reply. His hatred of the pretty hotel owner was evident. "Mrs. Mayo, if you choose to give free room and board, and who knows what other services, to the marshal, that's your business. You've told us that before. But the well-being of this town is my business. Two of my men saw Howard driving stolen cattle. Oh, Howard was clever enough. He even fooled his own deputies. But when he and Deputy O'Hara and Hiram Longstreet went out, supposedly looking for the cattle, Howard murdered Longstreet. One of my men was told that by Mr. Longstreet just before he died. I happen to know that a dying declaration is admissible in court."

Angelique glared back at the mayor. "And who is this person who supposedly heard this? I imagine he's a model citizen, like the gunslingers on your payroll who were searching for John the night another of your men murdered Reverend Hightower."

Pepper gave a triumphant smirk. "Oh, did I neglect to tell you my man's name? Well, rest assured that he is a solid citizen. But I'll wait until the trial to reveal his name. When I do, I think you will be surprised and disappointed, Mrs. Mayo." He wiped a stream of tobacco juice that had started to flow from the corner of his mouth. "And as for the unfortunate murder of Reverend Hightower, we all know that my personal assistant Ben Duff dealt with the man who committed the murder. And I trust it is not necessary to remind everyone that Chandler was operating on his own initiative. I had fired him earlier. He may have even been working with Howard and they had a falling out. I guess we'll never know. Now, back to the present matter. Gentlemen, let's discuss who we want to appoint to the grand jury. I want to ensure that everything is legal and proper. If Howard is indicted, then we also need to appoint a judge and establish a trial date. Naturally, I'm willing to serve in that capacity myself if we can't find another qualified candidate."

Angelique rose to her feet. Her pretty face was beet-red with anger. "Gentlemen, you know that any grand jury would be hand-picked by Pepper. Of course they would indict the marshal! And any trial presided over by Pepper would be a sham. If you want a trial, then get a real judge to preside."

Unknown to the council members, during the discussion, four riders came into town. All were capable-looking individuals. Two were strangers, but were distinctive, because the morning sun glinted off badges on their chests, identifying them as United States Deputy Marshals. The third man wore a dark gray suit and sported a gray beard. He had a stern expression and the air of authority about him that Pepper had unsuccessfully tried to emulate for years. The dark-complected man in the lead was no stranger, but Preston Kirby.

The group entered the hotel just as Angelique finished speaking. Kirby nodded toward the town council. "Well now, looks like we're just in time to make some medicine. These two Deputy U.S. Marshals are Mr. McCormick an' Mr. Barnes. The gent in the suit is Judge Robert Hampton. Judge Hampton's been appointed by the Governor to look into the trouble we've been havin' with murders and rustling."

CHAPTER THIRTY-THREE

The trial of John Howard overshadowed the upcoming Independence Day celebration plans for the town of Gold Valley. As predicted by Angelique, the grand jury indicted Howard. However, Howard was assured of a fair hearing because of the presence of Judge Hampton. Hampton had a well-deserved reputation for being tough but fair-minded. He had originally been a staff attorney for William Jayne, who in 1861 became the first Governor of the Dakota Territory.

When the trial began, the judge gave explicit instructions to the lawyers, jury, and spectators that left no doubt as to the seriousness of the trial and the fact that he was committed to see the law carried out fairly and impartially. Dozens of spectators jammed into the makeshift courtroom that was established in the main entrance area of Angelique Mayo's hotel, while countless others milled around outside.

The judge surveyed the crowded courtroom. "Gentlemen of the jury, ladies and gentlemen in the courtroom, my name is Robert Hampton. I've been tasked by the Governor to investigate problems in this area involving cattle rustling and murder. During my short time here, indictments have been brought against the town's marshal, John Howard. One of the crimes he is accused of is murder, which can bring the death penalty. Therefore, I charge the members of the jury to carefully and deliberately consider the facts presented to them during this trial. Please notice that I used the term 'facts'. We are not interested in opinion, speculation, or rumor, because the law is based upon fact. It is incumbent upon everyone associated with this hearing to remember that. I will not tolerate any disruptions or foolishness, because a man's life is on the line. The prosecutor is Mr. Wayne Lambert, of Pierre. The defense is Mr. Gaylord Adams, of Yankton. You will notice that there are two United States Deputy Marshals present. They will be assisted, if need be, by a unit of the United States Cavalry, who I see are now coming into the courtroom. Their job is to maintain order in the court."

Howard glanced behind him and saw several troopers of the Second Cavalry filing through the door. Walking in front of the men was Howard's friend, Lt. James Campbell. On closer look, Howard noticed that his friend now wore two bars, the insignia for the rank of captain. Captain Campbell smiled and nodded at Howard. Most of the soldiers with the captain had been with Howard during the fight with the Sioux the previous autumn. They also gave Howard friendly looks. The hulking figure of the last soldier in line was also immediately familiar to Howard as being Sergeant Reilly. On closer inspection, Howard saw that, like Campbell, Reilly's rank had changed. Some of Reilly's chevrons were missing. It appeared as though he was now a corporal. The look he gave Howard was anything but friendly.

Howard quickly returned his attention to the judge, who was addressing a small man wearing gold-rimmed glasses and an expensive black suit. The man was sitting at the prosecutor's table. To this individual, the judge asked, "Mr. Lambert, is the government ready?"

"We are, Your Honor," replied the prosecutor.

"Mr. Adams, is the defense ready?"

Howard's attorney stood before the judge. Interestingly enough, he also wore gold-rimmed glasses and had a suit identical to that worn by the prosecutor, leaving Howard to speculate if all trial lawyers in Dakota patronized the same tailor.

"Your Honor," he said, "The defense is ready."

The prosecutor spoke first. For almost ten minutes, he told a convincing tale that impressed everyone present. His eloquence could not be doubted, and he seemed sincerely convinced that Gold Valley's marshal was, in fact, guilty of cattle rustling and murder. During his speech, Howard noticed that many of the jurors appeared to be swayed by the prosecutor's arguments.

After the prosecutor finished, Howard leaned over and whispered something in his attorney's ear. His attorney grinned and stood up when it was his turn to speak. "Your Honor, my worthy opponent has enthralled us with his eloquence and style. Why, he was so convincing that my client just told me that he knew he was innocent before Mr. Lambert's opening statements, but that now he's not so sure himself. In point of fact, he's halfway convinced that he may have even murdered President Lincoln, and that John Wilkes Booth was merely a scapegoat."

Laughter erupted in the court. Judge Hampton banged his gavel for several seconds before the noise abated enough for the defense lawyer to continue.

When Adams began again, he said, "Your Honor, if it please the Court, we will establish not only that John Howard is innocent of the false charges brought against him, but with the Court's indulgence, we will prove beyond the shadow of a doubt who was really responsible for these heinous crimes."

The presiding judge lowered his glasses to glare at the attorney. "Mr. Adams, what pleases this Court is the proper administration of justice. Therefore, I'm willing to hear all pertinent facts, and even to try another case if need be. But I will not tolerate any more theatrics from you that result in disrupting these proceedings. So be very cautious about telling any more jokes, or the joke may be on you after you find yourself held in contempt of court. Do I make myself clear?"

"Yes, Your Honor," replied the defense attorney in his most contrite voice, although it was obvious that his ploy had succeeded. He had broken the spell woven by the prosecuting attorney. Howard was thankful that the Hightower girls had hired Mr. Gaylord Adams, Esquire, of Yankton, Dakota Territory, to defend him.

CHAPTER THIRTY-FOUR

The first witness called was completely unexpected by Howard. It was his old nemesis, Donald Reilly. Reilly testified that Howard was carrying stolen gold coins when they first met the previous fall. Reilly said that when Howard was changing the saddle-bags from his dead Appaloosa to the army mount, a gold double eagle rolled out of the bags. The soldier then said that he was able to covertly pocket the twenty-dollar gold piece without being noticed. He said he notched an "X" on the rim of the coin to identify it later.

While Reilly spoke, Howard whispered comments to his own lawyer, who scrawled notes on his pad. The note-taking grew more frenzied as the soldier told his story.

Under the skillful direction of the prosecutor, Reilly told how the Indians had appeared just after the troopers had spotted Howard and questioned him about the stolen gold shipment. Later, when Howard recognized the Indian leader, Touch the Clouds, the general consensus of the troopers was that Howard was hiding something. With a defiant look at Captain Campbell, Reilly also described how Campbell gave up a weapon to the Sioux at the behest of Howard, and that he refused to try to arrest Touch the Clouds when the war chief gave a stolen army mount to Howard. He also testified that Campbell had endangered the lives of his men by following the war party. Finally, he accused Campbell of letting a trooper desert the army; the same soldier who became a deputy of Howard.

Finally, the judge had enough. He stopped further testimony with a stern warning to the prosecutor. "Mr. Lambert, your witness will confine his comments to the matter at hand. I don't expect a noncommissioned officer to be familiar with criminal procedure, but I do expect you to be. I fail to see what bearing his testimony has on this case."

"If it please the court, Your Honor, I'm only seeking to give background information on Howard, to show his true character," replied the prosecutor.

"Very well, I'll allow his testimony to stand, for now," replied the judge. "Mr. Adams, do you care to question this witness?"

Mr. Adams stood and walked over to Reilly. "Do you know the penalty for perjury, Corporal Reilly?"

"I ain't sure what perjury is, but I done told you the truth."

"I see. I don't suppose you still have that coin, do you?"

"No, I don't. I give it to Lieutenant, I mean Cap'n Campbell. But it wouldn't surprise me none if he got rid of it so his Johnny Reb buddy wouldn't get in trouble."

Extracting a gold coin from his own coat pocket, Adams asked, "Is this the coin you gave Captain Campbell?"

Reilly's eyes narrowed. "Well now, I ain't exactly sure, but I think it is." Upon closer inspection he said, "Yep, that's the one. Say, how'd you get it?"

Adams turned to the judge. "Your Honor, we're willing to stipulate that this coin is the one Mr. Howard had on him at the time of the battle with the Sioux last October. For the record, the mint mark on it is from Chicago. We would like that information entered into the record."

The prosecutor stood. "Your Honor, I didn't know that defense counsel had that coin. That aside, what does the mint mark have to do with anything?"

Judge Adams glanced from the prosecutor to Howard's lawyer. "Mr. Adams?"

Howard's attorney answered, "Your Honor, the stolen gold shipment was from the Denver mint. As I said, this coin was minted in Chicago. Therefore, this coin could not have been part of that shipment."

The judge was satisfied. "Fine, Mr. Adams, now do you have any more questions for this witness?"

"No, Your Honor, but with your permission I would like to enter several facts for the record regarding the testimony of this witness."

The judge adjusted himself and folded his hands. "Since the prosecutor called the witness, yes, you may make a statement. However, I caution both defense and prosecution that future testimony will be directly related to this case."

"Thank you, Your Honor. Gentlemen of the jury, you just heard an interesting tale, practiced undoubtedly under the coaching of my worthy opponent. However, the facts are that Mr. Howard saved those troopers, including Corporal Reilly, from being killed that day. The United States Army has a full report from the commanding officer present during that skirmish. That officer is present today in this courtroom and can testify, if need be. The Army disagrees with the corporal's conclusions because the ranking officer received a battlefield promotion as a result of that engagement, something almost unheard of since the Civil War. Captain Campbell also received a commendation from General Sheridan himself for his part in causing Touch the Cloud's band of renegade Sioux to leave Dakota. Captain Campbell told the Army that John Howard deserved the credit for their victory and for the Sioux under Touch the Clouds leaving Dakota. I could also call several witnesses, in addition to Captain Campbell, who could testify that my client saved those troopers later, as well as several civilians."

Returning his attention to Reilly, the lawyer said, "I notice you are a corporal, yet it looks like there used to be more stripes on your sleeve. Were you ever a sergeant?"

"Objection, Your Honor. What does Mr. Reilly's rank have to do with anything?"

The judge directed his attention again to Howard's lawyer. "Mr. Adams, I was wondering the same thing myself."

Adams approached the judge and then turned slightly toward the jury box. "Your Honor, it has relevance because this witness is prejudiced against my client. After the fight with the Sioux I just told you about, this witness was demoted for insubordination, because he refused to obey orders from his commanding officer. I believe he frequently said that he wouldn't listen to anyone who was a friend of a rebel, meaning my client."

"Very well. The objection is overruled. Mr. Adams, you may continue."

Adams walked back over to the witness chair. "Just one final question. And remember you're still under oath. Are you still planning to kill Mr. Howard?"

Prosecutor Lambert's objection was loud and vehement.

"Objection sustained," said Judge Hampton, "Corporal Reilly, you don't have to answer that question."

"I don't mind answering, Judge. If he don't swing for murder, yeah, I plan on beating him with my fists. Mebbe he'll live through it and mebbe he won't. I don't much care one way or the other, just so long as I get to bloody him up and give him what's coming to him."

CHAPTER THIRTY-FIVE

After Reilly stepped down, the judge called a brief recess. After fifteen minutes, court resumed. The next witness called by the prosecution was William Pepper.

When he was sworn in, he gave his name and described his occupation as being the mayor of Gold Valley, the owner of the Gold Valley Bank, and owner of a cattle ranch. He added, "I also have some other business interests. For example, you may be interested to know that I'm also an attorney, although I'm not currently practicing. I left a very lucrative law practice in Chicago to assist in the establishment of this fine city. So I must say that I also see myself as a sort of a philanthropist, if you will. That is, I'm someone whom anyone can turn to in times of trouble. My job is really taking care of the people in my town. Everyone knows that, and I must say that my reputation for benevolence extends far beyond the town limits."

It was obvious that the obese banker was enamored with the sound of his own voice. It was equally obvious that Judge Hampton was totally unimpressed with the pompous arrogance of the witness.

The judge advised, "Mr. Pepper, if you are an attorney, then you should be familiar with criminal proceedings. Therefore, please answer Mr. Lambert's questions directly and as succinctly as possible. The government is only interested in any factual information that you might have regarding the murders of Hiram Longstreet and Jeffrey Hightower, and the theft of cattle from your ranch and other ranches in the vicinity. We are not the least bit interested in hearing about how highly you regard yourself."

Pepper's pockmarked face reddened so much that the color of the purplish veins on his nose became less pronounced. "Your

Honor, I disagree. I think it is important to know the position I hold so that proper weight will be given to my testimony. Furthermore . . . "

Pepper's speech was cut short as the judge banged his gavel and snapped, "The witness will be quiet! Now, you listen to me and you mark well my instructions. You will answer the questions, and will give concise answers, if that is possible. You will not attempt to lecture me or anyone else in this court again. If you try to, I'll have you immediately jailed for contempt of court. Do you understand?"

Under the stern reprimand from the judge, the arrogant banker meekly nodded his head in affirmation. Howard's attorney turned to the gunfighter and whispered, "Mr. Howard, if this old windbag is the star witness, we've got nothing to worry about. He's already alienated the judge, and unless I miss my guess, the jury as well."

As it turned out, however, the defense attorney's assessment was somewhat premature. Once the banker started answering the prosecutor's questions, he told a convincing story that clearly pointed the finger of guilt at Howard, beginning with the first question.

"Mr. Pepper," asked Prosecutor Lambert, "before the trial you told me that you have proof that John Howard murdered Hiram Longstreet and that he is behind the cattle rustling that has been going on. Are you prepared to present that evidence at this time?"

"Yes, I am." Apparently Pepper remembered his legal training now and was taking the judge's admonition seriously.

"And what proof is that?"

"My personal assistant, Mr. Ben Duff, saw Howard driving the stolen cattle. Later he came upon Hiram Longstreet on the trail the day Mr. Longstreet was murdered. Mr. Longstreet's last words were that Howard shot him. He had found out that Howard was behind the rustling that was taking place. Also, Mr. Longstreet said he had discovered that, how do I say this delicately, Howard was taking liberties with both of the Reverend Hightower's young daughters, one of whom is a minor child."

"That's a lie!" The voice was young, feminine, and very angry. It belonged to Consuela. "Your Honor, that is a filthy lie from the mouth of a hateful and evil old man!"

Her sentiments were echoed by several spectators present. The rising crescendo was loud and spontaneous and was accompanied by the shuffling of people and chairs, as those in the back and outside the door strained to get a better look at the proceedings.

Judge Hampton banged his gavel. "Order! Order! I'll have order in this court if I have to clear it!" When things quieted down he added, "Young lady, you will have a chance to testify in due time, but no more outbursts. Mr. Lambert, you may continue questioning your witness."

"Thank you, Your Honor. I have no more questions for this witness."

The judge shifted his attention to the jury. "Then I will admonish the jury to disregard everything this witness said regarding statements by Mr. Longstreet to the individual named Ben Duff, because it is hearsay testimony. Mr. Adams, you may cross-examine."

"I have no questions at this time, Your Honor."

The judge then gave Pepper permission to step down. As the fat man laboriously raised himself from the witness chair, Howard's lawyer stood and cleared his throat.

"Oh, Mr. Pepper, I do have one question. It must have slipped my mind during the excitement. Is the sum total of your evidence the statements of this Ben Duff, or do you have additional evidence?"

Pepper stopped, frowned and eased back into the witness chair. "Yes, it is. I have no other evidence aside from Mr. Duff's testimony. However, he's well-respected and . . . "

Howard's attorney interrupted the banker. "Just one more question, and I assure you it's my last one for now. Do you trust Ben Duff?"

"Of course, I trust him implicitly. He has been my right hand for almost two years now."

To the judge, Adams then said, "Your Honor, I'm through with this witness for now. As you noted, I could have objected to much of his testimony as hearsay, because he swore to what another person said when he was not present. Both Mr. Lambert and I know that's not admissible. However, I welcome all of Mr. Pepper's comments into the record. Is that satisfactory with the prosecution and Your Honor?"

A somewhat perplexed prosecutor nodded his head in agreement. He had thought to stall for time by having Pepper testify, because Ben Duff, his main witness, was not present. He did this although he knew that his opponent would have standing to object to most of what Pepper said. Now he was worried that Mr. Adams had not only conceded the point, but had actually seemed to welcome Pepper's hearsay comments. However, Lambert was a competent attorney and an honest man himself. Besides, he had called Pepper as a prosecution witness. He agreed to have Pepper's testimony stand.

Judge Hampton spoke. "Mr. Adams, the Court allows the witness's testimony to stand, and notes that the defense could have objected on the basis of hearsay, but opted not to do so." To Pepper he said, "You may step down."

CHAPTER THIRTY-SIX

Sitting in the defendant's chair, Howard found that anger and melancholy were starting to take a firm grip on his being. He reflected that things could not have been much worse. He mentally recited them. First, he had been accused of stealing cattle. To make matters worse, he was being charged with murdering Hiram Longstreet, a friend he had tried to help. And Ben Duff, a man highly regarded by everyone in Gold Valley, was apparently going to give false testimony against him. Duff's testimony would be particularly damaging, because he was known as a man of integrity. Not even his employment by Pepper changed that.

Howard felt somewhat better when a long line of character witnesses appeared on his behalf, including three members of the town council. The testimony they gave was explicitly favorable. On the other hand, several witnesses described the young marshal in uncomplimentary terms. They said he was ruthless and too willing to kill. Miss Bradford, the bank teller, testified that he appeared to know almost too much about how bank robbers operated. After over two hours of testimony, the judge banged his gavel for a one hour recess.

Just before declaring the recess, the judge addressed the courtroom. "I have heard conflicting testimony regarding the character of the defendant. It seems that different witnesses have diametrically opposing viewpoints regarding him. However, as I stated at the outset of this trial, we are only interested in facts, not opinion. The day is wearing on, and so far, no one has introduced any compelling evidence showing that John Howard has committed any of the crimes he has been charged with. Therefore, the prosecution has one hour to present such evidence establishing his guilt, or the case will be dismissed."

Just then an aide to the Territorial Prosecutor barged his way inside the courtroom and rushed to the side of Mr. Lambert. He handed the prosecutor a note, causing the lawyer to smile broadly before clearing his throat and standing to address the judge.

"Excuse me, Your Honor, but may I address the Court, before the recess?"

The judge answered in an irritated voice, "This had better be worthwhile, Mr. Lambert. I've called a recess."

"It is, Your Honor. The prosecution will not need another hour to prove its case. Ben Duff is on his way to court, as we speak. He should be arriving within a few minutes. In the meantime, I request to call another witness after the recess. This witness is a special agent with the Pinkerton National Detective Agency. He will be able shed light on other crimes that Howard has committed for the past several years, including bank and train robberies. He will also be able to establish Howard's true identity."

"Very well, Counselor. Court is now in recess. We will reconvene in fifteen minutes."

At the recess, Rosa and Consuela came to Howard's side. "It will be all right, you'll see," said Rosa.

Howard could only look at the woman he loved, because he was rapidly losing all hope. He was now certain that his past had caught up with him, and there appeared to be nothing he could do about it.

"Rosa," he quietly said, "regardless of what happens, you must understand that the love I have for you is real and that I've never lied to you. You must also know that in spite of what I've done in the past, I'm not the man I used to be. But it's too late. If the Pinks are here, it's too late. They've been dogging me for years."

Strangely enough, Howard's attorney spoke up before Rosa could answer. "John, we're going to win this thing. I know more about your past than you think. Just remember, the Constitution protects you against self-incrimination. You don't have to answer questions that might tend to implicate you in any crime."

Howard frowned in frustration. "You don't understand. The Pinks . . . "

"Hush, now," interrupted Rosa. "Things are not as they appear to be. It will be all right. You'll see."

CHAPTER THIRTY-SEVEN

When court reconvened a few minutes later, a middle-aged man wearing a brown suit took the stand. He looked competent and tough. He gave his name as Alan Whicher and his occupation as a special agent with the Pinkerton National Detective Agency, having been employed by them for almost ten years.

Prosecutor Lambert then inquired, "And what has been your principal assignment with the Pinkertons for the last six months?"

"I've been assigned to conduct an investigation requested by William Pepper of Gold Valley, Dakota Territory, to do a background check on the man who calls himself John D. Howard."

"And is there any particular reason why you were assigned to this investigation?"

"Yes. Mr. Pepper suspected that the marshal had a criminal background." The Pinkerton man then dropped a bombshell. "I was assigned to the case because for two years prior to this present assignment, I've been part of a team of detectives investigating the Jesse James gang. As a result of my investigation, I believe that the evidence shows that the man who calls himself John D. Howard, is actually a former member of that gang. In fact, I think he may be Jesse James himself."

The resulting furor from the audience caused the judge to bang his gavel so hard that it broke, causing the head of the gavel to fly ten feet or so in front of the bench. To the federal law officers in the back of the court, he commanded, "Marshals, you will clear everyone out of this Court if there is one more outburst! Captain Campbell, your men will assist."

After things calmed down, the judge spoke to the witness. "Agent Whicher, the Pinkerton National Detective Agency is well-known and respected. It's even recognized as an unofficial arm of the federal government. Therefore, I must assume that you have evidence to support such a charge. Am I correct in that assumption?"

"Yes, Your Honor, although most of it is circumstantial. Nevertheless, when all the facts are taken together, they are quite convincing."

"Very well. Proceed."

The Pinkerton agent then quickly ticked off several facts. "Your Honor, one of the members of the James gang rode an Appaloosa. It was seen in the vicinity of several of the robberies. John Howard rode an Appaloosa until it was killed during a fight with the Sioux last fall. Also, we know that the James gang attempted to rob the bank in Northfield, Minnesota on September seventh of last year. Two members of the gang were killed, and several were wounded. We tracked the gang to the Dakota Territory, where they dropped from sight. John Howard was seen riding in the Dakota Territory in October 1876, just a few weeks after the Northfield incident. It would have been enough time to have ridden from Northfield. Also, we know for a fact that the most commonly-used alias of Jesse James is 'J.D. Howard' or 'John D. Howard', which is the name used by the town marshal. In fact, I understand that the marshal signs his name as 'J.D. Howard'. Additionally, it is common knowledge that Jesse James is a deadly gunfighter, just as John Howard is known to be."

Howard's lawyer then spoke up. "Your Honor, Agent Whicher has admitted that the evidence is only circumstantial. Is that all he has?"

The Pinkerton man spoke to the judge. "There is more, Your Honor. I have saved the most convincing evidence for last. May I introduce it at this time?"

"Proceed."

The agent looked directly at Howard. "First, I admit that I have never seen Jesse James in person." Pulling a photograph from his pocket, he added, "However, I do have his photograph. You will also notice that I have a very accurate sketch made of the photograph."

He then handed the photo and the identical sketch of the photo to the prosecutor, who handed them to Mr. Adams and the judge. Then the Pinkerton agent said, "Your Honor, may I ask you to pencil in a moustache on the man in the sketch?"

Intrigued by the request, the judge replied, "This is irregular, but if Mr. Adams has no objections, I will do so."

Upon hearing no objections from the defense, the judge added the moustache, and as he did, his eyes widened in amazement. When he showed it to Mr. Adams, those near him saw why. The sketch was a very accurate likeness of John Howard!

Howard's lawyer was not impressed. "Your Honor, I could object to this parlor trick because that drawing resembles a number of people, including Ben Duff. I don't suppose Mr. Whicher is going to accuse the prosecution's star witness of also being Jesse James, is he?"

Counselor Lambert answered his opponent. "Agent Whicher has just presented evidence that must be considered. However, whether or not the man calling himself John Howard is a member of the James gang, or is in fact Jesse James himself, doesn't have to be decided right now. I see that Ben Duff has just arrived. His testimony is not circumstantial or hearsay, and will clearly establish whether or not the defendant is guilty of theft and murder."

Howard looked back and saw that Ben Duff had just stepped inside the courtroom. Duff wore a neutral expression. In contrast, Pepper had one of smug self-satisfaction. For some inexplicable reason, the Pinkerton man looked like he had seen a ghost when he saw Duff.

Rosa leaned forward and whispered to Howard, "Don't worry. Everything's about to come out in the open."

Agent Whicher was dismissed. Duff walked up the witness chair. His first words caused such a commotion that the accusation by Agent Whicher seemed mild in comparison. It was so astounding that Judge Hampton forgot his own warning that he would clear the courtroom if there were any more outbursts.

And what an outburst it was, because after being sworn in, Duff was asked to state his name and occupation. "I'm known locally by the name 'Ben Duff'. However, my true and correct name is Benjamin Franklin Hightower. I'm the younger brother of the late Reverend Jeffrey Hightower. Like Mr. Whicher, I'm a special agent with the Pinkerton National Detective Agency. I also hold a special commission as a United States Deputy Marshal. I can prove that John Howard is innocent of all charges made against him. I can also identify the man who is really responsible for the murders of Hiram Longstreet and my brother, and who is behind the rustling as well."

CHAPTER THIRTY-EIGHT

Almost everyone in the courtroom was stunned, including the judge, prosecuting attorney, and John Howard. The most shocked individual was William Pepper, who looked like he was on the verge of a stroke. The only people not taken aback by Ben Hightower's revelation were the Hightower sisters, Counselor Adams, Preston Kirby, Angelique Mayo, and the two U.S. Deputy Marshals. Had anyone noticed the federal lawmen, they would have seen them unobtrusively move to where Pepper was seated and position themselves directly behind him.

The prosecutor, normally never at a loss for words, required several seconds before continuing, "Mr. Duff, I mean Mr. Hightower, will you tell us what proof you have of John Howard's innocence?"

"Yes. First of all, I was told by the Macleod brothers, both of whom were employed by William Pepper, and was later told by Pepper himself, that the actual murderer of Mr. Longstreet was another bodyguard employed by Pepper. The man called himself Sonny Chandler. Chandler later killed my brother, after Jeff refused to tell him where John Howard was recovering. Chandler himself admitted to me in front of witnesses that he murdered my brother. I can also produce witnesses who saw the murder of my brother. However, Chandler was only a hired killer. The man behind the murder was William Pepper. Pepper also engineered the theft of cattle from the three ranches, including his own. I know this because Pepper himself used me as an intermediary to give the instructions to the rustlers so that he wouldn't be implicated himself. Also, Chandler told me just before he died that Pepper had paid him to murder Mr. Longstreet and Mr. Howard. I believe that a dying declaration is admissible evidence. Then Pepper told me to lie in court and say that Mr. Longstreet told me that John shot him."

"You Judas!" screamed Pepper. He sounded like a woman in labor. "I trusted you! How could you betray me? How could you betray me?"

His screams were loud enough to be heard over the loud commotion taking place in the courtroom. Pepper fumbled for a single-shot .41 caliber Colt derringer carried inside his coat pocket. He was too clumsy and too slow. In apparent anticipation of his action, one officer deftly snatched the tiny gun from his hand, while the other wrestled him to the floor. Within just a few seconds, he hands were manacled behind his back.

Although the lawmen brought him under control in a matter of mere seconds, it was several minutes before the judge could get things quiet enough so things could proceed. The judge had apparently reached the limit of his patience.

"Marshals," he growled, "you will keep Mr. Pepper restrained. If he makes any more noise, gag him. Mr. Pepper, you are under arrest for murder, attempted murder, felony theft of livestock, disturbing the peace, contempt of court, and any and all other charges that I can think of. You will sit quietly through the duration of this trial. I suggest you start thinking about finding legal representation for your own upcoming trial."

Pepper's breath was labored and wheezing. He was unable to speak. It was just as well, because one of the federal marshals had already taken out a soiled red bandana from his own pocket. The lawman appeared anxious to use it as a gag on the banker.

"You may continue Mr. Hightower. But first, I have a question. Why would Pepper steal his own cattle?" queried the judge.

"I don't know, other than I suspect he has an insatiable thirst for power and money. He told me that if he could bankrupt the other ranchers, he could have a monopoly on the cattle business in this part of Dakota." Hightower pulled a small black book from his pocket. "Your Honor, the testimony I gave can be corroborated by other witness and through this tally book. The book has a record of all the stolen cattle, including Pepper's. It includes notes on how he was planning to move them out of the area. Everything in the book is in Pepper's own handwriting."

"Fine. Is there anything else you wish to add?"

"The Macleod brothers can both verify that Pepper ordered me to hire men to steal cattle from the three ranches. They left Gold Valley after my brother's murder, but are staying in Deadwood, awaiting word from me. Philip Macleod also heard Chandler admit that Pepper hired him to murder Mr. Longstreet and John Howard."

"I don't think it will be necessary for them to testify at this time. They can testify later at the trial of Chandler and Pepper."

"Your Honor?"

"Yes, Agent Hightower."

"Chandler's dead. I shot him the night he murdered my brother. I tried to arrest him and gave him a chance to surrender. There were plenty of witnesses."

Now it was the prosecutor's turn to speak. "Your Honor, Agent Hightower is the principal witness for the prosecution. After hearing his testimony and observing today's proceedings, I ask that the charges against John Howard be dropped."

The judge nodded his head in agreement before speaking. "Before I render my decision, I will warn everyone for what I hope will be the final time that this is a duly constituted court of law and that order will be maintained. Does everyone understand?"

After seeing that the court was in order, the judge continued, "This has been a highly unusual case. Upon recommendation of the prosecution, I am ready to make a final ruling. The defendant will stand and face the Bench."

After Howard complied, the judge said, "I am not going to dismiss the charges, but rather to exercise judicial prerogative and decide the defendant's guilt or innocence. If I dismiss the charges, they could be brought again. Therefore, I'm going to render a final verdict at this time. In the matter of the murder of Hiram Longstreet and theft of cattle from the Longstreet, Kilcoyne, and Pepper ranches, I find the defendant John David Howard not guilty. However . . . "

The spontaneous cheering and applause from all sections of the courtroom drowned out the judge's next words. He started to bang his broken gavel, but upon further reflection, simply sat back in his chair with a look of resignation on his face, until the noise subsided.

When he resumed speaking, he looked at Howard. "You seem to have several friends in this courtroom, Mr. Howard. You are a free man. I was going to say, before I was interrupted, that in the interest of justice, I am going to allow Agent Hightower to continue testifying, so that these other matters that have come to light during this trial may be dealt with. We will take a fifteen minute recess. Marshal Barnes and Marshal McCormick, you will escort Mr. Pepper to jail, while I decide how to proceed. Mr. Howard, you will retrieve your sidearm and assist in maintaining security. Court is now in recess."

CHAPTER THIRTY-NINE

During the court recess, Ben Hightower walked over to where his nieces, Howard, and Howard's attorney sat. He ushered them to a back room where they could have privacy. Howard was still in a state of shock, and was trying to sort out the sudden turn of events.

Ben Hightower said, "Now you know why I spent time at Jeff's house. You also know why Rosa and Consuela were so fond of me."

Howard nodded mutely. Then he said, "I have to admit that at one point, I was jealous of the time you spent there. I feel pretty stupid about that now."

Hightower replied, "Don't think you're the only one who has been stupid. Do you know that I almost called you out just before Christmas, over a misunderstanding?"

Howard was totally dumbfounded. "What are you talking about?"

"I saw you hug Angelique the night she gave you the cross for Rosita. You left the door ajar. The only reason I even hesitated was because I trust Angelique completely. But I admit she didn't help things when she refused to tell me what the embrace was about, only saying that it was innocent. Finally, Jeff set us both down one night and told us we had both better start acting like adults, before we damaged our relationship. He even said he would wallop me like he used to do when we were kids, if that's what it took to get my attention. That's when Angelique told me about the cross. You can imagine how I felt."

Howard didn't answer at first, but was very thankful that they hadn't fought, especially over a misunderstanding. Ben Hightower was the only man he had ever met who he doubted he could beat in a gunfight. More than that, it looked like they were going to be related by marriage.

After a few seconds Howard asked a question that was nagging him. "Where did you go after the Parson was murdered?"

"I went to Deadwood. Pepper thought I was going there to set up the sale of the cattle he had stolen. I really went there to make sure the Macleod brothers were ready to testify in court against Pepper."

"So the Macleods knew you are a Pinkerton man?"

"Not at first. Other than my brother, nieces, and Angelique, the first person in Gold Valley to know my true identity was Preston Kirby. I sent him to Pierre with this telegram the night you were shot and Mr. Longstreet and Jeff were killed," replied the Pinkerton man, as he handed a folded piece of paper to Howard.

Howard unfolded the paper and read its contents. Printed in neat capital letters on the note were the words 'TO GOVERNOR AT YANKTON DAKOTA STOP CAN PROVE MURDER AND RUSTLING IN GOLD VALLEY STOP SEND US MARSHAL AND JUDGE STOP MEET DEPUTY PRESTON KIRBY AT PIERRE FIRST STOP SIGNED BEN HIGHTOWER PINKERTON DETECTIVE'.

Hightower added, "The Governor didn't reveal my true identity to the judge or prosecutor because we didn't want anything to prevent Pepper from giving a full statement in court. We thought that if everyone accepted Pepper's charges on face value, Pepper would be more likely to tell his entire concocted story, commit perjury and implicate himself. I also didn't tell Detective Whicher in advance for the same reason."

Howard handed the note back. He turned to Rosa. "Your family is full of surprises. How much of this did you know about?"

"All of it. In fact, Papa, Consuela and I came to Gold Valley after Uncle contacted us."

Agent Hightower interjected, "I sent for them after I received word that my sister-in-law and nephews had died. I had been investing money for Jeff for years. We own a number of shares in the First Strike Mine, as well as the Homestake Mine over near Deadwood. Angelique and I were planning to get married as soon as I arrested Pepper. I hadn't got to see much of my family over the last several years, and asked if they could join me. It happened that there were several orphans in Gold Valley, so that gave Jeff another reason for coming."

"Why were you going to arrest Pepper?" asked Howard. "Were you after him for other crimes?"

"Yes. I've been after Pepper since before the Civil War ended. I've been trying to prove that he was involved in the theft of over two hundred Henry rifles that were illegally sold to Southern troops. He was in business in Baltimore at the time, and also had a position in the federal government. He used his position to arrange to have the rifles stolen and sold to Confederate troops. Just before his assassination, President Lincoln himself commissioned Mr. Pinkerton to find out who the traitor was. You seem to be a well-read man, John. Perhaps you know that there is no statute of limitations where treason is involved."

Hightower continued, "I lost track of Pepper because he changed his name and ran. I got a break two years ago when he was in Yankton, trying to promote some land schemes involving the Black Hills territory. He made the mistake of advertising in the Chicago paper. I saw the ad and came to Dakota. I introduced myself to him, and worked my way into a position as his personal assistant. After a little while, he began confiding in me about his plans. Over the years, I've found that most criminals have at least one fatal flaw. Pepper's was assuming that he was smarter than everyone else, and that everyone was as crooked as he is."

Rosa then spoke up. "Uncle, what will happen now? Will you leave the Pinkertons now that Pepper has been arrested? Or will you stay with them after you and Mrs. Mayo are married?"

"I haven't decided yet. There are still a couple of loose ends I have to take care of. Now that Pepper's in jail, I believe I can have former Confederate officers identify him as the one behind the theft of the rifles. However, even if I can't prove treason, justice

will still be served, because he'll hang for rustling and for murder."
He placed his hand on top of Rosa's. "But there's another unresolved
matter, Rosita. It involves your fiancé."

At those words, Howard felt his stomach tighten. He knew
that Ben Hightower was shrewd and capable, like most Pinkerton
detectives and federal lawmen. He also had a good idea that
Hightower knew who he was, or at least what gang he had ridden
with for several years. He waited for Hightower's next words.

The Pinkerton man wasted no time. "John, you need to know
that Agent Whicher had a cousin with the same last name. This
other Whicher was also a Pinkerton man. He was murdered by the
Jesse James gang. They killed him after he infiltrated the gang and
they found out he was one of us." The Pinkerton agent loosened
his string necktie. "I'm talking to you now as the uncle of Rosa
and Consuela, not as a Pinkerton detective or Deputy U.S. Marshal.
But you've got to tell me the truth." He quickly waved his hand at
Howard's lawyer. "Don't object, Counselor. Trial hasn't resumed
yet. This is a family matter that is off the record, for now. John,
were you aware of the other Agent Whicher's murder?"

"Yes."

"Did you have anything to do with it?"

Howard never hesitated. "No. I wasn't even there when it
happened. I've killed several men, but I've never murdered anyone. "

Hightower breathed an audible sigh of relief. "Excellent. That
confirms what we know through other sources. Now, with Mr.
Adams' indulgence, I'm going to tell a story. It's very interesting.
Let's suppose that a young boy lost his family and everything else
in the Civil War. Then he joined a regiment commanded by one of
the finest soldiers in the world, Colonel John Mosby. He learned
tactics from Mosby and even though Lee surrendered, this boy
never did. After the war, he went west. He spent some time with
the Sioux Indians and later with distant relatives in Missouri. These
relatives hadn't surrendered either, and they thought that Yankee-
owned trains and banks were fair game. Let's say that his relatives
were named Frank and Jesse James. To make things even more
interesting, let's say that Jesse thought that it would be a good

joke to use the young man's name as an alias. Am I holding your attention, John?"

Howard could only nod. Both of the Hightower girls held his hands.

Ben Hightower continued, "If this certain young man rode with these outlaws and participated in most of their deviltry, he would be guilty of numerous crimes of robbery. Fortunately, he never shot anyone during the robberies. Now, let's suppose that everything went smoothly for several years. Then the incident at Northfield, Minnesota took place last year. The young man and the rest of the gang escaped into Dakota. Through a strange twist of circumstances, the man became a lawman, and was a good one from all accounts. Then, through the influence of an old preacher and the preacher's young daughter, the young man decided to change his ways. Do you think this hypothetical story has the makings of a Ned Buntline dime novel, John?"

Howard's neck muscles tightened. He said nothing.

"Well sir," continued Hightower, "now let's suppose that this young man had a chance to make amends for his crimes, and start a new life with the girl he had fallen in love with. Do you think he would be interested in doing that?"

Rosa answered for Howard, "Of course he would, Uncle."

"Good. Since he never murdered or even shot anyone during the robberies, and in the absence of witnesses and tangible evidence, suppose he returned his share of the stolen money. There would be no more investigation into his activities with the Jesse James gang."

Attorney Adams interjected, "You mean 'alleged activities,' don't you Detective Hightower?"

"Yes, of course, because they have not been proven in court. By the way, if it ever comes up in the future, I can prove that John is not Jesse James. We know that Jesse is no taller than 5' 9". John, you're as tall as I am, and I'm over six feet in my socks. So Mr. Adams, you will be pleased to know that John can't be Jesse. Also, contrary to popular myth, Jesse is not as proficient with a gun as he is reputed to be. He is certainly not nearly as good as John is.

Now back to my story and the matter of the stolen money. How much do you think that young man we've been discussing would need to return, John?"

"Almost eight thousand dollars," replied Howard in a voice barely above a whisper. "What if he hasn't got anywhere near that amount?"

"Oh, but he does," piped up Rosa. "He's going to marry a rich young lady, who has that amount, and far more."

"Then," said Agent Hightower, "if the money were returned, there would be no investigation and no charges. How does that sound?"

"It sounds too good to be true," replied a stunned John Howard.

"It's not too good to be true, I assure you. My brother believed in giving second chances and wanted you to have one. That's why the first night you arrived in Gold Valley, he convinced me to talk to Pepper and persuade him to hire you as town marshal. I had my doubts about you at first. I'm glad my brother convinced me otherwise."

Rosa put her arm around her uncle. "Then after we repay the money, John and I can move on with our lives and get married?"

"Yes, you can. But there may be more. I might want to recruit him for the Pinkertons. He's proven to be a smart and resourceful lawman. He would be a good agent. We need men like him. Of course, I wouldn't ask him to hunt the James gang because they're related. And there's no need to. The James boys' days are numbered."

"He might need to talk about that with me," said Rosa primly. "I might like him taking on safer work for a change."

CHAPTER FORTY

When the hearing resumed, Ben Hightower repeated his story to the judge. He left out the 'hypothetical' part about the former bank and train robber who became a lawman. He also told the judge that he had witnesses, former Confederate officers, who might be able to prove that Pepper was involved in treasonous acts during the Civil War.

As a result of Hightower's testimony, the judge ordered the Deputy U.S. Marshals to arrange to have Pepper transported to Yankton to await trial. After that, the judge brought the proceedings to a close.

People milled around after the trial. Several of them offered congratulations to Howard. The first in line to do so was Preston Kirby followed by Captain Campbell.

"Well, John," said Campbell, "it looks like justice was served today. Can you imagine a Southerner getting a fair shake in a Yankee court from a Yankee judge? Do you think that perhaps the Civil War is finally over?" His genuine smile kept the irony in his tone from being sarcastic.

"I never thought I would have seen this day, James. It looks like I've been wrong about many things. Sometimes things do turn out for the best, it seems."

Captain Campbell agreed. "In your case I would have to say so, on several counts. You've not only been cleared of false charges, but I also understand that you're getting married. Is that right?"

Rosa answered for Howard. "Yes, Captain Campbell, and the sooner the better. It's a good thing he didn't trade me to the Sioux last fall," she said laughingly.

Campbell and Howard laughed also. Then Campbell asked

Howard about his future plans. It seemed lately that many people were interested in his future.

"My only definite plan is to marry Rosa. After that, I don't know."

"What about the helping the Army?" asked the soldier. "There are still many small independent bands of Sioux and Cheyenne warriors operating in the Black Hills. The Army needs someone who could talk to the Indians, someone they would trust. If you agree to help, you could be employed as a civilian scout, and would receive the same pay as a second lieutenant. I believe that it would even be possible to get you commissioned as a regular officer, if you're interested."

Howard shook his head. "I'm not the man for the job. I have friends among the Lakota, and present company excepted, I still don't have much respect for the Army."

Campbell nodded. "I only thought I would ask. If you ever change your mind . . . "

"He ain't gonna change his mind." The voice was truculent. It belonged to Donald Reilly. "So, you got away with it, Reb? Well, me an' you still got some unfinished business, an' it'll be with fists, not guns."

"That's enough, Corporal." Campbell's tone left no room for argument.

"It's all right." Howard looked at Reilly with more pity than contempt. "You're wrong, Reilly. We've got no business. You're wasting your time hating me. It's time for everyone to move on. I no longer hate you. I don't even think about you. You ought to do the same thing."

Rosa squeezed his hand tightly. Her pride in him was evident.

"Huh?" Reilly knew that the marshal was not afraid of him, and therefore couldn't understand Howard's attitude. "You ain't willin' to fight me? Ain't you well enough yet?"

Howard didn't bother answering. He and his friends walked past the non-com to the hotel's private dining room. Everyone ignored Reilly, leaving him standing alone and perplexed.

On their way, Captain Campbell told the rest of the troopers that they had one hour of free time before they would ride out. The soldiers filed out of the hotel.

Howard's group sat down at the large dining table. It had been a long day and no one had eaten. While they were ordering their meals, Consuela began looking for her purse. She was unsuccessful finding it. "I'll be right back," she said. "I must have left my purse in the other room, where the trial was held. You can stay here, Ian. I'll be right back."

The men stood as she left the table. After about ten minutes, Ian O'Hara mentioned that Consuela had not returned. Nobody was overly concerned, because they were sure she was still in the hotel. Still, O'Hara insisted in looking for her.

O'Hara returned a few minutes later. His normally cheerful expression was altered by a deep frown line that creased his forehead. "Consuela's not in the hotel. Nobody knows where she is. I reckon we better start looking."

Ben Hightower quickly organized parties to search the town. Captain Campbell rounded up the troopers and ordered them to assist. One of the soldiers mentioned that Corporal Reilly was missing.

Howard escorted Rosa back to her house. She was visibly frightened. "Do you think Consuela's all right? I'm afraid for her. You don't think that awful soldier is with her, do you?"

"I hope she's all right. I have to admit that it concerns me that Reilly is also missing. It hasn't been long, though. We'll find her. You just stay here and keep the door locked, and make sure the guns are loaded."

Howard left Rosa inside. He tested the door after she locked it.

Once inside the house, Rosa noticed a muffled sound coming from the back bedroom. She opened the door and stepped inside, coming face to face with Corporal Reilly and Consuela. Her younger sister was tied and gagged. She had bruise on the side of her face, but otherwise appeared to be unharmed.

Reilly grabbed Rosa and yanked her inside. "Well now, look

what we got here. Now I got both of you. You two are mighty fine-lookin', that's for certain. I was fixin' to keep the little one just till I could get Howard to fight me. But after thinking about it, I reckon I'd rather have the two of you and forget about the Reb, just like he said." At Consuela's look of horror and disgust Reilly added, "Don't worry, sugar, you're gonna like it. So is your sister. I just got to decide which one of you gets to go first."

Rosa struggled against the viselike grip of the huge soldier as he talked, but the man held both girls easily. "Let us go or I'll scream! John is still on the street, and he'll shoot your heart out! You know that he won't take kindly to his fiancée and her sister being touched by the likes of you, and you've seen what he can do when he's angry!"

"Not as long as I've got you right here, girly. He's got to get through you to get to me!" Reilly chortled at the irony. "An' if you scream, I'll sure enough wring both your necks. I can snap 'em in two easy as anything."

As her sister's muffled sobs became more desperate, Rosa knew that her wits were her only weapon against this brute. She had heard how saloon girls got what they wanted from men like Reilly, and she decided that appearing to resign herself to the inevitability of her situation was her only option.

Rosa tried to mask her revulsion of Reilly and gave him a look that she hoped conveyed total defeat. She tried to make her tone match her look. "Please leave my sister alone. She's just a little girl. You can do what you want with me, just don't hurt her." Rosa stopped struggling in a further attempt to appear willing to surrender.

Reilly leered at his victim. "That's a good girl. It's gonna happen whether you want it to or not, so you might as well be quiet about it, and maybe, if you're good enough, I'll leave baby sister alone. Now get them clothes off."

Rosa began to undo the top button of her dress as Reilly watched her with an evil leer. He unloosened his belt as Consuela looked on in shocked disbelief.

By the time Rosa got to the second button, Reilly lost what

little patience he had. "You're going too slow. Get that thing off right now!"

"Of course. Just let me get this necklace and cross off first. I don't want to break the necklace. It would be faster if I could use both hands."

That seemed to momentarily satisfy Reilly. He let go of her arm, stepped back, and watched as Rosa gently pulled off her gold necklace and cross with her right hand. Reilly looked with admiration at the jewelry, thinking that since he was going to commit rape anyway, he might as well add theft to the charges, since rape was a hanging offense.

With his attention glued on the movements of Rosa's right hand, Reilly failed to notice the subtle movement of her left one. He failed to see her draw her double-barreled .41 Remington derringer from her dress pocket. When he finally noticed the gun it was too late. Rosa had already cocked the derringer as she drew it. The barrels were pointed squarely at the middle of Reilly's chest.

Rosa's voice instantly changed. No longer was it cooperative and laced with fear. It was as tough as steel, and brooked no argument. "Raise your hands and slowly back up to the other side of the room. If you move toward my sister or me, I'll give you both barrels."

The initial shock on Reilly's face began to fade as he backed away. "Hey, darlin' you're some actress. Fooled me for sure. Now you best put that little old pea-shooter up. It might hurt some, but I'll still get my hands on you. I been shot before with a bigger gun than that, an' I killed the man that done it. So you best put it away and I won't hurt you none."

Rosa hesitated, as if carefully considering her options. She started to lower the gun. Reilly smirked. He thought he had won. Then the gun's muzzle stopped. When it did, the huge would-be rapist stopped grinning. The gun was pointed directly at his groin.

"The Bible speaks of eunuchs, Corporal Reilly. How would you like to become one?" The girl's arm was as steady as a rock. It matched the hardness in her voice.

For one of the very few times in his sadistic life, Reilly began to feel uneasy. Then the feeling grew until the brutal soldier actually began to experience fear. It was a rare emotion for him, having always relied before on his strength and ability to intimidate anyone who opposed him. But this time things were different. He was loathe to admit it, but he knew that this beautiful girl would shoot him if he wasn't very careful.

He tried to talk his way out of what had rapidly deteriorated into a bad situation. "Okay, okay, missy. Tell you what. Why don't you just let me out of here and we'll forget the whole thing? I didn't hurt your sister much. Just slapped her once."

"We'll forget nothing. And you're not going anywhere but to prison or a hangman's noose."

Rosa moved over to her sister and used her left hand to untie Consuela's hands. When she was free, Rosa said, "Go get Papa's pistol. Fire it into the ground outside. It'll bring help."

"I can't leave you alone with him, Rosa. Come with me."

"Go on, Consuela. I'm in no danger. He is. If he even twitches a muscle, I'll shoot him first in the groin, and then in the eye. On second thought, if he tries anything, perhaps I'll just shoot him twice in the groin. He may not die right away, but I think he will wish he were dead. What do you think, Corporal?"

Reilly started to turn pale. Something in Rosa's voice and the direction where the gun was aimed made him believe her. Had he been a wiser man, he would have been able to identify the words as something John Howard might have said. Then again, had he been a wiser man, he would have never accosted her and her sister in the first place.

Once outside, Consuela fired her father's Walker Colt six times into the ground. The thunderous noise reverberated through the length of the entire town. It grabbed the attention of all of the search parties.

The first to arrive after Consuela fired was John Howard. He had already started to walk back to the house. He later said that he had the feeling that something was wrong when he left Rosa, and returned to search the house before leaving her alone.

He spoke briefly to Consuela and then sprinted inside with

his gun drawn. When he saw Rosa and Reilly, he cocked the hammer and aimed at the center of Reilly's head. From the bleak look in his eyes, both Rosa and Reilly guessed that the soldier was going to die on the spot. Some men might bluff in that situation, but not John Howard.

Even if Reilly had any doubts regarding Howard's lethal intentions, the gunfighter's next words erased all doubt. "Reilly, you've got exactly one minute to make your peace with God."

"No, John!" screamed Rosa. She echoed her father's words spoken the time of the incident at the Pink Palace. "He isn't worth it! Consuela's all right. So am I. Don't throw everything away because of him!"

Other people raced toward the house. They heard the gunshots and had seen Consuela when she went outside. Ben Hightower was the next person inside the house. He rushed into the room. The expression on his face matched Howard's. He heard the last of what Rosa said to Howard.

Hightower gave quiet instructions to his niece. "Go on outside, Rosita. John and I will handle it."

"Uncle, you can't shoot him! I told John already. Consuela and I are all right. Uncle, you and John are lawmen. You can't kill him without a trial."

Hightower had drawn his own gun. It was also pointed at Reilly's head. "Go on now, Rosita. We'll handle it," he repeated.

"Wait!" The voice belonged to Reilly. It was full of animal desperation. "Don't leave, girl. For God's sake, don't leave! They're fixin' to kill me if you do!"

Rosa started to protest but turned and walked out. When she left, in Reilly's mind, all hope left with her. He was convinced that he was going to die in just a few seconds.

Then Reilly's conniving mind tried to formulate a convincing argument to persuade the two lawmen to spare his life. For some reason unknown to him, he felt he could reason with the gunfighters more effectively than he could with Rosa. He seized on Rosa's words. "It's like she done said; if you shoot me, it's murder. Yeah, it's just plain murder. You're both lawdogs. You gotta follow rules. You can't just gun me down."

Regaining some of his nerve, now that Rosa was gone, he spat on the floor and cursed. "I reckon you want me to say I'm sorry or something. Well I ain't, not even a little bit. Listen, there's other people coming. There's gonna be witnesses. All I done was rough up the little one. Weren't no big thing. You can't shoot me for that."

By that time, Captain Campbell arrived with four troopers. The enlisted men stayed outside. Campbell entered the room.

Reilly exhaled a genuine sigh of relief. "Boy, I never thought I'd be glad to see you, Cap'n. These two gunslicks was fixin' to shoot me. That cute little tramp was gonna give herself to me and then changed her mind."

Campbell faced Reilly but spoke to Howard, Hightower and the soldiers in the next room. "I heard what you said, Corporal, about there being witnesses. But you're wrong. There are no witnesses." The officer partially turned toward the door. "You men in the other room, do you see anything?"

"No sir! We don't see nothing. Don't hear nothing, either. Fact is, we ain't even here."

Campbell turned to leave. "We'll be outside."

At that instant, Reilly roared and charged at Howard. Brute though he was, he was no coward. He was determined to die fighting. Besides, he preferred death to a life in prison.

However, John Howard had no intention of accommodating him. He didn't shoot. Instead, he tossed his gun to Ben Hightower, who deftly caught it in his left hand. Howard moved to the side and caught Reilly across the throat with his forearm. He ducked behind, and in a well-practiced move, began to choke the huge soldier, just as his teacher had done to Jackson. Reilly tried to pivot and elbow Howard, but was unsuccessful. Howard was weakened from his recent wounds, but had a perfect position. He pulled Reilly backwards to the floor and rendered him unconscious in a matter of seconds.

A few minutes later, everyone gathered outside the house. Reilly was led away in handcuffs that were supplied by the U.S. Deputy Marshals. Four troopers escorted him away.

As the rest of the soldiers walked away, Campbell said, "I knew you wouldn't shoot him. I just wanted him to squirm a little. I didn't know he was going to attack you."

"It turned out to be no problem at all. I'm glad I had a good teacher."

As Howard finished speaking, Rosa put her arms around Howard and kissed him. She looked at Howard, her sister, and her uncle. "He can't bother us again. I don't think he'll try to."

Ben Hightower agreed with his niece. "He would be a fool if he did, even if he ever gets out of prison."

"Because he doesn't want to face you or John?" asked Rosa.

Her uncle laughed. "Partially that, but mainly because of what you put him through, Rosita."

Captain Campbell added, "You're right, Mr. Hightower. You know, I've never seen Reilly show any fear until today."

Howard shared his friends' sentiments. He said to Rosa, "Consuela told us how you handled the situation before we got there. No one could have done it better. I'm very proud of you. And there's something else. I think your father is looking down on you. I think he's very proud also."

Rosa kissed him again. "I hope so. But why shouldn't he be? After all, I am my father's daughter."

Printed in the USA
CPSIA information can be obtained
at www.ICGtesting.com
LVHW041653190923
758692LV00012B/36/J